BLOOD REBELLION

BLOOD DESTINY SERIES

CONNIE SUTTLE

Print Second Edition (2018)
Print ISBN: 1-63478-052-3
Print ISBN-13: 978-1-63478-052-0
ISBN: 1-939759-20-X
ISBN-13: 978-1-939759-20-7

Published by:
SubtleDemon Publishing, LLC
PO Box 95696
Oklahoma City, OK 73143

Cover art by Renee Barratt @ The Cover Counts

To Walter, Joe, Larry, Lee, Dianne, Sarah and Mark.
Thank you.

ACKNOWLEDGMENTS

As always, this book is the result of collaboration. If it weren't for the support of my editor, my cover artist and my beta readers, it would be less than it is. All mistakes, as usual, are mine and no other's.

About the Author:
Connie Suttle lives in Oklahoma with her husband and a conglomerate of cats. They have finally banded together to make their demands, which has proven disconcerting to all humans involved.

You may find Connie in the following ways:
Facebook: Connie Suttle Author
Twitter: @subtledemon
Website and Blog: subtledemon.com

ALSO BY CONNIE SUTTLE

Blood Destiny Series:

Blood Wager

Blood Passage

Blood Sense

Blood Domination

Blood Royal

Blood Queen

Blood Rebellion

Blood War

Blood Redemption

Blood Reunion

Blood Destiny Series Boxed Set (Books 1-10)

Blood Recall

Blood Alliance*

Legend of the Ir'Indicti Series:

Bumble

Shadowed

Target

Vendetta

Destroyer

Legend of the Ir'Inditi Boxed Set

High Demon Series:

Demon Lost

Demon Revealed

Demon's King

Demon's Quest

Demon's Revenge

Demon's Dream

God Wars Series:

Blood Double

Blood Trouble

Blood Revolution

Blood Love

Blood Finale

Saa Thalarr Series:

Hope and Vengeance

Wyvern and Company

Observe and Protect*

First Ordinance Series:

Finder

Keeper

BlackWing

SpellBreaker

WhiteWing

~

R-D Series:

Cloud Dust

Cloud Invasion

Cloud Rebel

~

Latter Day Demons Series:

Hot Demon in the City

A Demon's Work is Never Done

A Demon's Due

~

Seattle Elementals Series:

Your Money's Worth

Worth Your While*

~

BlackWing Pirates Series

MindSighted

MindMage

MindRogue

MindMaster*

~

Black Rose Sorceress Series

The Rose Mark

Rose and Thorn

Black Rose Queen

Queen of Thorns and Roses

Future Wars Series

Buffer Zone

Black Zone*

Other Titles from SubtleDemon Publishing:

Malefactor

Transgressor

Underhanded*

by Joe Scholes

*Forthcoming

BLOOD REBELLION

BLOOD DESTINY SERIES, BOOK SEVEN

CHAPTER 1

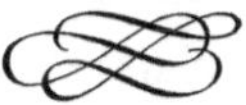

I lie inside a cage. It is bitingly cold here, and no respite from the chill will be offered. With bars all around me, there is no privacy. No place to hide. It has been thus for centuries and my captors will not change it, no matter how much I beg or the benefits I offer them in exchange. They merely laugh, as I am their prisoner and subject to their whims anyway.

Have I tried to better my conditions? Many times. At first, they made promises to placate me, but no promise was ever fulfilled. My mistake, I know. They have only taken from me of late—of my flesh and what remains of my sanity. They have asked no questions. That is their mistake.

The time is coming.

Soon.

I look forward to the ending of my misery.

Beliphar

"I didn't do it!" Davan shouted as he was dragged by two guards past rows of prison cells. His trial was a sham; without proper representation, he'd been sentenced (as so many others before him), to death by vampirism. Accused of stealing from the state, the sentence was the same for anyone convicted of that crime. Everyone was employed by the state; everything was owned by the state. There were managers and supervisors who thrived and prospered; nearly all of whom were corrupt upon the world of Beliphar.

Once, Beliphar had been a mighty world and a member of the Reth Alliance. No longer—a new regime had come to power, eliminating elected officials quickly. They claimed it was to reduce the amount of government in the Belepharans' lives, but it had come to mean the opposite. Those who'd risen to power had stayed in power and the world of Beliphar labored under their harsh authority.

The Reth Alliance had withdrawn membership quickly, leaving Beliphar to fend for itself. The Belipharans suffered and the small vampire population was quickly captured and condemned for trumped up crimes against the state. Vampires, like everyone else living on Beliphar, were now controlled by those in power.

Vampirism was dealt as a punishment for most crimes and vampires were held in check with special cuffs and chains. They worked in street crews at night or in the mines, did labor on state run farms or processed fuel, chemicals and pharmaceuticals. Anything that might be done at night that could prove harmful to humanoids was ultimately done with vampire labor, as environmental controls on Beliphar were all but abandoned.

Still, Davan proclaimed his innocence and his cries were truth, but he'd been sentenced anyway and was now being hauled down a long, sterile hallway toward a small, windowless room. A vampire waited there—a vampire controlled by the courts and its officers. Davan would be turned unless he died in the attempt. As a male, his chances of surviving the turn were very good. Any female convicted knew her punishment was a death sentence—perhaps one in twenty-five thousand females would turn. Every vampire on Beliphar was male.

Davan stepped up his struggles as he reached the small, sterile cube of a room. A cuffed and controlled vampire waited inside, accompanied by a supervisor with a controlling wand.

"No! In the name of the light, no!" Davan shouted. A blazer stick was pressed against his neck and current shot through his body. The resulting pain forced him to his knees as he howled in agony. Davan wept and cursed as the guards jerked him to his feet.

"Name?" The supervisor demanded coldly.

"Davan Falthis," one of Davan's guards replied; Davan was still weeping and unable to answer.

"Davan Falthis, you have been sentenced by the state. Your punishment is vampirism, after which you will serve the state that you conspired against," the supervisor droned in a detached voice. "Load him onto the table."

Davan could only moan and whimper as he was hefted onto the stainless-steel table and strapped down; body, arms, legs and neck. The two guards retreated to the corners of the room.

"Do your duty, vampire," the supervisor snapped at the cuffed vampire. He nodded and pulled a steel bowl from beneath the table. It would catch the excess blood when the prisoner's wrists were opened.

Tears ran down Davan's cheeks—he had no idea how his life had come to this—he'd trained as an accountant and had done his duty for the state for thirty years. Now he was in his mid-fifties and someone, a supervisor somewhere, had taken money, laying the blame on him. Davan had been sentenced for someone else's crime.

"You will not speak or cry out," the vampire laid compulsion. Davan was still frightened—the vampire had no control over that. Davan watched in terror as a sharp claw appeared on the vampire's finger, and then the claw slit his left wrist, three times—lengthwise. More tears fell as Davan heard his blood dripping into the bowl.

Can you hear me? A voice sounded inside Davan's mind as his right wrist was opened.

Hear who? Davan was terrified, thinking he was hallucinating during his final moments.

I am the vampire, the voice came again. *Do not be afraid. I will do my best to keep you alive. My blood is oldest upon Beliphar.*

Keep me alive for what? Davan still thought he was hallucinating.

We still have hope, the vampire replied. *Close your eyes, it is almost time.*

∼

Earth

"Something is going on with the Reldani," Dragon sighed and settled onto a barstool at Kiarra's kitchen island. Dragon and Devin had come for a visit—to let Kiarra know they'd gotten a whiff of strange events during a trip to Falchan to buy new leathers.

Dragon's dark eyes were narrowed in concern and his usual, enigmatic expression was missing, replaced by a few creases of worry on his forehead. Devin moved his long braid aside and rubbed Dragon's back as she sat next to him. If the former Dragon Warlord showed signs of worry, then there was definitely something going on.

"What's that?" Kiarra shoved white-blonde hair over a shoulder and handed Dragon a cup of Falchani black tea. Devin's cup was served next—she and Dragon both loved the dark brew.

"You know the Reldani can never agree on anything—especially when it comes to who's in command," Dragon sighed. "They have small principalities everywhere, commanded by whoever is strong enough to beat any contenders back. They raid across the borders constantly, when they're not fighting among themselves. Until now." Dragon sipped his tea and nodded in appreciation to Kiarra.

"So, what has changed?" Kiarra sat next to her adopted daughter Devin and pulled her close for a hug. Devin smiled and rested her head against Kiarra's shoulder.

"The Reldani are banding together, that's what. Under two leaders," Dragon grumbled. "That's unheard of. Something is wrong, here. I feel it."

"Something is wrong," Belen agreed, appearing in a brilliant flash of light. "I was on my way to warn you and the others."

Belen, Chief of the Nameless Ones, nodded to Dragon, First among the Saa Thalarr. "It is something that bears investigation," Belen went on. "And it would be prudent to send several of ours to help the Falchani army while you investigate. You have permission to join the Falchani army and act as you see fit in this," Belen nodded as he muted the light around him.

Dragon blinked in surprise—joining the Falchani army would be seen as interference under normal circumstances. Belen's permission merely reinforced his opinion of the unusual events on Falchan. Somehow, either an old enemy had resurfaced or a new one had come into being. Perhaps both. Dragon schooled his face as that thought crowded his mind.

"I can gather all our Falchani and sign up as a volunteer band from the hills—nobody will recognize us," Dragon agreed.

"I'll go, too," Devin offered. Devin, trained by Dragon and Crane in the art of the blade, was deadly with the Falchani swords she often carried.

"That goes without saying," Dragon smiled. "When should we go, Revered One?" he nodded respectfully to Belen.

"Soon." Belen inclined his head. "I will let you know when. There is one other thing, too."

"What's that?" Kiarra asked.

"Take the Vampire Queen with you. I care not how it is accomplished; I only know that Lissa's presence will prove essential." Belen disappeared quickly.

"Now how the hell are we going to convince Lissa that she has to go to Falchan?" Kiarra sighed, shaking her head. Belen had left before she could ask more questions.

"Mom, she's married to our boys," Devin grinned, pointing to herself and Dragon.

"Well, there's that, I suppose," Kiarra grinned back.

～

Campiaa

"Ranos grenades." Erland Morphis kicked the pile of formerly unbreakable transteel wall with a booted toe. Chunks of transteel littered the entry of the Sand Swept Casino, which Erland owned and operated on the gambling planet of Campiaa. Erland was so angry he hadn't bothered with a disguise, and those brave enough to withstand his anger were allowed to see what few on Campiaa ever witnessed—the most beautiful male they'd likely gaze upon in their lifetime.

Merrill and Adam, who owned the Moonstone Casino next door, stood beside Erland, examining the damage with the Karathian warlock. Their casino had been hit as well, but not as hard as Erland's.

"Ever since Divil San Gerxon was killed, his brother Arvil sees the need to flex his muscle, just to let everyone know he's in charge," Adam muttered, his gray eyes narrowed in anger. "And now, Arvil has managed to buy and smuggle in Ranos technology. If he ups his demands, we'll be forced to pay."

"He already gets twenty-five percent," Merrill pointed out. "Just for the privilege of putting up a building here."

"We still get good information," Erland sighed. "I wish there were a way to coax the wealthy gamblers away from here, though. The information would come with them—it can't be helped."

Erland, Merrill and Adam all had a common purpose in owning casinos in what was touted as the gambling mecca for the worst criminals—those who lived outside the Reth Alliance and its laws.

Campiaa saw its share of deals for drugs, weapons, assassins and any other illegal enterprise. Much of it, unfortunately, was aimed at the Reth Alliance. Drugs and weapons were shipped in, with the occasional criminal—all arranged and paid for through contacts that regularly visited Campiaa.

Wealthy gamblers from the Reth Alliance also found their way to Campiaa—it was a sign of their wealth that they could skirt Alliance laws and find ships to transport them. After all, anything could be had on Campiaa—for the right price.

One could get information on any illegal activity, if one knew where to listen. Adam and Merrill always listened for information that might affect the Saa Thalarr. Erland listened for other reasons.

"Follow the money, eh?" Merrill nodded at Erland.

"Precisely. Information and any illegal negotiations will always be near the funding. You can count on that. These gamblers may look legitimate—on the surface, at least. We know better." Erland agreed.

"Lord Morphis, I'll bring in the cleaning crew if you're ready," an employee approached Erland cautiously. The warlock now seemed calm enough to speak without blasting something to bits.

"Yes. Get those walls replaced by tomorrow."

"Of course, Lord Morphis."

∿

Le-Ath Veronis

I was doing my best not to get chocolate cake crumbs on a blue silk tunic. It was richly embroidered around the hem and cuffs and had matching trousers. I knew Giff wouldn't mind finding clothing to replace my outfit if I ruined it, but this was one of my favorites.

I was forced at times to wear dresses, and that was something I didn't like at all. They were such a pain and bother, since most of them were long and dragged the floor. I was constantly trying to move my skirts out of the way.

Drake and Drew laughed whenever I growled after nearly tripping over the damn things. Now I was sitting in the kitchen, eating cake while three comesuli cleaned up after a long day.

We'd entertained a committee from the Reth Alliance earlier—they were considering our application to join. We were jumping through the usual bureaucratic hoops, too. We had to have a working space station orbiting Le-Ath Veronis, and it was nearly finished and already operational.

We didn't tell the Alliance representatives that Larentii were putting most of it together for us. We'd hired work crews and some of our newly arrived vampires had expertise in that area, so all were working away to bring us into compliance.

Membership with the Reth Alliance would bring space travelers to Le-Ath Veronis and make it easier for the vampires living on Alliance worlds to come to us and petition for citizenship if they wanted it.

Kifirin, Connegar and I were in charge of the citizenship

applications from Alliance worlds. Those worlds recognized vampires as citizens in their own right; they were entitled to the rights granted by the law, just as any other citizen.

The Alliance worlds also had methods of tracking and controlling vampire criminals and they were treated just as any other criminal might be. Most of those worlds still had a hidden Vampire Council of some sort and they policed their own—up to a point.

We had nearly fifty thousand comesuli living on Le-Ath Veronis and many of them had become pregnant the moment they'd stepped onto the planet. Kifirin said the comesuli somehow recognized the need for more of their kind, as well as recognizing the fact that there was plenty of space and sustenance for them.

Merrill, Adam and Wlodek had (rather quickly) built a blood substitute manufacturing facility, to make up for what the comesuli couldn't provide to the resident vampires. They'd worked on the blood substitute itself, making it better—not just in taste but in nutrition. Our resident vampires were happy with what they were getting—fresh blood a couple days a month and a decent blood substitute the rest of the time.

The comesuli, too, had to be watched—they were a race that hadn't had sex before. Now they were anxious to have it (along with a vampire's bite), as often as possible.

We'd been forced to give them bracelets with two numbers. The months on Le-Ath Veronis were twenty-eight days in length and the two numbers on each bracelet indicated the two days a month a comesula could be bitten—giving them a two-week interval in between.

The taking of blood more often than that could weaken them. The pregnant ones were off-limits, too, both prior to the birth and for two months after. There were plenty of grumbling comesuli as a result.

Jaydevik Rath, King of Kifirin, the High Demons' planet, had brought Glindarok, his pregnant Queen, to stay at my palace. He didn't feel she was safe on Kifirin during her pregnancy.

The High Demons were having quite the trial getting their former Ra'Ak, High Demons and Elemaiya—Bright and Dark—to follow commands. None were willing employees, that much was certain. Many had deserted the city of Veshtul right away and Garde and Jayd had sent out hunting parties. When the deserters were found, they didn't live long.

Seventy thousand had been left on Kifirin when I finished with them, but now that number had been whittled down to sixty thousand. I got the idea that some of the newly humanoid inhabitants of Kifirin didn't take to cooking, cleaning, herding and farming.

Glinda, on the other hand, was about to deliver any day. Karzac, my Refizani mate and healer for the Saa Thalarr, was watching her like a hawk. Jeff, Merrill's son, and several other healers were doing the same.

"Is there any more of that?" Glinda waddled into the kitchen, rubbing her swollen belly with both hands. She was craving chocolate, so I'd instructed the cooks to make chocolate desserts as often as possible.

"I think so," I said, waving a hand at the comesuli, letting them know I'd get the cake—I didn't want to interrupt them. I pulled the keeper door open and pulled out the remaining cake and a knife.

I set a plate with a generous slice of cake on it in front of Glinda as she heaved herself onto a stool at the island. She was expecting twin girls and Jayd was a wreck whenever he was around her. Two female High Demons were cause for celebration, actually; they were almost as scarce as female vampires.

"I should have known," Karzac shuffled into the kitchen, closely followed by Rolfe.

"Do you want cake before I put it away?" I handed a glass of milk to Glinda; she was busy dipping into her cake.

Karzac pulled up another chair so I set a slice of cake in front of him with another glass of milk. Rolfe grinned at me and sat on the island. He was tall enough that it was like a bench to him.

"Do you need anything, Rolfe?" I asked while I was up.

"I've fed," he waved my offer away. I sat between Karzac and Glinda to finish my cake. No—I still hadn't gained all my weight back; Karzac grumbled about it, but my workdays were sixteen hours long. I didn't see how my situation might improve in the near future.

"How was your day?" I rubbed Karzac's back. He spent a few days every month with Devin and Grace; I had a calendar inside my closet with his schedule listed. With as many mates as I had, it was better to have a calendar. Otherwise, I'd never keep them sorted out.

Karzac always made sure I knew when he'd be spending the night. He was thorough about everything, I discovered. When he was with me, he was thorough about that, too. I held no doubts about his love for me.

He was also running a training program for the comesuli healers and was forced to bring them along slowly; they'd not had many improvements in their health care methods while they'd lived on Kifirin.

"The books Connegar supplied in the High Demon language are a big help," Karzac sighed. He and Jeff were working their tails off getting the medical facility built and supplied while they taught and oversaw others who were teaching.

Merrill's last turn, Joey Showalter, who'd worked as a healer for the Saa Thalarr, was teaching classes in anatomy and medical terminology, as well as computer technology. A few vampires were helping with that, in addition to many others who were taking the classes.

I'd even had a meeting with Griffin, Amara, Kiarra, Conner, Lynx and a few others about building a university. Well—we had vampires here who had lived through quite a bit of history—who better to teach something like that? Gabron could give lessons on Refizani history with his eyes shut, I think. Lynx sounded interested in putting the school for the arts together.

Jayd skipped in while we were talking and eating chocolate cake, Garde right behind him. Jayd lifted Glinda up the minute she finished her cake and took off with her. Garde sat in her vacated spot.

"I think there's one slice of cake left," I looked at him.

"I'll take it, but how about a sandwich first?" he begged. His dark hair was ruffled, as if he'd had a difficult day and hadn't stopped to worry about his appearance.

I got up and put a leftover meal together for him—it was roast beef and he was eating as if he were starved as soon as I set the plate down. I put the cake out for him, too, with a glass of wine.

"Let me guess—the kitchen help isn't all that great," I said.

"It's terrible—they burn everything," Garde grumbled around a mouthful of food.

"Maybe they'll improve when they get tired of eating it themselves," I said as I sat down again. Garde just snorted and kept eating. Jayd came back in a few minutes, so he received a plate of food.

Karzac and I left them in the kitchen—we were going to bed together and it was late already. Garde had a room at the palace if he wanted it, but I figured he'd go back to Kifirin when he finished eating —Jayd stayed with Glinda most nights and Garde wouldn't leave Kifirin untended.

"Karzac, do you think we should try to do something about the former Ra'Ak and Elemaiya on Kifirin?" I was yawning as I pulled pajamas from a drawer in my closet.

"Lissa, we don't need pajamas," Karzac was already undressed and putting his arms around me, nuzzling my neck.

"You look awful good," I turned in his arms and put my hands on his chest—it was lightly covered in crisp, brown hair.

"You'd look better without clothing," he murmured, letting a hand drop to the small of my back.

～

Earth

"Brenten, are you sure this is a good idea?" Amara studied Griffin's face. He seemed grimly determined about the idea, once he'd suggested it. Amara attempted to divert his attention, but he was obsessed with the whole thing. He was now claiming that his granddaughters and daughter should know as well. "Brenten, you may not like the information, once you have it."

"Love, I think they deserve to know, while she's still alive."

"But she treated you so poorly," Amara didn't finish her sentence.

"I know that better than anyone," Griffin ran fingers through his thick brown hair. "I tried to tell her when she was turning me out of camp that things would end badly for her. She laughed at me."

"There was no love in her," Amara came to put her arms around his waist. She gazed up into her mate's eyes. "Do you think it will do any good now, to take your daughter and granddaughters to see her?"

"At the most she has two hundred years left," Griffin sighed and hugged Amara tightly. "There is great unrest between the races that Lissa passed judgment over. She may not live the full two hundred years."

"You think any of those creatures will feel anything but contempt for those not of their race? If they had any compassion at all, they would never have turned their children away."

"I also wish to get information from her now," Griffin replied, leaning down to kiss the top of Amara's head.

"Do you think she will tell you, after all this time?" Amara murmured against Griffin's chest.

"I think Lissa can force her to tell me," Griffin murmured back.

Le-Ath Veronis

"Lissa Beth?" Don called my name.

My Don.

He only called me Lissa Beth when he missed me.

"Huh?" I realized I was dreaming as I said it, but it didn't alter the dream. Don was there and I was dreaming of him for the first time since he'd died. He was standing before me in our old living room, only he looked as he had when I'd first met him—with light-brown hair, brown eyes and an easy smile.

"I just wanted to see you again," he said. "Do you still love me?"

"Oh, honey," I said, trying to stop the sob that threatened. "I'll always love you."

"Lissa, I didn't mean to make you cry," he said.

"I know," I said, wiping tears away.

"You were always the strong one, Lissa Beth. I leaned on you for so long. I wanted to be a stronger man for you, be the one to support you, but it didn't turn out that way, did it?"

"We don't ever know what life is gonna hand us," I was still crying. "I don't regret a minute we spent together."

"Lissa Beth, I hope I get to hold you again, someday."

"Don't make me cry harder," I wept.

"I have to go," Don said. He winked out, just like that. I was crying when I woke and Karzac was cursing under his breath and pacing while Connegar held me in his arms.

"I'm all right," I wiped tears off my cheeks with shaking hands. "I just had a dream, that's all."

"Healer, go back to bed," Connegar was attempting to soothe Karzac and me. He was trilling when he settled me in the bed and Karzac pulled me against him, shushing me softly while Connegar sang the song that only the Larentii could sing. I was asleep again in minutes.

Drake and Drew were with me the following morning, along with three comesuli from the Queen's Guard. Yeah. Queen Lissa. Some days I wondered what I'd been thinking when I'd chosen this life. Of course, the alternative always reared its ugly head, so I sighed and kept walking.

We were inspecting the wheat crop, which was nearly ready for harvest. Early summer had come to Le-Ath Veronis and we stood near the equator, which meant there was daylight most of the time.

There was a wobble to the planet, so there were two hours of near dusk every day. The vampire cities were far enough south that they appeared to be in constant twilight—that magical hour after sunset.

The largest comesuli city was near the farms where we walked and it resembled what they'd had in Veshtul. Comesuli love color and the stones in the streets were many-colored, as were the walls of their dwellings.

Two smaller cities lay to the east and west of us, where the herders and tree farmers lived. Sernus, the farm overseer, walked beside me, chattering away about the wheat crop, which would be harvested in the next three weeks.

"Do you have plenty of storage for the harvest?" I asked. The crop looked to be a good one—the rains had been good and fields covered in ripening wheat stretched endlessly around us. I wondered briefly if Kifirin had a hand in that. I was just thankful the crops looked good so far and that we wouldn't be facing shortages.

"We have enough, Raona," Sernus smiled. "I have much experience in farming wheat. We will have more than enough to last us until next year's crop can be harvested."

"If you need anything, you only have to let me know," I said. Sernus was five-ten or so, one of the taller comesuli and he smiled down at me as I made the offer.

The harvest would be done by hand, but I wondered if I shouldn't ask for a meeting with my Inner Circle to see if we couldn't bring in equipment—I knew many worlds had solar-powered farming equipment and vehicles—the comesuli would probably appreciate the convenience.

It was my goal to make Le-Ath Veronis as self-sufficient as possible—I didn't want to depend on imported food to feed the comesuli. The sad truth is that we had hardly any industrialization at the moment; no manufacturing other than handmade goods, tools and such, aside from the blood substitute factory.

Equipment, better tools and vehicles would make things so much easier for the comesuli, who hadn't had anything like that before and therefore didn't know to ask for it. I made a mental note to send information to the comesuli overseers soon—as to what was available and how it might help them in their work.

Flavio and Gabron were also suggesting we allow tourism. I was having trouble with that—I didn't want a bunch of people on the planet looking for the thrill of the bite and I sure as hell didn't want any of them trying to get turned while they were here.

I had visions of the seriously ill—those wealthy enough to come, anyway, trying to find a way past their mortality. The comesuli would become vampire if anyone would.

"The farms are beautiful," I smiled at Sernus. He was beaming as we walked toward the barns. The plowing oxen were grazing peacefully in a field nearby; they would be used to pull the wagons when the wheat was harvested and hauled to the threshing floor.

I thanked Sernus for giving us the tour before turning to my Falchani twins. Drew gave me a slight smile as we folded to the next farm. Avocado trees, fruit trees, nut trees—they grew in huge groves and many had only the barest beginnings of fruit upon them.

My comesuli guards were exhausted when we finished our inspections for the day, but their counterparts were happy to see their monarch.

Those who worked the farms and weren't pregnant made their way to the vampire cities twice a month. They were already forming attachments to this vampire or that. They called the bite the rapture, since it gave them sexual release.

Drake folded us home after the inspections were over—I think I was as tired as the comesuli; I just didn't want to admit it. "Lissa, cara, you look worn out," Gavin said. He and Tony were waiting when we arrived.

Dinner was ready and most of my crew was there, as were Glinda and Jayd. The twins and I had to hurry and change; dinners were more formal and the only time when everyone at the palace would gather for a meal. It was only when I sneaked into the kitchen after hours that I could slump over the huge island and have a snack.

We were halfway through dinner when I noticed that Glinda was merely picking at her food. She stood when dinner was over and her water broke. Garde arrived swiftly, attempting to calm Jayd.

Jayd demanded that the babies be born on Kifirin, so that's how I found myself upon the High Demons' planet, sitting on a bench outside the royal suite and waiting for Jayd and Glinda's twins to arrive.

High Demon guards patrolled the hallways and outside the palace—Garde had no desire for any humanoids on Kifirin to attempt a murder or a coup while the royal family was in such a vulnerable position.

"Lissa, staying awake and fretting won't make those babies come any quicker," Tony sat on the bench next to me and draped an arm around my shoulder.

He'd traded places with Gavin—they were helping patrol the palace. Karzac, Jeff, and several Larentii were inside the royal suite, tending to the birth. I deliberately stopped myself from Looking—it was something that should be free from interference.

"You're awake," I pointed out the obvious. Tony grinned. I laid my head on his shoulder and closed my eyes for a moment.

~

Beliphar

"The substitute will always nourish you, but it will never taste the same as the real thing," Jeral informed Davan as Davan drank thirstily from the offered bottle.

Davan awoke on the fifth day to find his vampire sire with him inside the secured cell. Davan drank two bottles of the fluid before slaking his thirst completely. Once he was finished with his meal, Jeral set about teaching Davan how he should behave around humanoids.

~

Le-Ath Veronis

"Lissa, we can reschedule this meeting." Gabron had my elbow as we walked toward the library. I'd gotten two hours of sleep after Glinda's girls came—Gavin insisted we return to Le-Ath Veronis and he'd put me in bed himself. Karzac stayed on Kifirin to care for Glinda and the newborns.

"Let's get this over with," I sighed. I probably looked like hell—I hadn't paid attention to my face in the mirror and Giff had dressed me—I didn't care what I wore. Flavio was coming with the City Councils—all the members from Earth combined with the members from Refizan.

Council members from other cities were also coming, to hammer out the articles of governance. Gabron was going to help; Pheligar was sending a Larentii advisor.

"He's young," Pheligar said, describing the Larentii in question. "Only two hundred fifty years of age, but he is skilled at translating languages and has a feel for intentions behind words. He wants to work as a diplomat and this is the only world where Ferrigar will allow it—we do not involve ourselves in politics."

"His name?" I asked.

"Reemagar," Pheligar had replied. "You may ask Grace about his mother, sometime." I didn't know what Pheligar was trying to tell me and at the time, I'd been too busy to *Look*. I remembered his words now as we found the Larentii waiting for us outside the doors to the library.

"Reemagar?" I asked. He nodded solemnly to me and opened the doors using power.

We only broke twice during the lengthy day; blood substitute was handed out both times and I drank it with the rest of them, although it didn't do a thing to help with my exhaustion.

Gabron ordered that coffee be brought in and he, Flavio and I had a cup while we were debating what the age of adulthood should be for the comesuli.

"The comesuli consider a child an adult at age forty," I said for perhaps the tenth time.

"But that applies to apprenticeships and employment," Hervis of Refizan pointed out. "I have asked the comesuli that serve the City Council and they seem to think that age twenty-five is old enough for the bite."

This debate, once it was over, would establish the age at which a vampire could legally drink from a comesula, so there would be no doubt when enforcing the laws regarding drinking from a child.

"I still think that's the equivalent of a fifteen-year-old," I grumped. I needed my physician here, to give us information on when a comesula was completely grown and past their formative years, but he was off-planet at the moment. My brain was working slowly, though, until it finally hit me.

Mom? I sent to Amara. She'd been a healer for a hundred thousand years, and she'd been involved in children's hospitals and children's causes for a very long time. Maybe she could help me out with this.

Lissa? Her mindspeech sounded slightly surprised. Probably because I called her Mom.

We're having a bit of an argument over how old the comesuli are when they're fully-grown and capable of handling blood donation, I returned. *Can you help us out with this?*

She didn't reply, she came herself and knocked discreetly on the door. Gabron rose from his seat to let her in. Amara is so beautiful—I knew what Griffin had seen in her the minute I'd met her the first time.

Every vampire in the room stopped and stared as she entered the Library. Gabron offered her the seat next to mine and then sat beside her.

"This is Amara, who has been a healer for a very long time," I introduced her. "She is also my stepmother. She will be speaking truth to you when she answers your questions." I was being Queen, now, although I was exhausted and shaky as hell.

"In your opinion, Lady Mother, what is the age when a comesula is fully grown and capable of handling blood donation?" Hervis asked. He was the biggest proponent for the twenty-five year plan.

"Their bones and organs come to full growth around the age of twenty-nine," Amara smiled at the gathering. We had nearly a hundred vampires in the room—Le-Ath Veronis was growing nicely and the Councils from eight cities were represented.

"The comesuli are slow to come to adulthood, since their average lifespan is six hundred years, barring accidental death," Amara continued. "If you take blood from them between the ages of twenty-four and twenty-nine, it should only be done once every two months and that may be difficult to track. It is my suggestion that you place the mandatory death penalty for drinking from a child at age twenty-three and below. Perhaps a severe punishment could be handed out if a vampire drinks from a comesula twenty-four through twenty-eight years of age, as long as it is once only. More severe punishment, up to the death penalty, might be considered if the vampire repeats the offense."

Reemagar translated Amara's words for all present, one language at a time. It amazed me that he kept track of all of it so easily. When the last language had been delivered, I saw nodding around the room. Most of the vampires spoke Alliance common, but it was considered polite and they understood it better if their own language was employed.

"I'm pleased with that suggestion," I said, smiling at Amara.

"I am grateful for the explanation," Hervis nodded courteously to Amara. "I think I can come to terms with this."

"I will write up the proposal and send electronic copies to all of you," Gabron said. "Prepare any suggestions for revisions and return them to me. I hope to have this finished by the time we meet next week."

The meeting broke up after that; eventually, only Flavio, Gabron, Amara and Reemagar remained.

"Child, you are exhausted," Amara said as I rose from my seat.

"We had two baby girls born last night," I yawned as discreetly as I could. "Reemagar, I can't thank you enough—this would have gone on until midnight if you hadn't been here. Are you going to stay with us or fold back to the Larentii homeworld?"

Reemagar was only a bit over eight feet in height—one of the shorter Larentii I'd seen—and he smiled when I thanked him. "I wish to stay upon Le-Ath Veronis, but I will fold to the light half to feed. Where shall I sleep while I am here?"

"I'll find a room for you, just send mindspeech when you get back," I was yawning again.

"Come, you need something besides blood substitute," Amara coaxed, so we made our way to the kitchens after Reemagar folded away.

I only ate a light meal and Reemagar was back before I finished. Flavio folded away after the meal so Gabron, Amara and I found a room in the Royal Wing—there were fourteen suites in that wing. Reemagar was perfectly happy with his suite and set about enlarging the bed right away, to accommodate his height. "I will bring in sufficient clothing, Raona. Please let me know whenever you need my services."

"I appreciate your help," I said. "I need a nap now, before I keel over," I patted his arm. He nodded politely at me and we left him.

"Lissa, allow me to carry you," Gabron murmured in my ear as he, Amara and I walked toward my own suite.

"Lissa, I should go," Amara stopped and smiled at me.

"All right," I was yawning again. I was afraid I was going to crack a jaw, the yawn was so wide.

"Get some rest." Amara leaned in and kissed my cheek before folding away. Gabron lifted me the minute she was gone and I think I was asleep before he got me to my suite.

CHAPTER 2

*K*ifirin

"I hate this." Jayd paced before his oldest brother Gardevik for perhaps the fiftieth time. "She and my daughters should be enjoying adoration and pampering here on Kifirin, yet the servants we have are surly at best and murderous at worst. I cannot keep her here and our children are not safe."

"We knew there would be problems, I just had no idea how difficult these creatures could be," Garde agreed, keeping his voice soft.

Glinda was sleeping in the bedroom of the suite—he and Jayd were in the reception area. Cleo and Shannon had come to help with the twin girls, allowing Karzac, Jeff and Joey some much-needed rest after a long night.

"I can't rule from Le-Ath Veronis and I can't keep Glinda here. It is too dangerous," Jayd snorted, smoke pouring from his nostrils. His Thifilathi was agitated and threatening to turn.

"Perhaps we should ask Lissa if there is something she can do," Garde suggested, attempting to calm his brother.

"I hate to ask her for anything," Jayd muttered. "I know that most of this is our fault, but it still angers me that things are not better on Kifirin."

"Most of this is not our fault," Garde replied. Jayd looked up at his brother's words. "All of this is our fault," Garde added, causing Jayd to snort again. "Granted we were younger, brother, when Lendevik sat in his throne room and pronounced the doom of the Dark Realm with his indifference and lack of caring. We could have spoken up. Nedevik was the only one who did so and he was ridiculed for his efforts. We watched from our place of safety while all those worlds fell. We then reaped the benefits of Le-Ath Veronis' fall, in the form of the commons. We no longer had to do for ourselves, brother. They took all our tasks upon themselves while we wallowed in the luxury. The cost of that luxury has now come due and we barely have the skills to feed ourselves."

"You are paying for your continued indifference," Griffin folded in to join the conversation. He still felt animosity toward Jayd but attempted to overcome it. "You collected most of the profits from the labor of the comesuli, yet you never put any of that money toward improvements in manufacturing or anything else that might have brought this world into alignment with others. Even the cloth for clothing is still woven by hand. Nothing changed since Lendevik laid down the initial laws."

"So I'm supposed to just go out and build factories?" Jayd snapped.

"I did not say that, but if you expect to keep your world alive, you must turn your thoughts in that direction. Do not do anything in haste—these things must be carefully considered. My daughter is doing the same thing for Le-Ath Veronis—deciding what is needed now, what will be needed in the future and then asking for ideas and suggestions from the Councils now in place before acting. Do not tell me that your High Demons don't skip off this world for pleasure. They are aware of the amenities that other worlds enjoy."

"Do we have funds for this?" Garde looked at his brother.

"The accounts are in total disarray, brother," Jayd sighed. "The treasury was always in High Demon hands; none of the commons were allowed access."

"More than likely because Lendevik and Rorevik had no desire for the comesuli to see how they were taken advantage of," Griffin said. "That does not include the thousand years that Glinda's eldest brother held the throne and raped the planet."

"Then what do you suggest we do?" Jayd asked. He was annoyed and made no attempt to hide it. A bit of smoke drifted from his nostrils.

"I suggest you go to my daughter," Griffin gave Jayd a hard stare. "Ask her for one of two things—either to move the High Demons to Le-Ath Veronis and establish your kingdom there, or ask her to move your current humanoid population to the world once occupied by the Dark Elemaiya. They will never gate away from it and they will live or die there by their own efforts. That choice, of course, will require that either you send your High Demons out to farm and herd and weave and cook, or you will be forced to hire new servants and pay them a fair wage. That may also be the case upon Le-Ath Veronis, but the farms there could help support your population—I believe the comesuli would be happy to sell to you at a fair price."

"We need to find a way to bring in income, instead of paying it out," Garde suggested. "No matter what our choice is from now on, that is the way it must be."

"I think my daughter speaks fondly of the cheeses that were made here," a slight smile tugged at Griffin's mouth. "And she liked the cane sugar she had to work with when making desserts. Those are two viable exports."

"Beef is highly sought after by Reth Alliance worlds," Garde agreed. "All their planets are highly industrialized and their beef is not organic or high quality. Ours is both."

"All of your produce would be considered organic," Griffin's smile widened. "You merely have to find someone to tend the crops."

"Can we offer citizenship, perhaps, to a world in need of it?" Jayd asked. "If we must hire, I want those who desire to come and are happy with what we can offer."

"Perhaps. There are many worlds classified as not worth saving, though there is a small percentage of the population that is still good and decent. Perhaps you could ask Kyler, Kiarra and some of the others to bring those to you. Of course, you have to rid your planet of the ones you have now. They have not taken advantage of the opportunities they were given."

"I like this idea," Jayd nodded thoughtfully. Garde also agreed. "How quickly can this be accomplished?"

"I have to approach my daughter, first," Griffin's smile disappeared.

"She still has reservations, doesn't she?" Garde knew what Griffin's expression meant.

"Where I am concerned, she does." Griffin didn't elaborate.

"I will come with you, if you want," Garde offered.

"So we can share in the frigid indifference?" Griffin asked.

"Something like that," Garde nodded.

"I'll settle for that," Griffin agreed.

Le-Ath Veronis

"Raona?" Roff's voice was barely a whisper.

"Hmmm?" I was trying to swim up from the depths of a deep sleep. I felt his fingers on my face, gently stroking, and then the kiss.

"Roff," I wound my arms around his neck.

"Raona, your meal is ready and the others are waiting." I let my arms drop away.

"I don't wannoo," I mumbled, trying to force my eyes open.

"Raona, please speak clearly," Roff teased. "You know I have difficulty understanding your slang."

I blinked up at him. "You understand me just as well as anybody else," I touched his mouth with my fingers.

"Come, my love. We will eat with the others and then you may sleep again. We must also discuss off-days."

"Who wants off-days?" I sat up and rubbed my eyes. Roff was supporting me with an arm around my shoulders.

"We must discuss off-days for those who are not getting them," Roff said, coaxing me off the bed.

"Who isn't getting off-days?" I blinked at him, confused. Every comesuli was supposed to get two off-days in every seven-day week. If somebody wasn't getting them, their supervisor might get a personal and angry visit from the Queen.

"Come to dinner and we will discuss this over food," he pulled me to my feet. Giff, who'd been standing by (I just hadn't noticed her yet), had clothing ready.

"Giff, baby, are you all right?" I asked as she and Roff proceeded to pull my nightdress over my head. Giff and Gavin must have put it on me while I was asleep after the Council meeting; I didn't remember doing it.

"Raona, I am quite fine, as is Rolfe." Today was one of her days for the bite and I figured that had already happened. Giff was smiling too much for it to be otherwise.

I was dressed in a comfortable tunic and loose pants. Giff wanted to put shoes on my feet but I convinced her to let me out of the bedroom wearing socks that matched my outfit. Roff escorted me to the dining room.

We had guests, I learned, the moment we walked in—Griffin, Amara, Kiarra, Adam, Merrill, Kyler and Flavio were all there, in addition to my bunch. Garde had also come, I noticed.

"How are Glinda and the babies?" I asked, first thing. I'd only gotten a brief glimpse after they were born two nights earlier. Two long days of Council meetings had happened since then and I'd managed to get a brief nap before dinner this time.

"They are very well," Amara smiled at me. She'd gone to see them, I could tell.

Roff got me seated at the head of the table. The other end was for Kifirin, but he only showed up occasionally. Usually the seats to my right and left were for the ones who were scheduled to spend the night with me. Right was first, left for the night after that.

The soup course came and Garde spoke up. "I have a huge favor to ask, Lissa."

"You want an apple pie?" I quirked an eyebrow.

"That too," he smiled. "But Jayd, Griffin and I talked earlier and we came to the conclusion that the ex-Ra'Ak and the Elemaiya are not going to accept their current situation. Jayd fears for Glinda and his daughters."

"Yeah," I set my soupspoon down and stared into my fragile, china bowl of broth. "It's not working, I know. I messed up. I'm sorry."

"We have a suggestion," Griffin said softly.

"What is it?" I looked up at him—his eyes were more hazel than brown, with gold flecks in them. I'd gotten my blue eyes and my hair color from my mother.

"The Dark Elemaiyan planet is uninhabited," Griffin said. "I would like to send all of them there, with your permission. Jayd and Garde are asking Kyler and Kiarra to bring in humanoids from a few worlds listed as not worth saving. They'll only take the ones who still have redeeming qualities and the desire to work for their citizenship on Kifirin."

"I know it's not practical, but can we look for the ones who have children?" I begged.

"Kyler and I have already discussed that," Kiarra answered my question. "Those are the ones we will select first and we'll make sure they are prepared for the hardship and the massive changes. A few worlds are on the brink of self-destruction and we will target them first."

"Good," I nodded and lifted my spoon again. "When are you doing this?"

"Jayd wants what we have on Kifirin gone as quickly as possible," Garde was tearing into the bread set at his elbow.

We were served by comesuli and vampires tonight. A few vampires had experience in the culinary arts and didn't mind cooking or serving. Some, like Adam, had owned restaurants and were looking to do so again. They were the strongest faction promoting the idea of tourism.

"I think we can get them relocated beginning tomorrow," Griffin said. "It may take a few days to get all the transfers done. The new residents can be brought in after that. We may need to borrow some of the comesuli, though, to teach the trades needed. Glendes of Grey

House is begging for oxberry wine and has offered quite a bit for twenty cases. I think that oxberry wine, cheese, cane sugar and beef could be major exports," Griffin smiled as he cut into the quail served to him.

"You'll have to get Roff to teach them how to make wine," I said. "And tell Glendes I'll share what I have at the moment—Shadow can take it back with him when he comes for a visit."

"Raona, we are experimenting with oxberries here, but I do not know if the soil is the same to get the proper flavor," Roff informed me. I nodded at him—it probably wasn't the same. We might be forced to buy oxberries from the High Demons so Roff could make wine.

"The Reth Alliance will have to inspect all facilities before allowing export," Merrill said.

"We probably won't be ready for that for at least a year," Garde offered. "That may give us time to work the ash from Baetrah's eruption into the soil and plant cane crops. The barns and buildings on the cane farms will also have to be cleaned up—what still stands, anyway. It will take much work, but Weth and Foth have offered for those lands. If we put Lord Nedevik in charge, I think he will make his High Demons work just like everyone else. He knows how to plant and harvest."

"I like him," Roff said quietly. "He purchased oxberry wine from me many times and occasionally came to help pick berries."

"My brothers still run the cattle herds," Garde said. "We used to depend heavily on comesuli help, but we worked alongside them, much of the time. The beef supply has been uninterrupted."

"The wool that the rugs were made from was really soft," I said. "Orliff's parent made rugs and they were beautiful. That's something else you might be able to export."

"I think both planets should work together," Adam suggested. "Since Orliff's father and the other comesuli weavers know how to make the rugs, the wool could come first to Le-Ath Veronis and then the rugs could be exported from here. The oxberry wine as well—Roff could oversee his own winery, with the berries coming from Kifirin."

"I am in agreement with that—this would mean fewer facilities to be inspected by the Alliance," Garde said. "That would still leave us with cheese, beef and cane sugar as major exports, with the wool and oxberries offered exclusively to Le-Ath Veronis for wine and rug making."

"I'm good with that," I said and tore a bit of bread off in my fingers. It was herb bread and very good. I was going to have to introduce Cheedas and the vampires to olive oil and balsamic vinegar as a dip for bread.

"Roff, do you want your own winery? I think you could do very well with this. I can see exclusive restaurants offering oxberry wine as a specialty. I think you could be very wealthy in no time."

"I might like to try this," Roff smiled. Giff was nodding hopefully at her father. Little Toff was being cared for by another comesula, so Giff and Roff could have their evening meal.

"Adam and I would like to help put up the winery, as an investment," Merrill said. He'd tasted Roff's wine and thought it was exceptional. Merrill had an eye for good wines; he always kept the best cellar. If he wanted to invest, he knew it was a winner.

"Roff, you need to get with Adam and Merrill. When will the oxberries be ready for harvesting on Kifirin?" I asked.

"In two weeks on the Northern Continent," he slumped dejectedly in his chair.

"Don't worry about it, okay?" I rubbed his shoulders.

"We may be able to come up with something," Adam chuckled.

"Uh-huh," I said. "Roff, you may have your winery by tomorrow afternoon."

"Perhaps in two to three days—we'll consult with Roff and look into other wineries to see what is needed," Adam said. "It'll go up quickly after that."

"Hear that, honey?" Roff smiled at my words and leaned in to kiss me.

"Now, about the other business," Karzac sliced into his rack of lamb, which was the latest course. I was full after the quail and silently attempted to auction off my lamb to someone else.

Drew winked at me. I kept a little for myself and passed the rest down to him and Drake. They'd been out training the vampires and comesuli that made up our new palace guards and army, so I knew they'd be famished.

"What other business?" I asked, tasting the lamb. It was delicious, but I was about to pop and we still had dessert coming. The strawberry soufflé would have to wait until later.

"The off-days business," Gavin growled.

"Yeah, who isn't getting off-days? And why haven't I heard about this before? I may have words with the ones responsible," I grumped.

"Then you need to get a mirror," Tony snickered. "And I want to watch you chew yourself out." My fork was still in my hand as I gawked at Tony.

"Since when does the boss get a day off?" I said and busied myself with a forkful of lamb.

"Since the entire Inner Circle decided," Karzac said. "Lissa, you have yet to gain an ounce, you push yourself for sixteen hours or more at a stretch and are generally asleep the moment your head hits the pillow. I can't say I'm completely familiar with your power, but it isn't doing anything to keep you from exhaustion."

"When we confine ourselves to a corporeal shape, it drains us," Kifirin appeared and sat in his seat at the opposite end of the table. "I did that for a very long time and it almost drained me completely. That is why I slept, avilepha," Kifirin accepted a plate from a vampire server. "You will drive yourself into the same state if you are not careful. I have discovered that if I spend one or two hours each day in my energy state, it rests me and I can continue as you see me now."

"But I don't know how to do that," I said. Honestly, I was afraid to do it, since I was unfamiliar with the concept and afraid to go *Looking*.

"I know this, m'hala. I will teach you." Kifirin was devouring his quail, a satisfied smile playing about his lips.

"Back to off-days," Karzac grumbled.

"Karzac, I don't know when I could take any. And I've wanted to find a place in this palace for a pool and hot tub and I haven't even had time to go look."

Everybody at the table was staring at me, now. Gabron cleared his throat. "What?" I asked.

"You have a pool and hot tub," Tony said. "And if you'd take five minutes for yourself, you'd know that."

"I take time," I grumped, feeling embarrassed. "Where the hell is the pool and hot tub?"

"Between the Royal Wing and the Guest Wing," Gabron sighed. "I thought you had the ability to reach out for information, my darling."

"I do have that."

"She's *Looking* for other things," Karzac was at his grumpy best.

"I will clear your calendar for tomorrow and then we will decide on regular days off," Gabron went on.

"But what about the City Councils?" We were still hip deep in hammering out universal laws. With this diverse a population from eight different planets so far, everything had to be woven together into whole cloth. We weren't anywhere close, yet.

"We need days off, too," Flavio weighed in.

"All right, what do you suggest?" I glared at the third most beautiful man I'd ever met, daring him to complain. He gave me a lovely smile. While that might make most women swoon, it wasn't doing a thing for me at the moment. Kifirin was smiling and ducking his head to keep from laughing at me.

"A decree from the Queen, stating that the City Councils take the week endings off from meetings," Flavio said.

"A Royal Decree," Kyler nodded enthusiastically. I was only now realizing that I'd been cutting into her time with Flavio.

"Great. What am I supposed to do, wave my arms or something?" I grumbled.

"That would work for me," Flavio chuckled.

"You need a royal seal; you don't have one," Gabron offered.

"One that can balance a ball on his nose," Tony snickered.

"I'm coming over there," I threw my napkin down and misted toward Tony.

"Lissy, we can't wrestle on the floor, think of the neighbors," Tony said when I turned up right next to his chair.

"If the neighbors complain, I can put them in a headlock, too," I tugged on Tony's ear.

"Lissa, please be more circumspect," Gavin was seated next to Tony and chose to hand out the usual chastisement.

"Fine. Any other complaints before I leave? No? Good." I misted away.

~

"Now where the hell did she go?" Karzac demanded, standing and angry in an instant.

"She is tired. Now isn't a good time to draw attention to what you think of as her shortcomings," Griffin offered.

"Then there won't be a good time," Drake said. "And it probably wasn't a good idea to do this in front of everybody," he added. "She's good if you tell her with just the Inner Circle, but she gets embarrassed with others around."

"I should learn to hold my tongue," Gavin muttered.

"Where's Lissa?" Erland Morphis folded in.

"Have a seat, warlock," Griffin pushed an empty chair out with power. Erland sat and someone came to serve him. "We don't know where she went; she left a few seconds ago."

"Warlock, when you finish eating, we will visit the Dark Elemaiyan planet," Kifirin said. The Dark Lord was halfway through his rack of lamb. Erland was given the update on Lissa and current events while he ate.

~

Evensun

I walked through a field on Evensun, the Dark Elemaiyan world. Twilight was falling across the section of the planet where I walked and I wondered why they'd traveled away from it.

Stars were beginning to appear over the eastern horizon and they winked and twinkled over my head as I gazed about. I wouldn't have walked away from this place, I don't think. I did a little *Looking* and there was no construction anywhere.

Several thousand years had passed since the Dark Elemaiya had left their world. Had they found that gating to other worlds held more appeal than the world they'd stood upon, or did they have the desire to travel so much that staying in one spot was unbearable?

It mattered no longer; they were going to live out their days upon Evensun. I wasn't sure they deserved such a beautiful world, but they were getting it, nonetheless.

"Avilepha, do you think we need to build some sort of shelter for them?" Kifirin had come and was now taking in the planet and what it offered. Everyone else from the dinner table followed Kifirin; they appeared in twos and threes around us.

"Kifirin, my handsome love, they have had too much handed to them already. Let them worry over their own shelter. Let them fashion their own tools and find their own meals." I shook my head at the thought of providing them with anything other than what we had already.

"There are a few young among them," Griffin said, wading through the grasses to my side.

"Are there any that are quarter-blood?"

"No, those were sent away with the sixteen," Griffin replied.

I'd sent sixteen to another world—the handful that hadn't wanted to participate in the Elemaiyan attempt to grab Fox, who was a quarter-blood and the Ka'Mirai.

"Good. How old is the youngest among the others?"

"One is seven, another is fourteen and a third is sixteen."

"What do you suggest, then?"

"I'd like to speak with them and feel them out before we cast them to the winds with the others."

"Then we'll go tomorrow," I sighed.

"I wish you to speak with one other," Griffin said.

"Who is that?" I asked.

"You will see. I will come for you three hours after the sun is up on Kifirin."

"All right," I agreed.

"What do you think of this world?" Kifirin asked.

"I think it's beautiful," I said. "Why did they leave it? I don't understand."

"The Elemaiya were always afflicted with wanderlust," Kifirin replied. "They were never satisfied with staying in one place." It sounded as if he was withholding information, but I didn't press him on the matter.

"Too bad, that's what they're getting now," I said.

"Avilepha, I have my doubts that they will ever be self-supporting as a race. They have lived off other races for so long, now. The Ra'Ak, too. They have vague memories of what they were before, but as you have likely discovered, the Copper Ra'Ak only allowed the strongest and most dominant to live. The only one who did not fit that mold was Gilfraith and I have yet to determine how he managed to slip through and become Ra'Ak."

"I'm glad he did. I think the answer to your question is love, Kifirin. Gilfraith loved. Both in the past and in the present. All you have to do is watch him around Fox. He would die for her."

"I think you may be correct, my love." Kifirin put his arms around me and nuzzled my neck.

"This is very nice, I have never been here before," Connegar folded in and looked around. Reemagar folded in right behind him.

"Hi, honey," I went to take one of Connegar's hands in both of mine.

"Do I understand correctly that the ones upon Kifirin will be coming here?" he smiled down at me.

"Yeah. Seems like a waste, doesn't it?" I asked. The night sky over our heads was such a perfect deep blue and even more stars were winking and glittering now.

"We will see what they do with it," Connegar replied.

"If they do not recognize the gift, then I pity them," Reemagar remarked, coming to stand beside us.

"Me, too," I smiled at him. There seemed to be a sadness in him and I hadn't run into that before with a Larentii.

Before we left, though, I wanted to place a benediction upon the planet itself. Sort of an apology, if you will, before handing it over to those who would likely curse it instead of appreciating it for what it was—a lovely, unspoiled world. I sang *How Can I Keep From Singing*, while a light breeze rippled the tall grass around my legs and the stars trembled over our heads.

~

My nights with Roff were so restful—he was content to let me sleep with my head on his shoulder. Someday, though, he was going to be a winged vampire. In the meantime, he loved me and that was good enough.

Griffin was there, right on time, with Amara, Kyler and Cleo the next morning. Roff and Giff had gotten me up, showered and dressed me and then herded me off to breakfast.

Gabron canceled my meetings for the day and then sent out a decree (after I signed it), declaring the two days at the end of every week as off-days for all involved in politics on Le-Ath Veronis.

Gardevik and two other High Demons came with us, once we arrived at the palace in Veshtul. Yurevik Weth and Dremevik Greth had blades strapped to their backs and were prepared to protect us, although the weapons wouldn't be needed if they went Thifilathi.

"What do you want?" Those words greeted us as we walked up to the woman. Griffin had folded us to her—she was sitting on a bench outside what had once been a comesuli bakery.

My nose told me that the rising bread had soured and insects had invaded the flour and other grains. The woman, however, was beautiful and would be for years to come. One day, age would find her, though, and she would die—if she didn't manage to kill herself with inaction before then. Of course, with the murderous tendencies of the former Ra'Ak, she could always fall by another's hand.

"We wish to speak with your child," Griffin said.

"Callan!" The woman shouted. A young boy came running. He

looked too frightened to do otherwise. He already appeared malnourished.

"He is seven years of age?" Griffin asked. I could have answered that for him but held my tongue.

"I don't recall his exact age," the woman snapped. "It doesn't matter, does it?"

"Not anymore," I snapped back. The boy and I disappeared.

"Where are we?" Callan asked, as we landed on another world.

"On a world called Mendenath," I replied, taking his hand. "Some of your family is here and I'm going to leave you with them." I looked down into his cherubic face. He had his mother's dark hair and green eyes.

"Will they have food?" Callan asked. He was hungry, I knew.

"I hope so," I told him. We walked through an open field for a little way until we found a makeshift village. Someone was cooking; I could smell a simple stew boiling as we walked up.

"Callan?" A woman pushed back the flap of a tent fashioned of animal skins.

"Aunt Zela?" Callan let go of my hand and ran to her. She pulled him into an embrace.

"He's hungry," I called out.

"I know," the boy's aunt replied. "We'll feed him."

There wasn't any need for me to stay; I knew she'd take care of the boy. I folded back to Kifirin. "Sorry," I apologized. "I took him to his Aunt Zela."

"She always was soft," the woman snorted.

"Nothing wrong with that," I said. "We're done here." Griffin folded us to the next spot.

I knew right away that the fourteen-year-old was as hard as his mother. We didn't stay long. The sixteen-year-old was the same. It happened quickly with these, looked like. We left them.

Griffin folded us one last time. We were outside a shop that had once sold pottery. A few items remained—things the comesula proprietor hadn't bothered to take with him. Nobody was sitting out front at this one. Briefly, I wondered what Griffin wanted here. When the woman walked out the door and I got a whiff, I knew.

Kyler was about to go crazy and Cleo looked ill. Amara attempted to comfort both of Griffin's granddaughters. Griffin was angry, his arms crossed tightly over his chest. Gardevik and our two High Demon guards had no idea what was going on. They knew as soon as the woman opened her mouth.

"Well, Brenten, you brought this on us, didn't you?"

CHAPTER 3

*K*ifirin

I stared at my grandmother for a second or two before I let her have it. "He didn't have anything to do with this," I spat. "You did well enough, bringing this on yourselves."

"And who are you?" She dismissed me with a contemptuous blink of her beautiful, gold eyes. Kyler and Cleo had those eyes. It might explain the gold flecks in Griffin's eyes, too.

"The one who put you here," I answered her question, reining in my temper. One more step and she'd be within range of my claws. That wouldn't do—I had a feeling my father wanted something from her. I hoped it wasn't love or affection—she was incapable of either.

She called me an extremely unkind name in the Elemaiyan language. I didn't care. "You will answer all of Daddy's questions honestly, from this point forward," I laid compulsion and put power in it. I'd probably shocked the hell out of Griffin by calling him Daddy, but we needed to close ranks against this one. She blinked at me a time or two as my compulsion settled over her brain.

"You're his daughter." She said it flatly.

"Obviously. Daddy, she's all yours." I stepped back and motioned

Griffin forward. Garde was at my back, suddenly, his hands on my shoulders while Griffin asked his mother questions.

"Who is my father?" That was his first question and I wanted to weep. I'd only waited forty-eight years to find out who my father was. Griffin was over a hundred thousand and he still didn't know.

"You are fortunate that she placed the compulsion." My grandmother hissed, cutting her eyes toward me. "Your father—well, he placed a spell of his own, when I refused to stay with him and refused to bring you back to him. He told me I couldn't tell anyone unless I brought you back. I told him to go fuck himself." She laughed at the memory.

"Brenten, your father was Karathian. Wylend Arden was his name. A powerful Warlock he was—more powerful than even I guessed. Not many could place a spell on any of us and have it hold like that," she snorted at the thought.

"You are only half Elemaiya," Griffin went on, as if the information regarding his father was of no consequence. I knew better—he was rattled but refused to allow his mother to see how she'd upset him. "What happened to your parents?"

"My Elemaiyan mother died. As did my sorry Traveler father. They kept me away from my people until I was nearly twenty."

"You killed them—your parents." I gave her a hard look.

"They kept me away from my people," my grandmother snapped. "They deserved what they got."

"Do I have any sisters or brothers?" Griffin asked his next question.

"All are dead except for one half-brother and he may be gone soon," she laughed humorlessly. "I left him at an orphanage on Beliphar more than fifty years ago. Good luck on finding him."

"You are pathetic," Kyler growled. "I should release your particles."

"No, sister." Cleo stepped forward and she was shining. What I saw next even I wasn't expecting. Cleo had wings. Beautiful wings that spread about her, their shining whiteness glowing in the morning sun upon Kifirin. Cleo reached out and touched her great-grandmother on the forehead, causing the woman to shriek in agony and then drop, weeping, to the ground.

"You will now know what you have dealt to others and you will search for the love you denied but it will not come to you. Ask not for pity from those who were once your family. It will not be granted." Cleo's words held Power. I had to *Look* to see where it came from. Cleo had a direct connection to something on the other side.

"What's her name?" I almost whispered my question to Griffin.

"Narissa," Griffin's voice was also soft as he watched his mother weep. We left her there, folded up on the ground and rocking herself.

I think Kyler took us back to the High Demon palace; I wasn't sure Griffin was able at the moment. He was finally allowing the information his mother had given to sink in, with devastating results. His hands shook and he might have been close to hyperventilating. "Em-pah, what are you going to do?" Kyler and Amara led him to a chair once we were inside a suite at the palace.

Garde sent the two High Demon guards away and stayed with us. Griffin shook with shock and I wasn't prepared to console him. I did know what I could do, however.

"I'm calling Erland," I said, and sent out mindspeech.

"Lissa, my love, dare I hope you've changed your mind?" Erland appeared in seconds after I sent mindspeech. He looked so hopeful as he took my hand and kissed it. The smile he gave me was blinding, too. Most women would have fallen to the floor in an orgasmic faint at that smile.

"Erland, I haven't, that isn't why I called you," I blew out a breath. Amara was doing what she could for her mate and Cleo and Kyler were both sitting with Griffin. They each held a hand, squeezing it tightly.

"What has happened?" Erland knew something was up, now.

"Daddy just found out who his father was from his Elemaiyan mother," I took Erland's arm and led him from the suite with Garde on our heels. When we reached the hall outside, I asked my question. "Have you ever heard of a Karathian warlock named Wylend Arden?"

Erland stared at me in shock for seconds. "What's wrong, Erland?" I asked.

"Fuck me," Erland breathed, his beautiful face displaying shock.

"Yeah, you keep asking and I keep saying no. Who's Wylend Arden?"

"Perhaps it is better if I show you." Erland folded me away before Garde could protest.

~

Karathia

"Where are we?" We'd landed in an entryway that reminded me of the rotunda at Grey House—the one that held all the sculpture and artwork. Only this one was six times bigger and even more obscenely opulent.

Marble tiles were veined in gold and silver. Some of the sculptures were gold or appeared to be gold and depicted humanoids and animals in many poses. Some danced; some played musical instruments or leapt and ran against polished marble walls.

A uniformed man appeared quickly in the middle of a central, wide doorway. "Lord Morphis, if you and your guest will follow me," he bowed slightly, seeming unsurprised that we'd appeared from nowhere without an invitation.

Erland nudged me forward; I walked on feet that had suddenly gone numb. Recognition shone in our greeter's eyes—he knew Erland and knew him well. We followed our guide through a seemingly endless hall.

Paintings and priceless treasures hung on walls or rested on ornately carved furniture throughout its length. We reached another doorway eventually and our guide stopped before us, causing Erland to pull me to a halt as well.

Erland's arm was around my shoulders and his fingers gripped my upper arm tightly, as if he were afraid I might disappear. I was thinking about it, but the opportunity passed quickly.

"Lord Erland Morphis," our guide announced in a loud voice. "And guest," he added before moving away. Erland pulled me forward, although I was beginning to have second (and third) thoughts about all this.

The throne room (that's what it was, I discovered quickly) was magnificent. The value of the tile alone could have fed a Third World country on Earth for several years. Who had wealth such as this? I had no idea.

Small knots of men and women stood here and there inside that throne room and they gazed upon us in curiosity as Erland steered me through them, heading toward the throne and the man who sat there. Flanked by two warlocks in uniform, the man on the throne observed us with guarded interest as we approached.

When we reached the bottom step leading to the ornate chair and the man who sat upon it, Erland bowed low. He didn't ask me to bow with him, or kneel or curtsy (not that I would have). The man on the throne lifted an eyebrow at me when Erland straightened up from his bow. I already knew from the scent who he was.

"Explain why your guest does not bow, before I call my guards to imprison her," Wylend Arden asked Erland calmly.

"Even if she were not who she is, it would be foolish to attempt to imprison her," Erland talked in circles. One of King Wylend's eyebrows lifted higher.

"You bring me a puzzle to solve?" Wylend seemed quite happy at the prospect.

"If you wish it, my King," Erland flashed a dazzling smile.

"Let me see," Wylend stood and walked down the steps, the two Warlock guards remaining at his side as he descended. King Wylend Arden was beardless, wore only a simple gold band on his forehead, dressed richly in a silk shirt and trousers and wore a heavy gold chain that circled his neck.

His eyes and his height were Griffin's—there was no mistaking them, as well as the brown color of his hair. Narissa had been shorter —very close to my height. Kyler and Cleo had gotten their beauty and rich auburn hair from her.

I was staring at my grandfather. Had I ever thought to have one?

My mother always said her parents were dead and Howard Graham's were deceased before I was born.

"Let's see," Wylend examined me carefully as he circled Erland and me. He stroked his chin lightly as he considered the conundrum I presented. "Do I get the standard three questions?" Wylend was still walking around me, much like a large cat might consider its prey.

"If you wish it, my King," Erland repeated, grinning wider, now.

"Very well. Is she human?"

"Not human." Erland was enjoying this. I wanted to elbow him in the stomach. Instead, I was forced to stand there and bear the King's scrutiny. Honestly, I had no idea what to do or how he might react when he learned he had a granddaughter (or great-granddaughters, for that matter).

How was Griffin going to deal with this? He had a living father. I think he imagined his father was dead and merely wanted to know the name. Who knows—with his ability to bend time, he might have gone back and watched his father from afar. That wasn't necessary. His father was here and staring at me intently.

"Is she pregnant with your child?" Wylend asked his second question.

"I may hold hope in that direction, but no," Erland chuckled.

"I didn't think you'd switched allegiances again so quickly," Wylend said and came to stare into my eyes.

"I have not, my King, although I still have desires where this one is concerned." What had he meant by switching allegiances? I was going to have to do a little digging myself.

"Is this the new Queen of Le-Ath Veronis?" Wylend stood back, a look of triumph on his face.

"Yes, my King, but there is something else that you must know about her," Erland vibrated with excitement.

"I guessed correctly!" Wylend seemed quite happy with his skill at this game. "Welcome, Queen Lissa," he took my hand and kissed it.

"My King, may we retire to your study so I may give you the last part of my information in private?" Erland asked.

"Of course," Wylend pointed us toward a small doorway off to the side and the two uniformed guards led the way. Wylend strode before us and Erland and I followed at his heels.

The study was luxury itself, with priceless antique maps hanging on one wall while another wall held a huge painting of a seascape. It made me think of Edwin Church's depiction of Niagara Falls—the handling of the water was very similar. The painting was breathtaking; I wouldn't mind having something like it hanging on the walls of my suite.

Wylend sat and then asked us to sit in chairs before his huge, elaborately carved, dark wood desk. "Now, Lord Morphis, what news do you bring to me?"

"Do you remember Narissa?" Erland asked. How had he gotten that name? I hadn't given it to him.

Wylend's face went dark with anger. "I remember. She was such a temptress when I met her."

"And then she turned into the biggest bitch ever," Erland nodded in agreement. He was acting as if he knew her—had met her, even. I was now staring at Erland in alarm.

"Tell me what happened when she left, Wylend." Erland coaxed. I had no idea what was going on between these two. Erland was behaving as if he and Wylend were close—closer than I imagined. I was trying to sort that out without *Looking*—I felt it would be rude if I tried.

"That bitch was pregnant with my child," Wylend was even angrier, now. "I know what her kind do with their quarter-blood children. She was half; I determined that for myself. She took my child away. I cursed her for it, but she took it anyway, out of spite. I had no way to find it, they gate so often, and the Elemaiya are generally beyond even our skills to track. My child is dead, now, and I have not been able to produce another." Wylend was acting as if he truly cared about that. It made the breath catch in my throat.

"I have information for you, my King," Erland left his seat and knelt ceremoniously before Wylend's desk. "Your child is not dead," he announced. "I was not able to bring him immediately," Erland lifted his head and gazed up at Wylend. "But your granddaughter sits before you now."

I always knew Erland had a flair for the dramatic. He certainly pulled out all the stops for this announcement.

"Erland Morphis, get up from there this instant!" I smacked his shoulder, causing Wylend to roar with laughter.

∼

Kifirin

"Where is Lissa?" Amara asked Gardevik, who'd come back inside the suite.

"Erland Morphis came and squirreled her away," Gardevik didn't know how he felt about that. Griffin still looked pale, but Cleo was tending him and he was better than before.

"He took her to Karathia," Griffin leaned on his granddaughters as he stood. "If Cleo hadn't already handed out a sentence to my mother, I might be tempted to do something myself," Griffin heaved a weary sigh.

"Em-pah, this is no different from Lissa finding out she had a father," Cleo rubbed his back affectionately. "Or Kyler and I when we found out our father was still alive. We love Daddy and we wouldn't trade him for anything."

"I hope my father enjoys a good laugh," Griffin muttered. "His son, older than he is."

"How can that be?" Gardevik was curious, now.

"The ones who approached me with an invitation to become the first Saa Thalarr came forward in time, when I was dying. I was taken back to the time when the Ra'Ak began to take the worlds of light, over a hundred thousand years ago. My father, Wylend Arden, is King of Karathia and twenty-seven thousand years old. I am nearly four times his age." Griffin snorted at the irony.

"Did you ever have the abilities the warlocks have?" Gardevik asked.

"They have a rite, similar to that of any other Wizard clan. The ability must be wakened by an elder. Ask my granddaughters—they have both been through the ritual for the Grey House Wizards. This is so any stray children will not cause chaos if they are reared away from their family of Wizards or Warlocks."

Griffin rubbed his forehead as if he had a headache. "It also wakes the near immortality. Otherwise, they live a normal life span and die. No wonder Lissa exceeded all expectations," he muttered. "She was a quarter Bright Elemaiya and a quarter Karathian witch."

~

Karathia

"You are truly my granddaughter?" Wylend had moved Erland away and now sat in the chair next to mine, holding my hands in his.

"It looks that way," I said. "Griffin went into shock, I think, when Narissa admitted who his father is."

"How is he still alive?" Wylend asked.

"He was the first Saa Thalarr," I said, gazing into eyes that were so much like my father's, sprinkled with gold flecks.

"My child became the first Saa Thalarr?" Wylend sounded proud.

"He is now called the Oracle," I said. "Because he has foresight that none of the others have. He was a King Vampire before he was made Saa Thalarr."

"And you became the Queen Vampire of Le-Ath Veronis," Wylend nodded. Erland sat casually on the corner of Wylend's desk, swinging a foot leisurely as he listened to Wylend's conversation with me.

"Yeah. That's me, all right." I couldn't keep the sarcasm from my voice. I was thankful Gabron had cleared my calendar. The day was becoming more complicated than I'd anticipated.

"Can you set up a meeting with your father for me?" Wylend was almost begging. Here he was, King of Karathia and perhaps the most powerful warlock on the planet, begging for a meeting with his son.

I felt dizzy, for a moment. Things were turned upside down and inside out for a few fleeting seconds. Narissa, my grandmother,

47

should have been the loving soul and the warlock should have been the cold and indifferent parent. Exactly the opposite was true.

"Child, you look pale," Wylend said, his voice coming from far away.

"She's fainting," Erland's voice was even farther away and hands were reaching out to keep me from hitting the thick, expensive rug in Wylend's study.

~

"Did you think I wouldn't know how to treat my Queen?" Erland's voice was soft and his hands were gentle. "Just because I am in a female cycle doesn't mean I wouldn't want you, or wouldn't treat you properly."

The term female cycle caused my eyes to open faster than they wanted to and the light blinded me for a moment. I squinted as the light dimmed around me.

My grandfather sat on a chair beside a bed and Erland was propping me up on the bed, stroking my face and hair. "That's better," Erland leaned down and kissed my forehead.

"Erland," I raised a hand and rubbed the space between my eyebrows.

"What, love?"

"What are you saying? Female cycle?"

Wylend cleared his throat and I glanced over at him. "We are nearly immortal," he offered. "And we go through cycles—male and female. We can change our appearance and anatomy if we wish, but many of us do not. Therefore, every hundred years or so, our attraction to males or females changes. Erland is in his seventieth year of a female cycle, which means he is mostly attracted to males. He and I are generally opposites and yes, we have been lovers in the past."

"Erland, I always thought you were weirder than holy water in hell, now I know it's true," I mumbled.

"If we find a mate or mates, we still love them, no matter what cycle we are in," Erland lifted my chin and gave me a kiss. "Wylend and I have not been together in that way for some time. We lean on one another—that is true, but sex is no longer in the picture."

"Erland, this isn't awkward or anything," I shook my head in confusion.

"I will give up my friendship with Lord Morphis if it will make my granddaughter happy."

Uh-oh.

"Your granddaughter already has ten members in her Inner Circle and can't keep up with all of them," I admitted, feeling my face go hot. "And why should you give up your friendship with Erland? That's silly."

"Pfff," Wylend tossed an arm in the air. "Having that many mates or more keeps them interested," he was smiling. "The powerful always draw multiple mates. Erland and I have been close for a very long time. I am grateful you do not mind our relationship. Here," he did the warlock version of *Pulling* and suddenly had a drink in his hand. "Drink this, it will help."

"What is it?" I sniffed it, attempting to determine what it was.

"Fruit, berries and protein," Wylend smiled and convinced me to try it. It was a smoothie and very good. I'd barely had breakfast before Griffin hauled me off to Kifirin—the planet, not the Lord of the Dark Realm and mate to yours truly.

"Lissa my love, I am getting urgent mindspeech from nearly all your mates, demanding to know where you are," Erland grinned. I figured that grin was his way of saying, *I have you to myself right now, so I'm not answering the call.*

"Who is sending mindspeech?" I asked, slurping more of my drink.

"Karzac is the one who is most demanding—Gavin is cursing in multiple languages, Gabron is considering slicing and dicing and Drake and Drew aren't considering it—I think they're about to sharpen their blades."

"If Gavin is using mindspeech, it's time to go," I said, sliding off the bed. "He never does that unless he's forced to."

"Lissa, your continued absence may result in a national emergency upon Le-Ath Veronis." Connegar and Reemagar folded in. The Larentii could find me, even if nobody else could.

"I was just about to leave," I handed the empty glass to Erland, who caused it to disappear.

"Lord King, the Oracle is waiting at the palace in Lissia," Reemagar nodded to Wylend.

"Then I will come as well," Wylend stood and flicked imaginary lint off his clothing. "I wish to meet my child. Inform the others that I will be back shortly." He jerked his head in the direction of the two guards, who stood in a corner. I'd scented them earlier but hadn't paid much attention to them otherwise. They bowed to Wylend and left the room.

"I can't recall that I've ever had Larentii in my bedroom before," Wylend smiled. The Larentii in question folded us to Le-Ath Veronis.

~

Le-Ath Veronis

Griffin stood straight and tall as we landed in the library of the palace. Amara stood beside him; she was the one who gasped when she saw Wylend. "Brenten, you look alike!"

"Child, I wish I could have been a part of your life," Wylend said and that's all it took. Griffin was pulled into a huge embrace and both of them looked a little misty when they parted.

"Where have you been?" Karzac had fists on his hips, giving me the once-over.

"She fainted." Erland stood at my side, handing out information when he should have kept his mouth shut.

"Can somebody send to the kitchen and have drinks and snacks brought up?" I had to say it over my shoulder; Karzac was hustling me out of the library, closely followed by Reemagar and just about everybody in my Inner Circle.

"Karzac, are we gonna wrestle here in the hall?" I asked. I shouldn't have said it. Connegar pulled me into his arms quickly and all of us were folded to my suite. Kifirin was there, waiting for us.

"She needs to drop her corporeality or she will continue to faint," Kifirin accepted me from Connegar.

"But my grandfather is in the library," I said, or at least I got most of it said before Kifirin and I both disappeared. Actually, disappeared might have been an understatement. We were pure energy, floating over the surface of Le-Ath Veronis. Kifirin was in charge, now, spreading me out somehow until I was everywhere. It scared me.

Avilepha, do not be frightened, his voice came to me in the thunder over a valley on Harifa Edus—the werewolf planet. Night had fallen there and a full moon would have been shining across a portion of the planet, except for the rain.

We became a part of Evensun and I saw that the exodus from the High Demons' world had begun. The new occupants were busy fighting with each other, for the most part.

They should have been building shelters together and searching for food, but that behavior was foreign to them, it seems. We flew away from Evensun, skipping lightly over the world that held the black Ra'Ak.

So many empty worlds populated the Dark Realm; the only life they held was vegetation, insects and a few animals. No other inhabitants. None of the ones for whom the worlds had been created. I felt the sadness in Kifirin as we passed them by. He'd constructed those worlds so carefully, yet it had taken only one of his creations to destroy all of them.

We'll make it right, I sent to him.

Lissa my love, are you gathering energy? It is there for you to take, m'hala. Kifirin showed me how—I hadn't done anything except observe up to that point. I thought it might be similar to the Larentii feeding off sunlight, only we could gather energy from anything.

I was doing it now and realized how weakened I'd become. Maintaining a corporeal shape prevented me from drawing the energy I needed to keep going. I could only draw energy while I was energy; stuffing that much power into a fragile, humanoid body was like placing a flame inside a plastic container. If the flame became too hot, the container could be destroyed.

Kifirin pulled me along as I replenished myself. We even wandered into the worlds of light, scooting here and there. I heard voices—talking, laughing, crying, praying. Dark spots cropped up, too, now and then. Those dark spots consisted of worlds the Ra'Ak had taken; now empty of life except for the usual plants, insects and a few stray animals.

Other worlds we passed over were not quite dark, but growing increasingly dim. *Worlds not worth saving*, Kifirin's voice came to me. *I want you to see Beliphar—it is one of those, but there are vampires there, love. Some of those may be worth saving, but it must be done soon.*

Let's take them now. I was getting information from that planet; we were right above it and the vampires there were used as slaves. It was awful. They were controlled by electronic cuffs that boiled their blood if they misbehaved, or the cuffs were employed at times merely because their human controllers wished to see the vampires suffer. Some of the vampires were criminals, but many were not—falsely accused and turned as punishment. How had this gotten past me for so long?

Send mindspeech to the others and I will gather the ones that should come to Le-Ath Veronis, Kifirin informed me. I sent mindspeech to Gabron and Flavio, telling them that the city ten miles east of Lissia was about to be occupied.

Kifirin guided me as I assisted him in gathering the vampires who would be welcome on Le-Ath Veronis. Kifirin was the one who turned the others to dust—I couldn't bring myself to do it, although they were better off.

You should have heard the angry shouting as vampires disappeared across Beliphar. Kifirin and I rushed our vampire cargo to Le-Ath Veronis, where we dropped them gently in the wide, circular courtyard of their new city.

Roughly twenty-seven thousand vampires stared at Kifirin and me as we materialized before them. Flavio and Gabron were there quickly, followed by most of the Council from Lissia. Drake, Drew, Gavin and Tony were there in a blink.

"Where are we?" A vampire made his way through the crowd, which parted to allow him passage. Another, younger vampire was at his heels—he was only days old as a vampire; I could tell by the scent. The other was old—at least seven thousand years.

"You stand upon Le-Ath Veronis," Flavio replied. "That means Heart of the Vampire. Lissa, Queen of this world, and Kifirin, Lord of the Dark Realm, have found you worthy. This is your new home."

The older vampire pulled the younger one against him. "Davan, we are home," the old vampire wept.

~

"This is blood substitute? It tastes like blood," Jeral, the oldest vampire from Beliphar remarked as he emptied the bottle. Davan, his youngest charge, was also drinking happily.

We were poring over a map of the city with a committee of new arrivals—vampires that Jeral had handpicked. They were also quite old and I could see the City Council forming already. Davan was a baby vampire and I didn't want to interfere with his teaching at Jeral's hand.

"This blood substitute was developed here," I informed Jeral. "The manufacturing plant is just outside Lissia."

"Do vampires run this facility?" Jeral asked.

"Yes. They are extremely meticulous, since they will be drinking quite a bit of it themselves," I said. "It is owned by the crown but everyone who works there earns a salary. They seem happy with the arrangement."

I pointed out the spot on the map where the blood substitute plant was located. "We currently have nine worlds represented here—your world is the ninth," I said. Reemagar was standing behind me; Flavio and Gabron were on either side, helping explain things as much as they could.

"What about the vampires on the Reth Alliance worlds?" Jeral asked. "There used to be many of them."

"There still are," I replied. "But the Reth Alliance recognizes them as citizens and they are protected by Alliance laws. They are allowed to petition for citizenship here and we will entertain their requests as they are presented. Not all vampires will be accepted. I'm sure you see my reasoning in that."

"I understand that you may not wish to import a criminal element," Jeral sighed.

"Yes. That is exactly how we feel about this," I nodded. "I assure you, however, that if a crime is committed here, it will be dealt with immediately. I will not tolerate the breaking of the law."

"Are there copies of the laws?" Jeral's face held hope, something he hadn't experienced in a very long time, I could tell.

"As much as we have, at the moment. We are still hammering out some of them," I said. "Le-Ath Veronis, as it now exists, is barely seven months old. We are gathering vampires as quickly as possible but it is a slow process, as you might imagine."

Gavin, Tony, Drake and Drew folded in, with electronic copies of the current laws; some of those laws temporary, since we hadn't decided on all of them yet.

"What are the comesuli?" Jeral asked after reading the first law. The handheld devices could translate the laws into almost any language. The one spoken on Beliphar was common to the Reth Alliance, though it was no longer a member.

"Are you interested in history?" I gave Jeral a slight smile.

"In this case, I think I should be," he inclined his head. I explained what Le-Ath Veronis was in the beginning and what part the comesuli played. I described what had happened when the Ra'Ak attacked and how many of the comesuli had been sent to Kifirin, in order to save their lives.

"And now they are back?" Jeral was intrigued.

"Yes. How many of your vampires know how to take blood properly from a donor?" I asked.

"A few," Jeral said. "The oldest, here, all know. The younger ones have not been taught."

"Then teach them. I will not allow the comesuli to be harmed by an untrained vampire," I said. "They wear bracelets, with two numbers," I added. "Those numbers represent the dates on which they can be bitten and then only once on that particular day. They must be given two weeks to replenish their blood supply."

We discussed many things that late afternoon, which wore on into the evening. Every vampire we'd brought from Beliphar was fascinated by the fact that this part of Le-Ath Veronis was in constant twilight and the sun would not force them to find a safe place to sleep. Maps were readily available on all the small, handheld computers, and each vampire was given a key that unlocked the door to his new home.

No females were in this group of vampires and that was sad. I'd seen many of these vampires staring at me and I knew it was because they'd never seen a female vampire before.

Jeral, Davan and the other, older vampires stayed when the rest left to find their new homes. Sadly, the twenty-seven thousand only filled a fourth of the city.

"We need a Council from here—a governing body that will meet with me, Gabron and the other Councils to finalize the laws and the constitution," I told Jeral when the others left. "You can decide this any way you want—most of the others already had a Council in place before they came and they continue in that capacity. Since you had no official governing body, I will let you decide how to choose your representatives. I will only interfere if there is no agreement."

"We have made nearly every vampire transported here," Jeral indicated himself and the six others with him. Davan was excluded; he was much too young. "There will be no problem; this Council is at your disposal, my Queen."

"Very well, the next meeting is in two days. Gabron will send a reminder—there are comp-vids in each house. If you need help working them, you only have to ask. You have mindspeech, do you not?" I smiled at Jeral. I'd smelled the Bright Elemaiya about him—he was a quarter, as was Davan, at his side. That wasn't all I knew about them, however, but that information could wait. Davan needed more instruction from his vampire sire before anything else could be done.

"My Queen, it will be the greatest of pleasures for me to be able to communicate with you in this way," Jeral offered a half-bow.

"Don't bow, I don't expect it," I said, waving away the formality. Jeral straightened and smiled his first real smile since he'd landed on Le-Ath Veronis.

CHAPTER 4

Le-Ath Veronis

Karzac had his hands on me the minute I was back at the palace and grunted his approval. Kifirin had been correct—I needed to come out of my corporeal shape one or two hours a day, just to replenish myself. Maybe I could hook up with either Connegar or Reemagar, when they went to feed. I hadn't really explored the light half of the planet, yet.

"That doesn't exempt you from your evening meal," Karzac lectured as he, Roff and Gabron chased me around my suite, handing out clothing while I did my best to braid my hair. Giff and Rolfe had the day off and were out somewhere, I knew, enjoying each other's company.

Drake and Drew were sitting on my right and left tonight. I was getting both Falchani in my bed; I just knew it. They often held a tag team event and I'd go to bed with one of them and wake up with the other. Not that it was a hardship, or anything. Shadow, whom I hadn't seen in a few days, folded in wearing a deep frown. Karzac pulled a chair out with power and Shadow sat.

"Are you hungry?" I asked.

"I've eaten," he sighed. "I heard a rumor," he added.

57

"What rumor?" I set my fork down; I was done with my roast duck anyway.

"That you're part Karathian."

"Oh, that rumor," I said. "I didn't find that out until today. Daddy's bitch of a mother 'fessed up."

"Lissa, this could turn into a problem if we ever have children," Shadow rubbed his forehead. Karzac was up and relieving Shadow's headache right away.

"I'm vampire. I don't get kids." *Thanks for reminding me,* I silently added. I wasn't ever going to get kids. My fate had been decided the summer I was thirteen and barely having my first periods. Howard Graham had beaten my mother and me. He'd kicked me and pounded me in the abdomen. Then, when he was forced to take us to the emergency room, he claimed we'd wrecked the car.

Howard Graham wasn't a nice man and we were too afraid of him to say anything. I'd spent two weeks in the hospital, then. Mom got out in a few days, but she was at the hospital whenever he wasn't home. He didn't want her giving me any attention when he was home at night.

"I'm done," I tossed my napkin on my plate, rose from my seat at the table and misted away.

"At least she can't walk into the sun again," Gavin growled and rose from his seat, leaving the others behind.

"What did I do?" Shadow gazed about him.

"Female vampires have difficulty with the fact that they can't bear children," Gabron sighed. "A very high percentage of the few who are turned walk into the sun before they reach the age of one hundred, partly due to that fact.

"Lissa was unable to have children before she became vampire, because her stepfather damaged her," Connegar folded in. "Is there any other information I may provide before I begin searching for my mate?" When there were no other questions, Connegar folded away.

"Why would there be a problem if you were to have a child with Lissa?" Roff asked Shadow. He was troubled as well and wondered where Lissa had gone.

"The ritual," Shadow replied. "Grey House would demand the right, but the Karathians might want it too, since Wylend Arden is Lissa's grandfather."

"You're not likely to get a child with Lissa," Karzac pushed his plate away. "You worry over nothing."

"Well, I didn't think about that," Shadow said, running a hand through his hair.

~

"Little Queen, you should not be troubled." Reemagar had found me, somehow, and now sat beside me on the dome covering the palace rotunda.

"I know," I said, looking over the city they'd named after me. Lights twinkled everywhere. Merrill told me once that Grace supplied the crystal for the solar panels that were collecting sunlight and feeding all those lights. I sighed. We needed libraries, theatres and all sorts of things for the vampires who were collecting on Le-Ath Veronis.

Plus, we still didn't have the laws hammered out. I worried over the application to join the Reth Alliance—we were supposed to get that information the following week and it would be a major blow if we were turned down. I realized I was saying these things aloud after a while and Reemagar sat there, listening patiently while I let it all come out of my mouth.

"We need jobs and entertainment and ways to keep the population involved," I blew out a breath. "And as much as I hate to admit it, I think we may have to allow humans on the planet, at least to visit—these vampires are used to interacting with them and I think they miss it."

"These vampires were all humanoid at one time; of course they would miss it," Reemagar agreed. "Perhaps we should put up taverns so the vampires might socialize with the comesuli, or create sports teams of some kind."

"Maybe we should ask the vampires for suggestions," I said, leaning my chin on my knees. "Not just the Councils, but the vampires themselves. Ask them what they'd like to do or what kinds of entertainment they'd like to have brought in. We can't have a planet full of bored and restless vampires. That sounds like trouble in the making."

"Your next meeting is in two days; I think we can prepare ballots by that time and download them onto the handheld devices they all have. I'm sure we can sort through the information we receive and have a workable solution in a short amount of time."

"That's a good idea," I sat up straight and patted Reemagar's arm. He smiled down at me. "Your face is transformed when you smile," I told him. "You should do that more often."

"I will do my best," he replied.

"In the meantime, let's go to Kifirin and visit the babies." I stood and dusted off my clothes.

"I will be pleased to make that journey," Reemagar smiled again. I liked it. The blue of his skin was flawless. He folded both of us to the palace in Veshtul.

"Lissa, what are you doing here?" Garde was walking down the hall toward Glinda and Jayd's suite. I'd been about to knock on their door.

"We came to see the babies," I said.

"Then we'll see the babies." Garde rapped lightly on the door before entering the royal suite. Glinda was rocking one of the tiny girls; the other was sleeping in a crib close by. Jayd was sitting on a chair next to Glinda's.

"How are they?" I whispered, going to look at the one in her crib. They'd named the girls Jhase and Jheri, but I hadn't sorted out the scents, yet. It didn't matter; they were adorable.

"Fine," Glinda smiled. "All fed and no longer fussy."

"How's papa?" I looked over at Jayd.

"As fine as I can be at the moment," Jayd sighed. "We got the last of the troublemakers off—Kiarra and Kyler accomplished this for us so we wouldn't have to worry about the girls' safety."

"I'll bet Evensun is a wreck already," I muttered. "Those fools."

"They'll bring in some of the others tomorrow," Jayd went on.

"You'll have your work cut out for you, even with willing help," I said. "We'll help as much as we can—I'll try to get some of the farmers and such to come and teach them what they need to know. Surely some of the new ones will know how to cook and clean."

"Little Queen, I think you should not worry; they are going to Wresha tomorrow," Reemagar rubbed a hand over my shoulders. "There are many on that world belonging to the lower castes who know much about those things, including how to plant and harvest. It is the highest castes who have ruined the world and brought it to its current status."

"If you need something, let me know," I nodded to Jayd. He looked exhausted. "Did you get dinner tonight? Something decent?" I waited for an answer. "I'll be back," I said and folded away.

Reemagar came with me; we loaded up quite a bit of food from my palace kitchen and returned with it. I fixed a plate for Jayd, Glinda and Garde, then sat with them while they ate. Reemagar even helped me clean the dishes and the kitchen after they were done. I was familiar with Jayd's palace kitchen, after all—I'd worked there for a while.

"Lissa, you don't have to do this," Garde came in while I was wiping off cabinets and countertops.

"Yes, I do," I said, giving the counter one last swipe. "I took your help away. We just have to get you better help and get them settled. They'll have a big cleanup job to do in Veshtul; I can't imagine the others left it in good shape. I wish Jayd would let Glinda stay with us while you wrangle the new ones. You're all welcome to come for meals, if nothing else. Can Glinda use her power, now? She can fold those babies in and out anytime. Giff would be more than happy to help her. Has Jayd given any thought to bringing in a nanny or something?"

"Lissa, slow down," Garde placed his hands on my shoulders. "The universe's troubles aren't all yours. We need to stand up and take responsibility for ourselves. We got us into this mess; we have to get ourselves out."

"I just feel responsible," I said, rubbing my forehead to ease the tension.

"If you hadn't done what you did when you did it, imagine where we'd be right now. I don't think we could have beaten back what showed up on our doorstep, do you?"

I didn't answer—we both knew the answer was no. Garde's hand moved to the back of my neck and he massaged it gently, beneath my hair, which I'd left loose. "Thank you for dinner," his breath fanned my temple as he leaned down to kiss my nape. "Go home, Lissa, and get some rest. You look tired."

Reemagar folded us back to Le-Ath Veronis and I thanked him before he went toward his suite. "Connegar was going to come looking for you earlier," he turned back before I went inside my suite. "I asked him if I could come instead. He allowed it."

"Thanks. I appreciate what you did for me, tonight." He smiled gently, so I told him goodnight and opened the door of my suite. Drew was waiting for me when I walked inside.

~

"There's our girl," Dragon said, greeting me. He and Crane were waiting at the breakfast table when Drake and Drew herded me to the dining room the following morning.

"Hey, Dragon. What's up?" I went to give him a peck on the cheek. Well, I was fooling around with his boys and all. Didn't that make us in-laws or something?

"Belen has given permission for all the former Falchani and their mates, if they so desire, to join the army on Falchan right now. There's a problem and the Falchani need our help. Don't worry," he held up a hand when I started to tell him I was busier than a ping pong ball in a tornado, "It's temporary and we can fold you back to this moment in time if you're worried you might miss a boring meeting."

Dragon grinned at me. I didn't see him grin often, actually. He

62

must really be looking forward to this. "Belen said you were welcome to go if you wanted. I just thought you might like to spend some time on Falchan. Look at it as a sort of honeymoon."

"Uh-huh," I nodded. "Can I have breakfast, first?"

"Why? There's breakfast waiting in the cooking tents on Falchan."

"Tents?" I think my eyebrows must have risen alarmingly, because I was folded away before I could say no.

Falchan

Dragon wasn't lying (as Saa Thalarr, he couldn't). There were cooking tents, all right, and Falchani warriors were lined up to get breakfast in front of a long, makeshift serving table.

It was late summer there—I learned that much by *Looking*. After staring down at myself, I found I was now dressed in black leathers, just like everybody else. Dragon was making sure I fit in as well as I could.

I think every Falchani who had joined the Saa Thalarr was there with me—Dragon, Crane, Drake, Drew, Dragon Taylor, Crane Trevor, Pheran Tiger, Caylon Black, Veykan, Turtle and Rik. Devin had come along, too, I saw. I knew where she'd be sleeping.

"Did you get a chance to say no?" Devin sidled up to me, watching both Dragon and Crane. Stoicism aside, they were happy to be treading the soil of Falchan again.

"That answer would be no," I muttered. We both spoke the Falchani language; no need to arouse anyone's suspicions. At least my leathers were sleeveless, just like the men's did, and laced up the front. Devin's did, too—the guys just left theirs open—no doubt to show off multiple tattoos and sculpted abs.

"Is this your company?" Someone walked up to Dragon as we stood in line for breakfast.

"Yes, Lord Marshall," Dragon inclined his head slightly to the warrior. He had a long braid down his back, just as Dragon did, and wore his vest open like the other males. His chest tattoo was a snarling wolf and smaller wolves wound around his arms, chasing one another.

"Stop by the Warlord's tent after breakfast and we'll record the names," the Lord Marshall commanded.

"Yes, Lord Marshall," Dragon dipped his head a second time as the Lord Marshall strode away.

"That's Lord Marshall Wolf," Drake turned and grinned at me.

"Nooo," I said. "Really?" Drake and Drew were ahead of me in line, which was fine. Devin was standing with me, letting hers go ahead of her, too. I guess rank had its privileges. Former Warlords and Generals got to go first. I could understand that.

"So, who's Warlord now?" I asked, as we inched our way toward the serving line.

"The Eagle Warlord," Drew said. "The Bear General is his second-in-command."

"Why are we here?" I asked. I was stumped, I admit, and I hadn't gone *Looking* for any info, yet.

"You see the mountain range north of here?" Drake asked. I looked, bending down a little to do so; the sides of the tent had been rolled up so we only had a roof over our heads for shade.

"Yeah."

"On the other side of that mountain range are the lands of the Reldani barbarians. They've organized recently, instead of raiding in bands as they normally do. They have a huge army waiting on the far side of the closest mountain, due north of here," Drake continued. "We're here to help convince them that attacking the Falchan side of the continent is a bad idea."

"Oooh," I nodded.

"They'll take any excuse to go whack people with swords," Devin laughed. "Just so you know, we have tents of our own and your blades are there, with everybody else's."

"I don't recall having blades," I said.

"You do, now. Dragon got Shadow to ask Glendes to make them for you. Shadow put protection jewels in the hilts. They're ready to go."

"I'm still trying to figure out why I'm here," I grumped.

"Come on, baby, it'll be fun," Drew was grinning again. "We'll move out tomorrow. Don't you want to be with us?" He was doing his best impression of a pout.

"Hey, don't mess up that handsome face with a pout," I said, crossing my arms over my chest. "And I do want to be with you. You couldn't book us a nice hotel, somewhere?"

"You didn't leave the females at home?" A warrior elbowed his way past us, giving Devin and me a black look as he did so.

"Somebody needs an ass-whoopin'," I grumbled as soon as he was out of hearing. Devin snorted a laugh.

We went to register at the Warlord's tent later; there was a long line standing in front of us doing the same thing. "This is for the small companies and individuals coming from the hills and outlying villages," Drake whispered to me as we patiently waited our turn.

The afternoon sun was hot as it bore down on us, and my black leathers didn't help much with that. I wanted to fan myself, but it wasn't in the *Stoic Falchani Warrior Manual* to appear weak or uncomfortable.

Therefore, I sweated and suffered in silence. The grass was dead and the ground was dry and dusty beneath our feet. It made me wonder when the last rain had come.

"Thirteen of you?" The captain at the table had already counted us as Dragon gave him our information. He said we were of the Wildcat tribe, whatever that meant.

Veykan's lending us his tribal affiliation; Dragon Taylor gave me mental details. *If Dad used his, it might raise suspicions.* Well, I could see how that might be a problem. Former Warlords who'd been dead to these people for thousands of years didn't just pop in on a normal day.

"Are the females sufficiently trained?" The captain asked Dragon, squinting critically at Devin and me.

"I'll match either against anybody here," Dragon replied, signing his name on the register. "They deserve the black they wear."

That sounded like a challenge to me, but then I wasn't Falchani, so what did I know?

~

"You did not say anything about riding a horse." I was giving the horse the same look the horse was giving me—if horses are capable of incredulity. Drake stood at my shoulder, trying to convince me to get on.

"Haven't you ridden a horse before? I thought you were from Oklahoma."

"I am from Oklahoma and believe me when I say that not all people in Oklahoma are experts on riding horses."

"You don't think you can stay on?" Drew walked over, grinning as usual.

"I can stay on. I just don't know what shape my ass is gonna be in when I get off." I slapped Drew lightly on the arm.

He and Drake had dressed me that morning, showing me how to strap on my new blades, which were beautiful—the workmanship was amazing. I almost hated to use them; I didn't want to mess them up. I also had throwing knives—three of them—in side sheaths. I'd never thrown knives and I always had my claws if I needed to slice something.

"We'll take care of your ass," Drake's hand was now on said ass. They'd seen to it the night before, too. "Now, get on your horse."

"Fine." I jumped onto the horse without using stirrups. Drake cleared his throat at my inappropriate antics. "Hey, you didn't say how you wanted it done." I stuck my feet in the stirrups and nudged the horse with my boots, as I'd seen the others do. He moved off. Drake and Drew climbed into their saddles and came after me.

Dragon arranged us in neat rows of four each, riding behind him. Crane, Caylon, Devin and Pheran Tiger rode in the first row, Turtle,

Veykan, Dragon Taylor and Crane Trevor were in the second row. Rik, Drake, Drew and I came last.

We were a smaller army somewhere in the middle of the Warlord's much larger one, and rising dust became a problem quickly. All of us had kerchiefs over our nose and mouth before long and the horses didn't like it much either, I could tell. My horse was a gelding, a bay, Drake informed me as we rode along.

"We'll be stopping to water the horses in a little while," he added. A wagon pulled by oxen rumbled along behind us, and much of their burden was water barrels. "We won't get to a river for two days, so we won't get baths, either. Just a wet cloth to wipe ourselves off at the end of the day."

"And you wanted to come," I shook my head in disbelief.

"Don't you want to know how your ancestors did things?" Drew chided.

"I think I could bend time a little, if I wanted to know that."

"Well, you're stuck here, now," Drake was grinning under his kerchief—I just knew it.

The horses were glad to get a drink at midday, as was I. I'd taken Kifirin's advice earlier—before breakfast, in fact, and turned to energy. I'd floated away, going here and there before coming back to Falchan and going off to the cooking tents. Devin drank the strong brew that Falchani called tea at breakfast—I settled for water.

A thick layer of pale, brown dust covered all of us by the time we stopped for the night. I was wishing for a bath when I slid off my horse. My ride stood patiently while I learned how to groom him that night—he got cared for first and was eating while I brushed the dust off him and cleaned my tack.

Crane came along and showed me how to check his hooves. I was stiff from riding all day, too—just as I thought I'd be—but it could have been worse.

My grooming came next—I unbraided my hair and got as much dust out of it as I could with a brush and then wiped my face, arms and leathers off. I had two more sets of leathers in a small saddlebag that someone brought for me; they'd thought of everything, looked like.

I also had underwear and several thin cotton tanks to wear under my leathers. I was grateful for the underwear and tanks—it kept the leather from sticking to important parts. After the horse was cared for and picketed, Drake and Drew showed me how to raise our small tent and that's where I sat to clean myself up. They did the same.

Dinner was simple—some sort of stew. Devin got vegetables and rice; there were a few vegetarians in the army, it seems. "We're going to spar after dinner," Dragon announced while we were eating. He lifted an eyebrow in my direction.

Joy.

"Come on, baby, strap those blades back on," Drew hugged me inside our tent later. Honestly, I wanted to just flop down on my flat mattress and close my eyes for a while. I strapped on my blades.

"Come," Caylon Black was crooking his finger at me. Caylon wanted to take me on? He'd taught Dragon and Crane. I heaved a sigh and went toward him. I learned quickly where Dragon and Crane learned the tactics of rushing their opponent immediately—Caylon had taught them that. I was barely able to block his first blows.

Caylon was like a shredder, too, and we weren't playing around with wooden practice blades. Oh, no. This was the real thing and the metal rang out as we sparred. The others were standing there, watching Caylon push me around the little square he'd drawn out in the dust. I was going to have to wipe off again. For nearly half an hour, he whacked away at me. Eventually I wondered whether he was going to tire soon. I yawned.

"That's it." Caylon stepped back, holding his blades out to the side, indicating he was done.

"Thank goodness, I thought you were going to go all night," I said, lowering my blades. Now I was going to have to clean and oil them. I was already checking them over, making sure there weren't any nicks or scratches.

"It's not polite to yawn at your Sursee," Drake chuckled as he herded me toward our tent.

"We've never landed a blow either," Dragon hid his grin in a cup of tea. Devin wanted to elbow him but held off. Caylon was cleaning his blades around the campfire. Some of their neighbors had come to watch the bout and stayed to watch Dragon and Crane spar afterward. "It's the vampire in her, but Merrill says it's also the Queen in her."

"Do any of the other female vampires fight like this?" Caylon asked.

"Merrill says no. He says he has seen Susila fight and she's better than most. Lissa was humoring us, tonight. She was tired."

"It's as if time moves differently for her," Crane added. "She can see our blows coming and has time to correct her grip on the blade, even, if it isn't in the right position to take the hit on the flat of it."

"Has she ever gone on the offensive?" Caylon asked. Lissa had only blocked his blows earlier.

"Not often, unless I forced her to come after me," Dragon replied. "When she helped me three hundred years ago on Refizan, I convinced her to spar with me a few times after she cleaned the dojo. If I taunted her enough she'd come after me, but only long enough to beat me back and then she'd settle for blocking blows again."

"But you weren't the enemy," Crane observed, sipping his tea. "If you were, I think she'd have your head in a blink."

"Time to get up, baby." Drake's whisper was soft and warm against the skin of my collarbone as he planted a kiss there. I'd gotten up earlier to turn to energy, but had gone back to sleep once I returned. Now, Drake and Drew wanted me to wake up. I wanted to sleep a little more.

"If you want breakfast, you need to wake up, pretty girl." That was Drew, and he was rubbing a thumb gently over my lower lip.

"What is it with you guys and early mornings?" I was grumbling and stretching at the same time.

"What is it always with guys and early mornings?" Drew bent down to kiss me.

"Okay, I'll get up," I forced my eyes open. Yeah, if both of them are leaning over me in the morning, I feel like I'm seeing double for a moment. My ass was sore and my thighs were worse. "Maybe I'll carry the horse today," I grumped as I pulled my leathers on.

"I hadn't thought about that," Drake grinned. "You could, couldn't you?"

"Yeah, but I saw the looks he was giving me yesterday. I don't think he'll sit still while I haul him around."

I laced up my leather vest after slipping my cotton tank on over my bare breasts. I was herded off to breakfast, right behind Crane, Dragon and the others. We ate together on plank tables and Crane and Dragon were deep in some discussion with Pheran, Caylon and Turtle when we were approached by three female warriors.

"Warrior," the tallest of the three bowed respectfully to Dragon.

"Warrior," Dragon nodded to her.

"We wish to join your company," the woman said.

"Will your company not be offended?" Dragon wore the usual scowl on his face. At least it wasn't the deep frown—that could scare children and small animals.

"Our company will not care," the woman replied.

"Who leads your group? If he verifies your request, I will consider it," Dragon replied.

"As you say," the woman bowed again and walked off. She was nearly six feet in height and muscles rippled in her arms, which were bare. A white eagle with black-tipped feathers was tattooed on one arm, but I could see no other tattoos.

The two women who followed her also had the same eagle on their arms. The eagle's black-tipped feathers made it different from any eagle I'd ever seen—except for one. That Eagle was a giant Eagle—a member of the Saa Thalarr.

We were almost finished with our breakfast and I was about to go clean my teeth when the three women came back, accompanied by a male. It was the same man who'd brushed past us on the first day, asking why the women hadn't stayed home. Now I knew why these three wanted to get away from him.

"If you're fool enough to allow these three into your company, you may take them with my blessing," the man grunted and stalked off. I realized then that I hadn't seen that many women among the Warlord's army, but then I hadn't seen much of it, yet.

There had to be twenty thousand troops or so, divided into groups, each with an accompanying set of supply wagons. Our group was made up of the add-ins—the ones who weren't regular army, I guess. I figured the Warlord had pulled in as many extras as he could, since the enemy was organized, now.

"Your names?" Dragon asked, as soon as the man was out of hearing.

"Tava," the tall one introduced herself. She had the black hair and Asian features of most of the Falchani I'd seen. The next one was five-eight or so, had dark-brown hair, didn't look completely Asian and gave her name as Hart.

The third one was the shortest—perhaps five-five or five-six, also with black hair and dark eyes and identified herself as Nima. They'd brought their clothing with them, plus a rolled up tent and a few other belongings. Their horses had been left outside the breakfast tent, already loaded and ready to go.

"Have you had breakfast?" Crane asked, first thing.

"We have," Tava nodded.

"We will expect you to keep in shape and spar with the others when we stop in the evenings," Crane went on.

"We would welcome that," Tava bowed slightly, as did the other two.

Dragon lined us up in three rows of five after that and Crane, Caylon, Devin, Pheran Tiger and Turtle now rode in the first row behind him, then Veykan, Dragon Taylor, Crane Trevor, Rik and Drake followed in the second row, leaving Drew, Tava, Hart, Nima and me in the last row. I rode next to Drew; the other three women were riding at my side.

"How long have you been a warrior?" Tava, who rode next to me asked after a while. Crane had introduced all of us to the three women when we saddled up to continue our journey.

"That depends," I said. "If you're asking how long I've been fighting with blades, not long at all. I've fought before that, though."

"Crane will test you tonight," Drew got in on the conversation. "He will see what you have."

"Then we will thank him and offer to do for him," Tava nodded.

"He will not expect that," Drew replied while I sat there on my horse, wondering what *do for* meant. "He merely wants to know what your level is, so he can teach you if necessary."

"If he expects no more than that, then we are most relieved," Tava smiled. I think that was the first smile I'd seen on her face. That made me go *Looking*, although I didn't like doing that very much—it felt like prying.

Those three women had been expected to prostitute themselves for whatever they could learn from the men of their company. I thought I might have a stroke when I got that information.

Lissa, calm yourself, Drew sent. Drake's mental voice wasn't far behind. I got mindspeech from Dragon, too, trying to calm me down. I was about to go give the ass-whoopin' to the man who deserved it.

We cannot interfere in that way, Dragon informed me. *That is the Warlord's business and he is ignoring things of that nature at the moment. We cannot get involved.*

Then maybe the Warlord needs the ass-whoopin', I snapped back mentally. Drew frowned at me. Yeah, I was being grumpy with dad-in-law.

We reached the river shortly after nightfall—the Warlord wanted to keep pushing until we reached it. I had no argument with that decision; I wanted a bath in the worst possible way. The horses were cared for first, the tents went up and then we all trooped down to the river, where a horde was already bathing communally.

At least the bathing was taking place past the point where the drinking water was dipped out and the horses drank. What freaked me out most was that everybody was naked and cleaning up and doing laundry at the same time. I backed up when we reached the riverbank—it was mostly men bathing and I'd never seen that many penises in my life.

"Come along, shy little flower," Drake laughed at me as he and Drew each grabbed an arm and hauled me along. Tava, Hart and Nima were already undressing to go into the water. Devin didn't like the circumstances either and was getting the same treatment from Dragon and Crane.

"You know those guys are farting in there, don't you," I hissed as Drew unlaced my leather vest.

"Or worse," Drew nodded as he worked on my laces.

"You could have kept that to yourself," I muttered.

"Come on, the current is carrying it away," Drake said in his best, don't be a wuss voice.

"Unbelievable," I said, as Drake pulled my leather pants off and hauled me over his shoulder. Yeah, the twins were already naked. I noticed that we got space when Drake hauled me into the water. Well, hauled is the wrong word—it was a big leap off the bank, dunking us under as we went in. Drew jumped in right beside us. I learned why we got plenty of space, too. Anybody with a full complement of tattoos got respect. They didn't get the tattoos unless they'd earned them and most of the guys around us only had a few. I hadn't seen Devin's tattoo before, either—she had a red dragon tattooed on her back left shoulder. It was really nice and about eight or nine inches long.

"Want a tattoo?" Drake whispered in my ear.

"Nope. You guys have enough for several people," I smacked his chest. "Are we getting clean or what?" I tried to get the soap away from Drew, who grinned and held it over my head. I was scrubbed. By both of them. Of course, they expected help getting their hair washed and combed out.

"There," I finished braiding Drew's damp hair after we climbed out of the river. Drake's had already been done. I kissed Drew on the back of his neck, too. He grinned at me.

"Let's go find dinner," he said.

~

"Lissa, I'd pay if you'd make biscuits," Crane didn't like the flat bread he'd gotten with dinner. He, Devin and Dragon had beaten us to the cooking tents.

"Do they have anything to use as leavening?" I asked.

"They have baking powder," Crane said. "I just don't think they know how to use it."

"You think they'd mind if I used their portable kitchen?" I asked. "I made Gardevik biscuits in a skillet over a campfire."

"Come on," he stood and led the way. I found everything I needed in the camp kitchen and about forty-five minutes later, Crane had a skillet full of biscuits. I gave the cooks a few, since they'd let me use their supplies. Crane was more than happy and hauled the skillet out to our table, the handle wrapped in a thick pad.

"What are those?" Tava asked. She and the other two women were sitting at the end of our long table.

"Biscuits," Crane grinned and offered them one. They used the bread to dip up their stew.

"These are wonderful," Hart smiled happily. There was enough for everybody to get one and Crane to get two. The skillet was huge.

"If you have honey to go with them, they're even better," I said.

The following morning I was hauled away early—the cooks had come calling, asking me to show them how to make biscuits. We made biscuits and Crane got as many as he wanted, with a little honey.

I also learned that we'd be getting close to the mountain range by nightfall and things were going to be tighter, security-wise, after that. Until now, we hadn't done any night guard duty, but each company would be asked, so our time was coming. Dragon talked to us about it over breakfast.

"Guard shifts are four hours long," he said, "two shifts per night.

Six companies guard the perimeter every night and walk a portion of it. You're responsible for getting to the perimeter on time to relieve the previous watch. Do not fall asleep—it will be strokes if you do."

"And you made me come here," I grumped at Drake. Dragon cleared his throat. *Time to shut up.*

"If you see or hear anything suspicious, alert the others," Dragon went on, ignoring me. "Your superior on the night watch will decide whether it bears further investigation."

"Don't worry, Gavin is exactly the same," I told Devin later. She'd explained that Dragon didn't mean the chastisement personally. He'd chewed me out after the meeting because I wasn't treating everything more seriously. Considering I hadn't volunteered for this assignment to start with, I thought I was displaying amazing restraint.

~

"If that were one of my boys, I'd force them into a sparring match and drive them into the ground," Dragon grumbled, pacing. Crane and Devin watched as he vented his frustration. "If I pull her onto the sparring square, she'll just block all my blows and yawn while she does it."

"Dragon, she isn't military and hasn't ever been military," Devin said. "This is all new to her. If you wanted a specific behavior from her, you should have been talking to her from the beginning instead of jumping her now, when she interrupted you."

"I've given Drake and Drew a dressing-down; they should have been giving her instruction," Dragon muttered.

~

"You get the second guard shift." Crane had been sent to hand out my assignment—Dragon was still seething, I figured. I just nodded at the former General. Drake and Drew were pissed at me, too, since Dragon had yelled at them after he yelled at me.

Well, the end of this little vacation couldn't come soon enough. I set my internal clock for half an hour before I had to relieve the first guard, who happened to be Drake. He, Drew, Rik and Pheran had all gotten the first shift. Pheran Tiger was point man on that shift for us.

I was going out on the second shift with Tava, Crane Trevor and Dragon Taylor. Dragon Taylor was chief cook and bottle washer on the second shift for us.

"Lissa, if you see or hear anything, let me know," Dragon Taylor was driving his point into my head, almost. I wanted to tell him I got it the first time, but my mouth had gotten me into trouble to begin with. I just nodded and went to walk the perimeter.

Each of us had a hundred yards to guard and we walked that hundred yards. The second shift is the hardest—the time when most people are sound asleep. Or, if they're awake, wanting to be asleep more than anything. Except for vampires.

I felt more comfortable in the dark—I didn't have the hot sun glaring down on me and making me wish for the darkest of sunglasses. The night was cooler, too, and I could listen better—the noise of thousands of horses clopping along wasn't confusing everything.

Scents carried better on the breeze, too—everything was quiet except for a few guards walking the perimeter. The wind was blowing past me that night, which meant I got the scents from the camp instead of what was in front of me. More than anything, I wanted to turn to mist and check things out that way, but figured I was in enough trouble as it was.

Roughly two hours before dawn, when I'd been walking my little section of the perimeter, I caught a sound, although the wind was doing its best to carry it away from me. I stopped still, trying to catch it again. While I stood there, wondering if my ears had played tricks on me, my skin began to itch. Then I heard it. I'd heard that sound before—René had died shortly after.

Arrows! I sent the mental shout to anybody with the talent to hear me. I didn't wait, either; I knew where that sound originated and I misted in that direction as quickly as I could.

The camp was boiling behind me as the first volley was released.

Falchani fought without shields. Arrows could be swift and deadly if something wasn't done about them.

I found the archers in a ravine roughly two hundred yards north of the Falchani camp. The enemy sent a second volley while I'd misted like a bullet in their direction. Twenty archers had been sent to attack; they all died, trying to fight an enemy they couldn't see. They'd hit me in the upper arm, though, when I materialized enough to take heads.

The camp was still boiling over when I walked back inside the perimeter, wondering what the best way was to remove an arrow from my arm. The metal point had gone clean through and was sticking out on the other side, making it difficult to move my right arm, in addition to hurting like hell.

Dragon was suddenly in front of me, the usual scowl on his face. "They're all dead," I muttered, stalking past him.

"Lissa, you have a fucking arrow in your arm," he snarled.

"Like I didn't notice?" I kept walking.

"Baby, we have to get you into the tent," Drew was beside me—Drake too, and they were hustling me toward our tent. Dragon had probably sent them mindspeech. I didn't really give a damn at the moment. I was ready to break the point of the arrow off myself and jerk it out—it hurt. All I had to do was reach the fucking point to begin with.

"Lissa, what happened?" Amara was inside the tent waiting for me. Griffin was there, too, but he was standing back to allow Amara the healer to take over.

"About twenty archers, two hundred yards north of here, that's what happened," I grumped. "They were downwind; otherwise I would have smelled them long ago. The wind was carrying the sound away, too, until I heard the bowstrings being pulled back. That's how René died, you know. He was shot through the heart with a wooden arrow, when the Dark Elemaiya came through the gate in Kansas City." I was babbling and hadn't realized it. "Where's Karzac?" I asked. I figured if any healer was going to show up, it would probably be him.

"Karzac's busy," Griffin said. I blinked at my father.

"Gracie's pregnant; Karzac is going to get his child, after all these years," Amara said softly while she sheared off the arrow point using power. Well, if anybody wanted to deal a blow to my system, along with the arrow through my arm—that would be the way to do it. Karzac had gotten Grace pregnant. I couldn't get pregnant. Ever. I went completely still.

"Amara, that should have waited for another time," Griffin said. Amara was pulling the arrow out of my arm; she was left staring at the bloody shaft in her hand as I misted away.

CHAPTER 5

arth—past

I hadn't tried to bend time before, but I did it then. My arm was still bleeding sluggishly while I stood outside Howard Graham's cell at the Oklahoma State Penitentiary in McAlester.

It was late afternoon there and sunlight shone through the tiny window in his cell. He looked a lot older than when I'd last seen him inside the county courthouse. Now he'd been sober for a while and had six months left before a stroke would kill him.

"Who's there?" The sunlight was glaring, keeping him from seeing me clearly. He'd been sitting on his bunk so he stood and moved to the other side of the cell to get a clearer view.

"You should know who it is," I snapped. He walked forward, then, so he could peer at me through the bars of his cell.

He didn't say anything for a long time; he just stared. Finally he spoke. "You look like your mother," he said.

"I don't. My mother was beautiful. They had to keep the casket closed because her face was nothing but a bloody pulp." I wasn't going to mince words. Howard Graham and I hadn't spoken since he'd nearly killed me when I was nineteen.

"You weren't mine." Well, some things would never change.

"I know I wasn't yours," I said right back to him. "I didn't find out until recently, but it's true. If you had a child, you shithead, he would probably be sharing a cell with you, right now. Your less than honorable attorney paid under the table for a DNA test and bribed somebody to draw the blood during one of my doctor visits," I said. "I got the information from his legal files."

"He told me," Howard Graham agreed, nodding his head. At least he didn't stink of gin, now. That's one of the things I remembered about him—the smell of gin on his breath when he'd yell. He'd had to dry out when he went to jail.

"I have a couple of friends here and we talk when we're allowed out of our cells to exercise," Howard Graham went on. "One of them has a son, who's eleven. All he talks about is that boy. I asked him once what he'd do if he found out the boy wasn't his. He just looked at me like I was crazy. And then he told me this; 'Howard,' he said. 'I was beat up when I was a kid. Went to bed hungry, too, lots of nights. I don't want any kid dealing with what I lived with, growing up. I don't care if that boy belongs to the mailman or the neighbor next door. He's not gonna suffer, if I can help it.'"

"So, he's a decent man, as far as kids go, then," I muttered. "What's he in for?"

"Dale's in for involuntary manslaughter. Ran a stop sign while he was drunk. He'll be out in six months."

"So, I'm supposed to believe that because some friend of yours you met in jail turned on the light, you're a changed man, now?" He wasn't going to convince me of that.

"No. I still get upset about it," Howard Graham said, sighing and shaking his head. "I couldn't help it. Still can't. You have to believe me when I say I did love your mother. I just didn't know how to handle this." He gestured toward me.

"That makes me feel so much better, especially since you killed her and all," I retorted.

"What are you doing now?" he asked, changing the subject. I just stared at him for a moment, shocked at the question. "I'm Queen of Le-Ath Veronis," I said. "If you don't know what that means, watch this." I gave him the best hiss I could with fangs, claws, red eyes and everything. I turned to mist, too, right in front of him, while he screamed his lungs out for the guards.

∿

Falchan

"What?" I wasn't a pleasant sight, I'm sure, when I became myself inside the tent. Only a few minutes had elapsed since I'd disappeared, but now Dragon, Crane and Devin were inside the tiny tent with Drake, Drew, Amara and Griffin. I still had fangs, claws and red eyes when I got there, so I had to pull all that back to normal.

"Lissa, where have you been?" Dragon was trying to keep his voice civil.

"Well, I hear Grace and Karzac are about to be parents, so I went to visit Howard Graham inside his jail cell. The only thing different about him was that he was sober."

"Lissa, is he still alive?" Griffin asked softly.

"Oh, yeah. The old bastard was still alive when I left him," I grumbled. "Is there any more pleasant news you'd all like to drop in my lap to make my life complete?"

"Lissa, I'm sorry. I shouldn't have said anything," Amara told me, looking at my arm. I'd forgotten about it during my conversation with Howard Graham.

"Why should you be sorry? You don't have to apologize to me," I told her. "We're in the same boat, you and I. We're not getting kids. All you got was a Queen bitch vampire for a stepdaughter. There's no justice in that for you. You deserve better. You deserve a child of your own, Amara. Don't you think so?"

"Lissa." Dragon said right beside me.

"What?" I turned to look at him. His fingers touched my forehead before I could stop him and I collapsed like a sack of grain.

∿

"Every one of them, decapitated. Quite neatly, too, Warlord."

"What happened?" The Warlord studied his Lord Marshall while he sipped a cup of tea inside his tent.

"The girl gave a warning to her superior, as I understand it, and since she was closest, went after the archers herself. I spoke with her tribal leader earlier. He said the arrows were going to do a great deal of damage if we waited until we had men gathered to go after them. The girl ran to the ravine where they were hiding and stopped them after only two volleys. She took an arrow in her right arm—thankfully, she's left-handed—and managed to kill the archers while they were scrambling to get away. All they'd brought with them were their bows. They couldn't fight her in close quarters."

"We need to find out if they have more trained archers. It will not be good news if they do. Granted we have some shields with us, but not nearly enough and many of the warriors do not know how to use them." The Warlord set down his cup and frowned.

"We've only dealt with a few archers here and there—this is the first time they've banded together," Wolf, the Lord Marshall acknowledged. "The General is out visiting the wounded—we're lucky we only lost one man in the attack."

"Are the wounded able to travel? I'd like to go on in the morning."

"I believe so, Warlord. We can leave them with the cooking tents if the attacks come soon." The Lord Marshall examined the map lying on the small table between himself and the Warlord. They'd been plotting strategy.

"Good. Spread the word; we'll leave first thing in the morning."

I wasn't speaking to anybody. Drake and Drew had given up, after a while. Dragon still walked around with a deep scowl on his face, but that was nothing new. I wanted to be happy for Karzac. He'd delivered so many babies; it was time he got one.

I berated myself for not feeling better and more cheerful over the whole thing. Had Dragon known before they'd taken me on this little jaunt into the wilderness? I wasn't about to go *Looking*. My life was miserable enough, thank you.

My arrow wound was already closed up and almost healed but I still wore the bandage. Amara said no sparring for a day or two. What we did in the evenings, now, was watch Crane train Tava, Hart and Nima.

Crane Trevor and Dragon Taylor were helping and they'd spar with the women. Veykan sometimes helped out, or Turtle, even. I was bored and depressed. There wasn't a rooftop to sit on or that's where I would have been, pondering the difficulties of my life.

"Lissa, there's nothing we can do to change things," Drew sat beside me while I watched Crane put the three women through their paces. I'd heard from Drake that they hadn't been trained properly at all. I wasn't surprised—I figured the men had cut corners with their training, just so they could have an easy lay out of it. Yeah, I wasn't in a charitable mood toward anybody, nowadays.

"Well, I'll just feel this way for a while, then," I muttered.

"Lissa, we love you. Drake and I. Karzac loves you. We've been afraid to tell him that you know already. I think he'd come if he knew you were gone."

"Oh, yeah, the whole time-bending thing," I grumped. Nobody was listening to us—Crane was shouting at Tava, who was doing her best to block Dragon Taylor's blows while their blades clanged in the early evening quiet. "Besides, Karzac needs to stay with Grace. That's his baby. No way he needs to come haring after a neurotic Vampire Queen."

I was trying to come to grips with this—Karzac needed to stay with his baby until that baby was grown. He or she was going to need a stable home life and a permanent father in residence, as far as I was concerned. The poor kid was going to have to get used to the idea that his mother had multiple mates, even if they were the best guys in the universe.

"What did Howard Graham say to you, baby?"

"He said a lot of things but the words I'm sorry have never passed his lips."

"I wish we'd known each other, growing up," Drew said, putting his arm around me. "Drake and I got into all kinds of trouble. If we'd had a friend that needed looking after, well, we might not have raised so much hell."

"I'm glad you got to raise hell," I said, bumping my forehead against his arm. "Somebody needed to. I was afraid to breathe, most of the time. It was a relief to go to school in the mornings. Nobody could touch me there."

"Gracie is our second mom," Drew said suddenly. "If Mom was gone on assignment, Gracie was there. Or Gram. We knew, early on, that we had an extended family. We still call Mack Daddy Mack, and the others, too. They were all dads for us. Of course, Dad had the final say if he was in, but Uncle Crane stood in for him if he wasn't, or one of the others. Karzac certainly did. We knew we could go to him for anything. Radomir helped teach us hand fighting. We had to work to get to his level, he's so fast. Lisster and Rush taught us how to fish. Justin and Mack taught us how to ski and surf. Grampa Adam and Grampa Martin showed us how to build things. Lynx, Russell and Will taught us how to gamble. Behind Dad's back, of course. Grampa Merrill taught us how to manage money and he and Grampa Adam help us with our portfolios."

"It's good you had all those people to depend on. I'm happy for you," I sighed.

"Lissa, what I'm trying to say is that you're part of that family, now. Karzac didn't expect this. Neither did Grace."

"I know. I'm just trying to come to grips with it. I'm going for a walk, now."

"Baby, no. Don't go off by yourself. Or let Drake and me go with you. We need to know how to fix what bothers you."

"There's no fixing some of what bothers me," I said and stood up. Drew didn't like it and his dark eyes were narrowed in concern, but I walked away from him anyway. The clashing of swords grew dim as I made my way toward the edge of the camp.

There wasn't any place else to go, so as soon as I was out of sight, I misted away, heading toward the river. It had a few days to wash itself clean since we'd been there, so I took a dip and then let the last heat of the day dry me off. Reemagar was sitting on the riverbank when I was dressed again.

"What are you doing here?" I asked. I might have expected Connegar, but he wasn't the one to come. I didn't have a comb with me so I had to run fingers through my hair to get the tangles out before braiding it again.

"I came to see you. The others do not know you are gone since Dragon will bend time to get you back again right after you left. I know, as do the other Larentii."

"That is an amazing gift, to be able to know things like that," I said, looking up at his solemn, sky-blue face. His eyes crinkled a little when he smiled at me and the blue of those eyes was incredible to see.

He was one of the Larentii who had dark-blond hair—almost a brown. It looked good on him. His wrists hung over his knees as he sat beside me, so I lifted the hand nearest me and examined his palm.

Larentii have different lines running through their hands—swirls and circles that humans don't have. "It's almost like cloud patterns in a blue sky," I smiled up at him. It was the first time I'd felt like smiling in a while.

"Little Queen, you make me happy," Reemagar removed his hand from mine and placed it around my shoulders instead, hugging me against him. I remembered that I was supposed to ask Grace about his mother, but Grace was pregnant with Karzac's child. I wasn't sure how welcome I would be anywhere near Grace. Maybe I could get Pheligar or someone else to explain things to me.

We sat there on the riverbank for a long time—Reemagar and I, not saying a single thing. Eventually I laid my head against his chest, listening to his even breathing. It finally put me to sleep.

~

"She fell asleep, sitting next to me by the river," Reemagar handed Lissa over to Drake inside the tent. Reemagar had to make himself smaller; he wouldn't have fit inside the tent, otherwise. "I placed her in a healing sleep so I could transport her back to you."

"Thank you. We were getting worried and Dad was about to come looking for her," Drew stood next to his brother, gazing down at Lissa's face. She looked so peaceful in the healing sleep.

"She will wake after a short time—I do not wish to put her in danger by keeping her under too long." Reemagar said. "I must go." He nodded to Drake and Drew and folded away.

"At least she got a bath," Drew said. "She hates the dust."

"You know she would have qualified for a tattoo after taking out the archers," Drake murmured, rocking Lissa gently in his arms.

"Brother, she would qualify for fifty full sets after what she did on the High Demons' world," Drew replied. Drake nodded in agreement.

I hadn't been up early to become energy for a couple of days, so I went that morning. I stayed that way for a while, too, before bending time to get back when I should. I didn't go looking for Kifirin, although I thought about him during my trip.

"It's about time; we were about to go to breakfast without you. The Warlord wants to move out quickly after we eat," Drake said.

I was standing between Drake and Drew in line to get our food when Tava's former commander brushed past us. He could do that to us but he knew better than to try it with Dragon, Crane or one of the others.

Caylon gave him a black look as he settled in front of Tava. She, Hart and Nima stood in front of Drake, Drew and me. The interloper had a full set of tattoos—badgers decorated his chest, back and arms. I wasn't impressed. Maybe he didn't know it, but badgers belonged to the weasel family.

Devin didn't like the fact that he'd cut in line, either, but she didn't say anything. If we'd been anywhere else, I might have taught him some manners.

Dragon kept the seat across from him empty and pointed me there when I got my breakfast. That meant I was sitting between Caylon and Pheran. Now what had I done?

"Lissa, I don't want you going off by yourself again like you did last night," Dragon pointed his chopsticks at me. "I am thankful one of the Larentii came—I was just about to come looking for you myself."

I didn't say anything; I just stared at my plate. When he was on Falchan, he was the Warlord. It didn't matter that another Warlord was supposedly in charge. Again, I wondered why they'd brought me.

I wanted to tell him to banish me from the planet—I'd be happy to go home. Roff was there. And little Toff. Instead, here I was, head bowed before the Warlord, taking the drubbing. I wasn't hungry when he was done with me, either.

"Lissa, you're just pushing your food around," Crane said. I dropped my chopsticks. I wanted to cry, only this wasn't the place to do it. Falchani warriors were everywhere, talking, laughing, eating. The sound was almost overwhelming. The scent, too, was overpowering. Too many bodies pressing close.

"Lissa, don't you dare pass out," Caylon was holding me up. I blinked at him stupidly. Drake and Drew were about to have a fit and Dragon had already issued the command for them to sit back down. They sat but they didn't like it.

"Lissa, drink this," Pheran had his cup of tea at my lips. I drank. I felt dizzy.

What's wrong with my baby? Drew's voice, so soft, inside my head.

"I feel dizzy," I said.

"Because you're not eating," Dragon's voice rumbled. *When did you have blood, last?*

Don't remember, I returned his sending.

You don't take from the boys?

I've never taken from them. It was an insult that he'd even suggest it. I only drank from Roff or my vampire mates and only then when they demanded it. Roff was bitten twice a month, at his insistence. I'd drank from Shadow, once, but I'd begged him not to ask for it again.

"Fuck," Dragon sighed and rubbed his forehead. "Somebody see that she eats." He left the table and stalked off. Devin started to get up and follow him, but Crane held her down.

Eat something, love. Drake was sending, now. *We have a long ride ahead of us. You won't make it if you don't eat.*

The food tasted almost as much like sawdust as it used to, when I ate food as a full vampire. I forced as much down as I could, remembering my lessons with Merrill. All that seemed like a thousand years ago.

Tava, Hart and Nima sat at the far end of the table, near Drake and Drew. They'd watched the entire episode, not saying anything. I thought I saw contempt in their eyes, though. Maybe that's how Dragon saw me, too, now.

We'd almost reached our camping spot for the evening when the attack came. The enemy had somehow gotten there, even though the scouts hadn't found them. I didn't know how that could be but I didn't waste any time, just like the others.

We were in the foothills and archers had been placed carefully somewhere above us. The entire army was in turmoil, getting horses out of the way so they could handle the enemy's ground troops. Then the arrows came raining down. I misted in the direction of the arrows; I didn't care what Dragon had to say about it and didn't ask.

Nearly a hundred archers attacked us, this time, all equipped with long bows. I wondered if the Falchani army was going to take the hint soon and train archers of their own.

I started with the back row of archers and worked my way forward. It took a while for them to realize that something was there, killing them. These had swords with them, but I was more careful, this time. I barely let my hands and claws materialize as I took heads.

It might have taken fifteen or twenty minutes, with the last five or so spent while they hunted me with their blades. One whacked a blade against my claws and screamed when the blade was sheared off. That one died, just like the others.

I sped down the mountainside, then, to join the other troops. Materializing beside Drake and Drew, I lifted my blades from the sheath at my back and went to work. If Dragon wanted to see me go on the offensive, well, he might have gotten his wish that night.

I had better night vision than anyone there; I knew that for a fact. Heads flew as I whirled through the enemy in a blur. I had no idea how many died that night at my hands. A lot, I suppose.

When the last ones I could find had been dispatched, I stood on the blood-soaked grass, panting from the exertion. There wasn't anyone alive around me when I stopped and I wondered where the Falchani army was. I turned to look behind me.

The nearest person was perhaps a hundred yards behind me, and that was Dragon. Caylon, Pheran and Crane were a short distance behind him and they were walking in my direction.

Now what? Was he going to yell that I needed to appear more human? He hadn't said anything about that to me. Somebody should have gone over the ground rules with me before this whole thing got started.

"Lissa." Dragon walked up to me slowly.

"What? What did I do wrong this time, Dragon?"

"Lissa, come back with us, now. They're all dead." Dragon was holding out a hand in a calming gesture. He and the others were stepping over dead bodies, some two or three deep. I reached down and ripped off the clean portion of an enemy's tunic to wipe my blades—they were covered in blood.

"Lissa, come." Dragon's voice was even and calm. Calmer than I'd heard it in the past few days, anyway.

"I'm coming, keep your shirt on," I grumped. That was a joke—he was bare-chested and his tattoos were visible to me in the sliver of moonlight that shone down.

I hadn't realized that the camp was so far away. We walked for almost a mile. Wounded were being tended when we got back and tents had been erected hurriedly so the healers could get to the ones most in need.

"Thank goodness." Drake and Drew were waiting for us around a campfire and a quick meal had been brought from the cooking tents. "Lissa, sit down."

I was waiting to see what all the fuss was. I was fine—nobody had touched me. I held out my bare arms just to make sure. Nope, not a scratch.

"Here, baby." Drew handed a bowl of rice with beef and gravy to me. Drake offered chopsticks, so I dipped in.

"Have you two had something to eat?" I turned to each of my twins.

"We ate." Drake was nodding. "Here," he handed a cup of rice wine to me.

"Where are Devin and the others?" I asked.

"Doing a bit of healing," Dragon said, seating himself on the opposite side of the fire. Caylon, Pheran and Crane settled down around the fire, too, and Crane passed around a large bottle of rice wine.

"Lissa, what do you remember about the battle?" Dragon asked after a while. I looked up from my food. I had to think for a minute.

"Not much, I guess. I just remember when it started and when it ended, I think. What time is it?"

"Around three hours before dawn. You were fighting from just after sunset until only a little while ago. The enemy was running away after a while. You saw where they were when you finished them off."

"That's bad." I put my bowl down.

"No, baby, eat the rest of it. Dad's not finished." Drew picked up my bowl and smiled encouragingly as he handed it back.

"The ones we fought tonight—at least half of them, anyway, were altered in some way. They were all faster and stronger than they should have been." Dragon sighed and shook his head as if he were having trouble with that information.

"That's how they managed to engage us so quickly. I know you're not aware of everything the Dark Elemaiya did before you came along, or even during the three hundred years of time you missed," Dragon went on.

"They've allied with the Ra'Ak before and at one time they had one among them called the Khos'Mirai, or Dark Mirror. He's the opposite of the Ka'Mirai—the True Mirror. I'm thankful he's no longer alive—the Bright Elemaiya killed him centuries ago. We were seeing the results of the Dark Mirror's alliance with the Ra'Ak tonight."

"What are you talking about?" I stared at Dragon in alarm.

"Somehow, the Khos'Mirai must have convinced the Ra'Ak long ago that it was in their best interest to splice Ra'Ak DNA with that of the Elemaiya, instead of making them spawn as they would normally have done. We were facing an army of those creatures, tonight. They were difficult for a regular soldier to kill—all these Ra'Ak-enhanced warriors were much stronger and faster. Our company took out its share, but we would have lost this battle except for you, Lissa. I see now why a Queen Vampire is as important as she is. I've never seen anything like that. Pheligar was here just a short while ago, telling us where to find you since we can't track you in any way. I think you had some sort of battle rage going and you took every one of those fuckers down."

"No wonder I'm so tired," I sighed. "Please tell me I can sleep in a bed soon."

"We will see that you sleep in a bed soon," Dragon replied, his dark eyes focusing on my face. "Crane and I will go to Kiarra and let her know what we found here. The Ra'Ak may have seeded these creatures everywhere in the past three hundred years, building up a widespread army and waiting for the opportunity to strike. There was more than twenty thousand of the enemy here. Likely more than half of them were Ra'Ak enhanced—enough to take down the Falchani army. Who knows when they were left here to breed? As it is, the Falchani lost more than a third of their numbers."

"They can breed?" I stared at Dragon in alarm.

"Just as the Ra'Ak spawn can breed," Dragon nodded. "The seed is in their blood or saliva."

"Are you sure we got all of them?" I felt like hyperventilating.

"You got the last of them on Falchan, Belen and Pheligar have confirmed it. There could be more, perhaps in the millions, scattered across the universes. This bears thinking about," Dragon leaned back and shook his head. "They instructed the Reldani archers that came against us, too, so they have weapons training."

"Then I hope you tell the Warlord to start training archers," I sighed, eating the last of my beef and rice. "I killed a hundred of them first before I ever drew a blade."

"I'll try to pass that message along."

~

"Remind me never to spar with her again," Caylon muttered, after Drake and Drew hauled Lissa off toward their tent.

"We still haven't told her about Tava," Pheran said.

"It's just as well; Tava approached Drew the other night while Lissa was at the river."

"As if he'd be interested," Crane huffed.

"He wasn't, but she wasn't complimentary toward Lissa. She told Drew that he didn't need to be with, in her words, that tiny, weak excuse for a warrior. She offered to bed him while Lissa was gone."

"What did Drew do?" Pheran was just as interested in gossip as anyone else.

"He told her to get out of his sight or he'd toss her out of our camp."

"That tiny, weak excuse for a warrior just took down half the enemy," Crane said.

"More than half," Dragon agreed. "Let's go find Devin before she wears herself out."

~

Drake and Drew let me sleep in (for a little while, anyway), before getting me up and off to breakfast. The others were already eating at the table when we got there. The Badger dude was banged up but standing in line ahead of us. We got our plates and headed for our seats. Tava was missing—only Hart and Nima were there. They didn't look at me—they just kept eating.

"What happened?" I stared at the empty seat on the bench.

"Tava didn't make it," Devin said. "Lissa, sit down and eat. It was a clean, swift kill. She didn't suffer."

I sighed as I set my plate on the table; the cooks had made biscuits again. The cooking tent was noisy and warriors were trading battle stories already.

"We're going to Gram's after we clear up our campsite," Drake whispered as I ate. I was feeling tired and out of sorts, but I didn't want to tell him that. At least I'd be able to clean up at Kiarra's before heading back to Le-Ath Veronis and whatever was on the schedule for the day. I felt bad about Tava, too. If stupid Badger-man had trained her properly, she might still be alive.

"Take us with you," Hart begged Dragon later, as we took down the tent and packed up our belongings.

"I have no place for you," Dragon informed her. "I am sorry."

"But we wish to continue our training," Nima said. The look of disappointment on her face was heartbreaking.

"We will not be a bother, such as Tava was," Nima blurted. That caused me to raise an eyebrow.

"It was nothing, we sent her on her way," Drew assured me. Well, that didn't sound good. Nima and Hart, though—I figured they'd had more than their share of crap at the hands of the males on Falchan.

"Where I'm going, you might not like it," I turned to Nima. "It stays dark there, most of the time. Like it is right after sundown?" I was trying to describe the lighting conditions on Le-Ath Veronis, and that didn't include the vampires. Well, Nima and Hart might like that, actually. "You're welcome to come with me, if you want."

"It's your call, baby. Drew and I can put them with the others and train them together," Drake looked thoughtful. Well, Le-Ath Veronis was begging for women. Nima was already nodding her head enthusiastically and Hart looked hopeful.

"All right, but if you don't like it, you have to tell us and we'll bring you home," I agreed. Nima almost giggled with relief.

I can't begin to describe the looks of shock and wonder on Hart and Nima's faces when they were folded to Gryphon Hall.

"How did we get here?" Nima finally worked up the courage to ask.

"Like this." I pulled a sheet off a pad of paper at Kiarra's kitchen island and borrowed the pen sitting nearby. "This is where we were." I drew a dot on one end of the paper. "This is where we are, now." I drew another dot on the opposite end of the paper. "Now," I said, "we did this." I pushed both ends of the paper together, causing the middle to bow upward until the two ends of the paper met.

"That is frightening," Nima breathed.

"But true," I said. "I want a bath. How about you two?"

"I think we can find an empty shower." Kiarra walked into the room and introduced herself, along with Adam and Merrill, who'd followed her.

"Little girl," Merrill leaned down and kissed my cheek. Well, he and I had declared a truce. It was the only way, I guess. Now, he was treating me as if he were still my surrogate sire. I sighed. Punching him in the face would only cause problems. I ignored that thought.

"Careful, I'm sure I taste like dust," I warned him. "Falchan is covered in it, right now." Merrill's bright blue eyes lit up and he smiled —he knew what I'd been thinking. The schmuck.

Dragon, Devin and Crane had gone off to their villa to clean up, before talking to Kiarra about what we'd found on Falchan. Drake and Drew were with me. I knew Karzac was at the villa, too, but I still didn't know what to do about that. Caylon and the others had gone off in search of mates.

"You're taking those two for guards?" Merrill lifted an eyebrow after Kiarra took Nima and Hart down a hall to show them the guest bath.

"They begged us to take them with us and I have to tell you, female warriors aren't being treated well on Falchan right now. Besides, I told them if they didn't like where we're going, we'll take them home. Simple fix."

"Lissa, Erland Morphis came to Adam and me two days ago and

gave us a proposal. I'd like to come and discuss it with you and the others sometime soon." Merrill was smiling.

"All right. How is the winery coming along?" I couldn't argue too much—he and Adam were building Roff's winery and I didn't want Roff to be disappointed if I reignited what I'd come to think of as *The Vampire Family Feud*.

"We're almost ready to build and Roff has gathered a group that can be taken to Kifirin to harvest the oxberries on the Northern Continent. He's quite excited over the whole thing."

"Good. I sort of love Roff. A lot."

"As if we couldn't tell," Merrill teased. When did he start doing that?

"Geez, Merrill, I never expected that from you—teasing, I mean."

"You might be surprised at what I can do. Frank, Shane and Tomas want to come for a visit, too." Was he trying to get back in my good graces? I couldn't tell. Well, he could keep that crap to himself. I wasn't falling for it. But Frank—and Shane—I loved them. Tomas, too.

"Frank is welcome anytime, as are the others. In fact, I'll name a guest suite after them and they can live there if they want. I love Frank. I've loved Frank since the first minute we met, I think. He's the brother I never had. Just like Charles, actually."

"Conner might have a fit but I'll tell them. Charles loves the house he has in Lissia. He lives next door to Flavio and Dalroy and Rhett are nearby. Kyler spends most of her time there, now, and she has even built a home on the light side, near the ocean."

"Wow. Maybe I need to do that—build a summer home near the ocean." I hadn't even thought of that.

"Adam and I can help put it up for you, if you'll let us use it from time to time."

"Merrill, you can do whatever you want, I don't care. How's that?" I held my arms out in sweeping gesture.

"Lissa, I do love you. I hope you know that. It might not be the kind of love you wanted once, but it's there anyway."

"Merrill, there's a lot of things I have to deal with, including

Karzac becoming a father. You and I both know I'll never get children, so that's been a bit of a blow. I'm dealing with it the best I can."

"I know, sweetheart." Merrill touched my cheek. "You are covered in dust," he said, when he drew his hand back. "Go clean up. We'll talk later."

I went to clean up and Kiarra had set some of Fox's clothes out for me when I stepped from the shower. I washed my hair three times, I think, just to make sure I got all the dust out of it. Drake, Drew, Hart and Nima were waiting on me when I walked inside the kitchen. I was the one who bent time and folded space to Le-Ath Veronis.

CHAPTER 6

*L*e-Ath Veronis

"Raona, you are not dressed properly for your meetings."

Those were Giff's first words to me when we arrived at the breakfast table. Those of us who'd come from Kiarra's were getting breakfast (again) for lunch. Hart and Nima looked around them, both with stunned expressions on their faces.

"Sit down, another breakfast is on the way," I said. Gabron was already there with Gavin, Tony and Roff. I went to give each of them a kiss.

"Lissa, why do I get the idea that you have been somewhere?" Gabron eyed my clothing with a critical glare.

"It's a long story. We'll talk later," I said and followed Giff so I could change clothes.

***

"We went to Falchan," Drake shook out his napkin after getting Hart and Nima settled at the table. He introduced the two women and informed Tony and Gavin that they would be training them to add to the palace guard.

"This is where Lissa lives?" Nima asked.

"Lissa is Queen here," Gabron replied. "All males here are members of her Inner Circle and mated to her. She has other mates, but they are absent at the moment."

Nima stared at Hart, her eyes wide. "We thought at first she was only a warrior and Tava held her in contempt because she seemed so small and weak," Nima said, turning back to Gabron. "We have seen her fight. We no longer think this."

"Have I mentioned that all here except Drake, Roff and I are vampires?" Drew smiled wickedly. "Don't worry, you are in no danger. Although I hear the bite can be quite pleasurable."

"I can arrange a trial bite for them," Gabron offered.

"We'll save that for later," Drake grinned.

"What's this about a trial bite?" I was frowning when I returned to the table, dressed properly this time, according to Giff. At least she'd let me wear a silk tunic and pants in an emerald color with gold embroidery on the cuffs and hem.

Giff also insisted I wear the simple gold coronet I had instead of the heavy claw crown, after she'd dressed my hair. I preferred to go without a crown or coronet, saving both for more formal occasions, but Giff had her way this time.

"I offered to arrange a bite, if these two young women are interested," Gabron said.

"I think you should explain it carefully before you let them decide," I said. "What's on the agenda today?"

"We are hammering out the final law on the age limit for the comesuli to receive the bite, plus a few other things."

"Great. Another day of fun-packed meetings. How many people did I kill, yesterday?" I asked Drake as I cut into a sausage link.

"More than ten thousand, I think," Drake said. "I just want to tell you how much I love you, baby."

"You speak of these things at the table?" Hart asked, staring at Drake.

"They speak of everything at the table," Gavin growled.

"Honey, that growl almost sounded good-natured. Is something wrong? Are you feeling all right?"

"I hear you have been gone from me for days, while it is only seconds for me. I am happy to have you back, cara."

"Where has my granddaughter been?" Wylend Arden and Erland Morphis folded in, causing Nima to shriek. Griffin folded in immediately after, followed by Amara. Amara was smiling. I got a good whiff of her and found myself standing, suddenly.

"Daddy, what the hell have you been doing?" I asked.

"What are you talking about?" Griffin turned his gaze on me.

"Mom's pregnant, that's what I'm talking about. How did that happen?"

"What?" Griffin and Amara said at the same moment.

"Check for yourself," I grumped. Griffin did a little *Looking*, as did Amara. Amara was shrieking and throwing herself into Griffin's arms. Wylend was beaming while Erland came to return me gently to my chair.

"Love, it is fine—Wylend needs an heir and Griffin has already declined because of his Oracle status." Erland was making sense, I knew, but really. Now two people were pregnant. I blew out a frustrated sigh.

"Are you a vampire, too?" Nima asked Erland, who was busy searching for an empty seat at the table. She was staring at the second most handsome man I'd ever met and liked what she saw, I could tell.

"I am a Karathian warlock," he announced with an imperious wave of his hand and then laughed.

"Did you leave any for us?" Garde folded in with Jayd and Glinda, each parent holding a tiny baby. Amara went to Glinda immediately and lifted the baby girl from her arms. They sat at the table, too, and the servants soon had plates of food in front of them.

"How are the new ones working out?" I asked.

"We only got them yesterday," Garde smiled. "I hear you were gone," he held up a hand before I could explain my unplanned stint on Falchan.

"Then eat something before you cave in," I said.

Should I tell Gavin you were shot with an arrow? Drake teased mentally.

You want me to suffer, don't you? I sent back.

"Lissa took an arrow through her arm," Drake announced. I wanted to throw my napkin at him. Maybe a few plates and the salt and pepper shakers, too.

Gavin was sitting next to me, as was Tony. "Lissa, tell me what happened," Gavin demanded, helping himself to another sausage. Drew was the one who told the story; I wasn't in the mood.

"These are the plans for the new theatre and the shopping district," Flavio unrolled architectural plans and laid them out on the conference table. I was hearing quite a bit, today.

The age vote had been approved unanimously—the legal age for the comesuli had been set at twenty-nine. Then we turned to other things. The vampires wanted entertainment. They wanted work to keep them occupied and they wanted female companions.

"This just came from the Reth Alliance," Roff stepped quietly into the room and handed an envelope to me. The room went still. I opened the envelope, frightened of what it might contain.

"The High Council of the Reth Alliance has approved the application for Le-Ath Veronis to join the Alliance," I read off the first sentence of the document. The entire room of vampires cheered. Reemagar, who was there to help translate, smiled at me and gave me a hug.

"I've missed you." I brushed a lock of hair off Gavin's forehead.

Gavin was half-covering me, doing his best to convince my body to open up to his. "Cara, my body wishes to speak with yours—intimately," Gavin growled.

"Well, you just need to move a little," I muttered. I was the one who ended up doing the moving and little Gavin slid right into home plate.

"That is what I waited for," Gavin nuzzled my neck, giving me a gentle thrust. "Oh, yes. This is what I want." He nipped my neck. Another thrust. Fangs were in my throat and I was crying out and lifting our bodies off the bed with the climax that was taking us both.

"My love. Cara mia. My beautiful rose." I went to sleep with those words whispered against my temple.

~

"You think this could work?" I'd set up a meeting with Adam, Merrill, Erland, Gabron and many others, including Flavio and most of the Council of vampires from Earth. They all wanted in on this.

"Campiaa is not a part of the Alliance," Erland was almost crowing with excitement. He wanted this very much, I could tell. "The Alliance allows gambling, as you likely know, so this will not be a stretch for them. The ones who come to Campiaa are already used to the process of preapproval before they set foot on the planet. Gambling is all they do and they have no Alliance to oversee the payouts. The San Gerxon clan has been raking in money for centuries. I think it's time they had a little competition." He and the others wanted that competition to be on Le-Ath Veronis. They wanted to set up a gambling city on my planet.

"I will take charge of setting up the brothels," Gabron offered.

"Gabron," I slapped a hand over my face. I knew the Alliance recognized it as a legitimate business and had laws in place to protect the employees, but the thought of it made me grind my teeth.

"Lissa, only the ones desiring that profession will be allowed," Gabron said. He knew how I felt about it. He had no such qualms. "And a suitable retirement allowance is mandated by law. They will not suffer."

"Fine," I muttered. "But I want to see a list of written laws handed to me in the next two weeks, protecting everyone involved, from the employees to the vampires to the gamblers. I do not want a criminal element to establish itself on Le-Ath Veronis. I swear I will lop off heads myself if that happens. Do you hear me?"

"We feel the same. That is why Erland, Adam and I wish to move our casinos here and shut down what we have on Campiaa. Our casinos have become very popular with the gamblers because the payouts are better and we treat the guests better. The San Gerxons screw everybody." That word, coming from Merrill's mouth surprised me greatly. He winked at me. He knew and had probably used the word deliberately.

"Are these casinos going to have hotels attached? And are they going to be here in Lissia?" That was my next question.

"I propose we open a new township, just west of Lissia." Dragon and Crane had come along—they wanted in as well. Dragon made the suggestion.

"We can build a transit system, to take guests to the light side of the planet, if they wish to spend time on the beach," Crane said. "More casinos can be built there. I believe both will thrive—this side because of the vampire element—the sunny side because of the lack of the vampire element."

"You've thought of everything." Charles slapped Dragon on the back. Well, they'd all been discussing this. I had a feeling they had an ulterior motive in setting up casinos on Le-Ath Veronis. I sighed.

"A few other casino owners from Campiaa wish to build and invest here, if we do this," Erland went on. "I have already priced work crews and I believe we might be able to forego the cost of transporting materials."

Of course, he could say that, since members of the Saa Thalarr were interested in building and Erland was no slouch in the power department. They could bring in supplies in a blink if they wanted and put up buildings in a blink, too, if they wanted.

"Well, Roff might have a built-in market for his oxberry wine," I sighed. Alcohol generally flowed freely in any casino.

"Raona." Roff was nodding and beaming at me. I would have

reached out for his hand if he weren't sitting across such a wide table at the moment. He was looking forward to this, I could tell.

"Garde and Jayd can have a market for all their exports," Charles said. "In fact, we may be able to hire a few High Demons to work the light side casinos. I wonder if they'd be interested."

"I wish to be in charge of the entertainers who come to perform," Susila spoke up. I lifted my head to look at her—she was down the table, sitting next to Oluwa. His smile was huge and flawless. "I would like to work with Susila," he said.

"Fine. You get to be in charge of that. Is somebody writing all this down?" I was about to get a headache. I was just as aware as the next person that Le-Ath Veronis needed entertainment, but even I hadn't gone in this direction. Now everybody, including the Saa Thalarr and Heads of Councils, wanted to turn Le-Ath Veronis into a gambling mecca.

"That headache is there because lunchtime has come and gone," Kiarra sat between Adam and Merrill but hadn't spoken before now.

"Okay, we need to do something about that," I sighed. Roff went to the door and shouted for someone to go to the kitchens for us.

We hammered out more details over plates of fruit, vegetables and turkey sandwiches, while the vampires enjoyed bottles of blood substitute. I had a bottle with my sandwich. It actually tasted good. Merrill was suggesting that we set up a method whereby any vampire might invest in the venture. Charles agreed.

"Then I wish to purchase shares for all the vampires from Beliphar," I said. "They came to us with nothing, although they deserved more. They have been little more than slaves for a very long time. This will be my gift to them."

"I'd like to contribute," Kiarra nodded. "I'll sell off a bit of Tiralian crystal for this." She could do that—she actually owned the deserted planet of Tiralia and had it warded, so any new crystal mined there was hers to sell or give away.

"I'm getting all this down, Aunt Lissa," Kyler was off in the corner, acting as my chief of staff. She was recording the entire meeting on a handheld computer device. "We're already being swamped with requests from Alliance vampires who wish to relocate here."

"I know it's not good for the environment, but can I get hard copies on all those requests?" I sat up taller in my chair so I could see my niece in the corner.

"I'll have them ready for you tomorrow," Kyler grinned. My nieces weren't gorgeous or anything.

"The Wolf contingent wants in on this." Weldon, Martin and Mack all appeared. Wlodek scooted over so Weldon could take a seat. Flavio moved things around so Martin and Mack could sit down. If anybody else showed up, I wasn't sure where we could put them. Of course, others showed up. Lynx, Will and Russell appeared as if they'd been called.

"All right, if there's more mindspeech to send out, do it now, so we'll know how many chairs to bring in," I said. I went to the door this time, motioning for Roff to remain seated. The room was extremely crowded now—even Glendes Grey, Eldest of Grey House, had come with Shadow, and I think every one of the Saa Thalarr were there, with their healers and Spawn Hunters.

Karzac and Grace had come together. I made sure a comfortable seat was brought for Grace. She wasn't showing yet, but she was pregnant. Conner had arrived with Lynx, Russell and Will. Griffin and Amara had also squeezed in and sat next to Erland and Wylend. This was going to be the multicultural venture to end all multicultural ventures and I still had my doubts over the whole thing.

"I am wiped." I let my head fall onto the tabletop when the room cleared out. Everybody had an assignment. Karzac, Joey, Franklin, Shane and Jeff had all volunteered to get the health facilities completed and coordinated—there would have to be some on the light side, too, if the plans went through. The usual application had to be sent to the Reth Alliance, just to get their approval on all of it.

"Lissa, we came to stay for a few days; I hope you don't mind." Frank sat on the chair next to mine.

"Frankie, didn't your dad pass my message along?" I sat up and looked at him.

"He said something about your naming a suite after me or something." He winked at me.

"You lunatic," I swatted at him. "I'll have your name on the door, spelled out in Tiralian crystal if you'll stay as much as you can."

"Then we will. I hear the food's decent, even for a vampire planet."

"Oh, crap—we forgot about that," I slapped my forehead. "Gamblers like to eat almost as much as they like to gamble. We have to import chefs."

"Don't worry about it—we can put out the word when the time comes. I think you'll have more applications than you can possibly imagine." Frank put an arm around me.

"Thanks, Frank," I sighed.

"Lissa?" I was getting dressed when I heard his voice. Well, it was time, I guess.

"What, hon?" I walked out of my bathroom and found Karzac and Grace inside my suite. "Are you all right, Grace?" I asked, first thing. "That meeting was long—do you need to lie down or anything?"

She looked fine, her honey-blonde hair was swept back from her face and she was dressed in jeans and a silk print blouse. As I'd never been pregnant, I had no point of reference as to how tired she might be.

"No, I'm not even two months, yet. Don't you start, too."

"Who's starting?" I forced a smile. Grace didn't answer; she just pointed a thumb at Karzac.

"Well, that's his baby." I was trying to get earrings into my ears and that was always a problem if I wasn't standing in front of a mirror while I did it.

"Let me help," Karzac came over and took the earrings from my hand. He had a wire slipped into my right ear in no time, then did the other ear for me.

"Thanks," I looked up at him. His mouth quirked into a crooked grin.

"We know this is hard for you," Grace said, coming forward. "More than a little, according to Dragon."

"I'm dealing," I said. "Karzac deserves a child, if anybody does. Amara's pregnant, too, did you know?"

"What?" Grace had just gotten juicy news.

"Yep. I smelled it this morning. Griffin is about to dance on the roof, I think."

"Oh, my gosh—two at the same time. Maybe we can school them together." Grace was already thinking about all this.

"Talk to Amara—I think she's in heaven, right now."

"Lissa," Karzac's hand cupped my cheek.

"Don't." I pulled away. "You guys go on—I'm sure they're waiting dinner on me." I made a shooing motion. They walked out the door of my suite, closing it softly behind them. The tears that hadn't come before came now; I dropped to the floor and sobbed.

"Someone else needs to go," Karzac's face looked haggard when he and Grace made their way into the dining room.

"What's wrong?" Shadow and Tony were both standing at the same time.

"She's crying," Grace said. "We didn't want to upset her. It didn't work."

"I will go." Roff was out of his seat quickly.

"I will do this." Connegar appeared in a brief flash of light and just as rapidly disappeared again.

"Little Rose, come here." Those were Connegar's first words to me as he lifted me off the floor. Giff had dressed me in expensive blue silk for dinner, since so many people had stayed to eat with us. I probably wasn't doing it any good by lying on the floor and crying all over it.

"I'll get over this," I wiped my face with the heel of a hand.

"My love, I will not say you should not weep. This is difficult for you, I know."

"Amara is pregnant because of you, Lissa." Kifirin appeared in my room; I caught his scent before I heard his voice.

"What did I do?" I sniffled. Connegar caused a handkerchief to appear in his hand and he offered it to me so I could dry things up a little.

"You told her she deserved a child. There was Power in your words. Perhaps you did not realize it at the time; nevertheless, it is so. She became pregnant right away."

"Great." I leaned my head against Connegar's chest. He'd settled on the bed and was holding me against him. Kifirin strode into my field of vision but his face was enigmatic as he studied me.

"Avilepha, do not upset yourself further. Come to dinner with me. I will take my seat and we will entertain our guests." Kifirin held his hand out to me.

"But I look like crap," I said, sliding out of Connegar's lap, still wiping my face with the handkerchief he'd given me.

"It does not matter. Hold your head up, as the Queen that you are. We will do this, you and I."

Kifirin is the most beautiful male I have ever seen. His angel's face now looked worried, though, as I took his hand. He tucked my fingers into the crook of his elbow and folded me to dinner.

Conversation hushed as we walked into the dining room and the servants—vampire and comesuli, rushed away to bring out the first course.

Dinner conversation dealt mostly with casinos, the Reth Alliance, Campiaa and the current conditions there. "I want this so bad I can taste it," Erland said. "We've been dealing with San Gerxon scum for a long time. I'm hoping that if we leave the planet and take at least half the gamblers with us, they'll feel the bite after a while."

"Well, it's a cinch the San Gerxons aren't coming here," I grumped.

"I thought we had the head off the snake when we took Divil San Gerxon down a while back," Adam said. "Unfortunately, it was a hydra and not a snake. His brother Arvil has taken over and he's just as bad as Divil was."

Adam was angry over this, I could tell. I also got the idea that Adam weighed everything carefully before he made important decisions, and this was an important decision.

"Then we'll do our best on this," I gave him the biggest smile I could, attempting to hide my concerns for Le-Ath Veronis.

"I'm just worried about what they'll do if things don't work out for them. I know we'll cut into their profits, if not take the business away from them. They could get nasty over this." Adam was still frowning.

"Well, we can always send my newly formed Enforcer Squad out after them," I said.

"What newly formed Enforcer Squad?" Drake lifted an eyebrow at me.

"The one I'll form if I need it," I said, wrinkling my nose at him.

"Just so you go through channels," Tony teased. "I think Gavin and I would have to approve the recruits."

"I have some out of work Enforcers, now," Flavio offered. "And an Assassin who's about to go stir crazy. Trevor asks every day if there's anything he can do."

"We'll work this out," I sighed. "In the meantime, do they like to play baseball or football or anything?"

"Get Brock, bubby loves baseball," Grace said.

"Bubby?"

"Grace and Brock knew each other before he was turned," Merrill coughed into his hand. "They worked together and are like brother and sister. She's the reason I had to chain him up for two months after I turned him."

"Of course," I nodded, although most of it defied my understanding. "I hope he had a shower within easy reach." Both times, my prison cells had been decidedly lacking in the area of personal comforts.

"And a fridge full of blood," Adam agreed.

"Lissa, we can issue a formal apology for locking you up. Twice." Flavio smiled.

"Too late, dude. That boat left the dock long ago. How would Trevor feel about being Sheriff?" I asked. "I mean, we have to have a lock-up—you can't expect everybody to behave one hundred percent of the time."

"Yeah, sending in the palace guards or the army might be a bit much," Tony agreed.

Flavio whipped out a communicator and had Trevor on the line in no time. "How does the position of Sheriff sound to you?" Flavio didn't waste any time.

"That sounds perfect," Trevor replied. Yeah, we all listened in.

"Have him check in with Gavin," I said.

"Tomorrow," Gavin nodded. "In my office." Gavin and Tony shared a good-size office, Drake and Drew did the same. Kyler had her own, as did Roff, and he was very pleased with it. He was already complaining that he needed artwork for the walls.

"Do we have vampires with artistic talent, architectural experience or anything like that?" I asked. "The palace needs decorating and I'd be happy to share any plans they might come up with on the whole casino city thing—both light and dark side."

"I wouldn't mind looking at a few ideas," Adam said.

"Good, you're in charge of that. Is Griffin still here?" We'd moved to the drawing room, for lack of a better title, and coffee and dessert were passed around.

"I'm still here, baby." Griffin came forward.

"Your brother that Narissa mentioned is here, with the Belipharan vampires," I said. "Davan is his name and he's being instructed by an older vampire. I just thought you should know."

"Lissa, that makes him your Uncle," Griffin came to hug me. "How long have you known about this?"

"Since Kifirin and I brought them in. I just didn't want to interfere with his instruction—he's brand new as a vampire. Turned because somebody framed him for a crime. He's a quarter Bright Elemaiya, as is his sire, Jeral, and both have mindspeech. I wanted to talk to both of them, though, and see if they have other talents."

"I want to be in on that meeting. You don't know who his father is?"

"No, Daddy. I don't. I didn't try *Looking*, either."

"Perhaps I should pay another visit to your grandmother," Griffin leaned down to kiss my forehead.

"My murderous bitch grandmother? I can't believe she killed her own parents," I shuddered at the thought. "I mean, I might have wished Howard Graham dead lots of times, but I couldn't do it."

"I know, baby." Griffin gave me a squeeze before he let me go. "I'm taking Amara home—she's had a long day."

"Sorry I let the cat out of the bag, Mom," I waved at her across the room. She just laughed as Griffin folded her away.

"Jeral," he smiled as I acknowledged him the following morning.

"Thank you for the clothing order," he said.

"We pulled you out of there without an extra stitch to your name— it was the least we could do," I said, as he and Davan made their way to assigned seats.

The Belipharan Council held seven members and Davan came along to keep records for them. He'd been an accountant before, after all. I wondered if he'd liked his job. We might be able to find something for him, if he were interested.

"My Queen, many of our vampires grow bored," Jeral said as I gave the indication that it was all right to sit in my presence. Making somebody stand was just dumb.

"Well, that may be about to change—the Reth Alliance has approved our membership and we'll need crews to work shifts on the space station. I woke this morning and found more than ten thousand requests from Reth Alliance vampires waiting on my approval, for either visits or relocation. And this is just the first day." I breathed a troubled sigh.

"Are all these requests from vampires?" Jeral asked, sitting down. I sat in the seat next to his; that particular Council member hadn't arrived yet.

"No. Some are just thrill seekers, wanting to see vampires. Some are vampires who wish to see what Le-Ath Veronis is before they make a decision. Reth Alliance vampires are generally fine where they are, but they can still be treated differently."

"I understand that very well," Jeral gave me a small smile. Jeral and Davan both had dark hair and golden-brown eyes. Jeral was the handsomer of the two, but Davan was no slouch.

"And my father and I wish to speak with you and Davan after the meeting today," I said. "Can we get you anything before the meeting starts?"

"We have fed, my Queen. We are quite fine, today."

Once all the Councils were assembled, we discussed more laws, stopped for a blood break and then went after it again. We tabled what we couldn't reach a decision on and rescheduled. And, as the Heads of Councils were the only ones notified before, Gabron, Adam and Merrill gave a presentation on the gambling planet proposal, including the brothels and other business concerns, to everyone present.

The Refizani contingent would be commandeering the brothels, but there were others who wanted in, so they agreed to hold a separate meeting the following evening. I really didn't want to get involved in that if I didn't have to.

Most of the vampires were quite excited that humans and other races might be coming to visit, and they were very interested in buying shares in some of the businesses.

"But what if the vampires have no funds to invest?" Davan held up his hand. Though he wasn't a member of the Council, I dared anybody to challenge me when I answered his question.

"I have already thought about this," I said. "I and one other are buying shares on your behalf, if all this comes about," I told him. "These shares will be placed in the names of all the vampires from Beliphar. Meanwhile, if any of your people have experience in architecture, plumbing or building of any kind, please have them contact Adam and Merrill if they're interested in that sort of work. We are looking for help and are prepared to pay for good, experienced employees."

Flavio, Gabron, Wlodek, Adam and Merrill came with me as Jeral and Davan followed me to my private study after the meeting. Yeah, I had one, but I didn't get to spend much time in it.

"This is the first time I've seen this," Wlodek said, admiring my study. It was quite large and the Vermeer hung on the wall behind my desk. The Corot held a place of honor on the opposite wall. Merrill had placed both paintings in stasis when he hung them for me. They would never deteriorate while the stasis spell lasted.

"This is lovely." Jeral zoned in on the Vermeer right away. "I remember sunlight like this," he sighed. Yeah, I knew that feeling, except he'd been without sunlight a hell of a lot longer than I had.

"A master artist from my home world painted that, around seven hundred years ago," I said. "I was very lucky that this came my way."

Griffin folded in at that moment. I had a few snacks laid out, including a few bottles of blood substitute. Davan took one of those after asking Jeral. Davan looked to be in his twenties, although the records that Drake and Drew had pilfered from Beliphar said he was in his mid-fifties—slightly older than I was.

"Please sit down," I said, going behind my desk. Plenty of seating was scattered against walls and in corners inside my study. Griffin came and sat on the edge of my desk.

"I asked Lissa to bring both of you for this meeting," Griffin informed Davan and Jeral, after introducing himself. "Jeral, are you aware of your heritage—what gives you mindspeech?"

"I am, but I may be alone in that knowledge, at least among the Belipharan vampires," he said. "My father was a quarter Bright Elemaiya and he was dropped off on Beliphar more than seven thousand years ago. He could mindspeak, as can I. He told me of the Elemaiyan race and how cruel and cold they could be. He despised them after they forced him out. I was handed to him only a month later, after I was born to one of the half-Elemaiyan women. My father raised me when he was only sixteen and had little knowledge of rearing a child." I shook my head at Jeral's tale, but it was something I'd already begun to suspect.

"Davan, do you know anything about your parents?" Griffin asked.

"No. I was raised in a state orphanage. My records said I was three months old when I was left there. No records of which parent left me there were made. I'm not sure they ever knew."

"I know who your mother is," Griffin sighed.

"Who was she?"

"No, who is she." Griffin corrected Davan gently. "She is very much alive."

"And the biggest child-abandoning bitch in the universe," I muttered. "Griffin, Narissa gave us the information she had at the time. Jeral and Davan are both your brothers."

CHAPTER 7

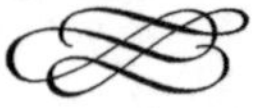

*L*e-Ath Veronis

Griffin whirled to look at me, a shocked expression on his face. "You're joking?"

"No, Daddy. They're brothers. That means they're your brothers. Well, half-brothers, anyway. Davan is definitely your mother's son, as is Jeral. You're both my uncles," I had to lean around Griffin to see both of them, now.

"We are related to the Queen?" Davan didn't understand. Well, I was a card-carrying member of that club.

"Yes, you're related to the Queen," I sighed. "And I can take you to meet your mother if you want. Be prepared; if that is what you want. Jeral, Narissa had to seduce your father before he turned sixteen, because that seems to be the time when the quarter-bloods are all cast out."

"That is true," Gabron agreed. Griffin, who was still coming to terms with all this, nodded mutely. "That would make him more than a quarter-blood, wouldn't it?" Gabron nodded toward Jeral, who seemed stunned at the information he'd been given.

"Yeah. Don't ask me to calculate the math," I said.

114

"I have no wish to meet her," Jeral said. "You may go if that is your desire, Davan."

"Is she truly that cruel?" Davan asked.

"She killed her own parents," I informed him with a shrug.

"So, that's patricide, matricide, seducing a child, child abandonment," Gabron ticked off her crimes.

"I don't want to know what else she did," I muttered. "I know too much as it is. I can't help but think Daddy was abused growing up; he just won't say anything about it." He and I had that in common; I just didn't know how severe his abuse was at Narissa's hands.

"Daughter, she is paying for her sins, now," Griffin muttered.

"Yeah, well," I didn't finish my sentence.

"What does this mean, though?" Jeral sounded confused.

"It means that you have a place here, if you want it," I said. "Or we can find you another home, somewhere in Lissia, or you can go back to the house in New Beliphar." They'd named their new city after their old planet. Go figure.

"As members of the Royal House, it might be wise to stay here, at least in the city. While most of the vampires here have good intentions, it wouldn't be the first time members of a royal family were kidnapped or threatened to achieve certain objectives," Merrill said dryly.

"I probably need someone to watch over the books; Kyler is doing what she can with help from Charles, but neither is able to keep up with all of it." I smiled encouragingly at Davan.

"Rolfe could use some help as well," Gabron suggested.

"Rolfe?" Jeral looked up.

"I'll get him," Gabron offered and slipped out the door. Rolfe was there with Gabron in a matter of minutes, a worried crease on his forehead.

"I'm not in trouble, Rolfe," I held up a hand. He breathed a relieved sigh. "Rolfe is my personal guard," I told Jeral. "But he can't be in all places at all times—he gets days off."

"She forces me to take days off," Rolfe grumped.

"I would be more than pleased to guard your life," Jeral stood and bowed.

"Please, don't bow. I'm not that important," I motioned for Jeral to sit down. "You'll be compensated, and I want to set up accounts for both of you. I think Adam and Merrill have our first bank open, now."

"We do—Flavio moved the last of his assets from Earth two days ago. We're doing quite well." Adam laughed. That didn't happen often—even I knew that.

"Am I missing something?" Erland folded in.

"Erland, Erland, Erland," I said, leaning my chin on a fist.

"You are lovely, Lissa," he gave me a smile that would make just about anybody experience an orgasm.

"Uh-huh. What's grampa doing?"

"Ruling with an iron fist," Erland laughed. "Or an iron spell, take your pick."

"Jeral, Davan, this is Erland Morphis, an emissary from my father, the King of Karathia," Griffin said.

"A Karathian warlock?" Jeral asked. Davan was unfamiliar with the term. That didn't surprise me—Beliphar had become an isolated world.

"Yes," Griffin nodded. "Lissa, if you wouldn't mind, I'd like to take Jeral and Davan with me tonight, so we may get to know one another. I've never had brothers before and hardly know where to start."

"Go ahead—I won't expect them back until I see them again. If you wouldn't mind, though, would you make sure they both have everything they need and charge it to my personal account?"

"We must make sure the others from New Beliphar know where we are," Jeral rose from his chair, followed by Davan.

"I'll take you there first," Griffin said and all three disappeared.

"Sheesh," I dropped my face into both my hands.

"Is that any way to be?" Erland came to sit on the desk beside me.

"How should I be?"

"You can come to bed with me and I'll show you."

"Erland, you keep saying bed to me, like you can't get in bed with anybody else. We both know that's a lie." I looked up at Erland—he was frowning. Adam laughed out loud. "Erland, I don't think I could handle being a disappointment to the second most beautiful man I know," I swatted his leg.

"You have such a terrible opinion of yourself," he smiled at me.

"And you have such an inflated opinion of yourself," I snipped.

"Come to bed with me and find out," he was still smiling.

"She could come to bed with me, instead." Garde skipped into the room. High Demons didn't fold; they skipped, like rocks on a pond. One skip was all it took to get from Kifirin to Le-Ath Veronis.

"Garde, I have scars from one set of teeth already. I don't think I need any more," I said.

"My Thifilathi longs for it."

"I'm sure it does. Forget I said anything. Are you hungry? I was thinking about putting an apple pie together. I'm a little too restless to sleep right now."

"I'll definitely come to watch, and I'll eat anything you cook," Garde smiled. Word got out fast. Just about every mate I had, plus Garde, Erland, Adam, Merrill, Gabron, Frank, Shane and Tomas was in the kitchen after a while, waiting for eight apple pies to bake. They had warm slices with ice cream afterward.

"Lissa, this is exceptional." Gavin loved it, as did Tony. I hadn't realized they hadn't had my apple pies before. Winkler had loved them, too. I wanted to weep at that memory. Instead, I picked up half a pie in a pie plate. "I'll be back," I said and folded to Grey House. Shadow was completing a protection jewel when I arrived, so I didn't disturb him until he finished.

"Lissa?" He looked up at me.

"I made apple pies, so I brought some for you," I said.

"Great. There's ice cream downstairs in one of the freezers," he said and folded both of us to the kitchen. I had a small slice of pie and a scoop of ice cream with him and watched as he devoured the rest.

"This is so good, baby. Will you stay with me, tonight?" He kissed me and the kiss tasted like pie and ice cream.

"If there's more where that came from," I said, kissing him back.

"Yeah. Plenty. How much do you want?" He murmured against my mouth.

I had to send mindspeech to Gabron, saying I'd be back in the morning and let Shadow take me to bed.

~

"Hey, my two favorite misters." Henri and Gervais had come with Susila and Oluwa.

"Should we bow to you now?" Henri smiled.

"You do and you'll be in trouble," I teased. "What's up?" The daily meeting was about to start—with more questions about the entertainment district and Gabron's plan to build the brothels coming first. I'd rolled my eyes at breakfast when Kyler handed the agenda to me.

"We asked to come and see a meeting for ourselves. Susila gave permission."

"You're welcome any time," I said. "And I think we need a larger meeting room. It might not be a bad idea to allow some of the public inside. What do you think?"

"I think that is an excellent idea—many are wondering what goes on and they would not mind getting a closer look at you, my Queen." Gervais agreed with my assessment.

"Brock is forming baseball teams among the younger vampires," Henri informed me. "He is making different rules. Anyone hitting the ball over the fence will be considered out. The ball must remain inside the playing area. It is the only fair way, with vampires playing."

"I see," I said. "How many are interested?"

"Many. He had to bring in metal bats and cases of balls. Also, there are basketball leagues forming, football leagues forming, both American and European, as well as cricket, tennis and many other sports. Other communities are anxious to put their own sports leagues together."

"When they start playing croquet, I'm there," I teased. Oluwa laughed. "Do you know where Brock is at the moment?" I asked.

"I do not," Oluwa shrugged. I sent mindspeech. *Brock, are you available?*

I am.

Can you meet me at the palace for a minute?

I'll be right there. And he was. He appeared in less than five seconds.

"Brock, get with Kyler and take money to buy sports equipment," I said. "Get with somebody in every community and find out what they need. Tell them I will take it all away if they get into fights over this."

"You got it," Brock grinned broadly as he folded away.

"We'll need umpires and referees, now," I sighed and walked into the Council Chamber.

~

"It's not the same without hot dogs and sodas," I said, two evenings later. We were watching the first baseball game on Le-Ath Veronis. Brock was having a great time and Drake and Drew decided to get in on the action.

There weren't any lights either—they weren't needed. Everybody had to pull back on their strength; a ball knocked over the makeshift fence was an out. The game was fun to watch and there was only one friendly argument—the ball had bounced and then rolled under the fence by only a fraction of an inch.

It was settled after the benches emptied and vampires were on the ground, their faces pressed to the grass as they examined the position of the ball and the line of the fence. I buried my face against Gavin's arm and did my best not to guffaw.

~

Campiaa

"I don't care if they leave. We will take the property and put it to our own use. The gamblers will not desert us. They will remain loyal, as they always have." Arvil San Gerxon snapped at his assistant.

Theos had fretted over bringing the news to Arvil to begin with, as

Arvil was so mercurial over these things. It could be much worse, however, if Theos failed to turn over the information that Le-Ath Veronis had submitted an application with the Alliance to build casinos there. That would mean that Erland Morphis' casino, as well as the one owned by the A & M Consortium, would likely leave Campiaa.

"My brother spent years trying to rid this planet of those two, and now they will leave us freely if this application is approved? I see that as a great day for the San Gerxon clan," Arvil snorted.

"As you say, Lord Gerxon. I merely wished to keep you informed." Theos bowed low and hurried from Arvil's private study. "Stupid vampires," Arvil muttered and turned to other matters.

Le-Ath Veronis

"We're approved." Kyler stuck the letter from the Alliance in front of my face the minute I woke up. It had only taken the Reth Alliance three weeks to process our application to set up gambling on Le-Ath Veronis. Nearly everyone had anticipated our approval, so buildings and businesses were already going up.

"Did you tell Adam and Merrill?" I asked, trying to get my eyes open. Roff was snuggling against me, still. Even he didn't want to get up this morning. Two more days and it would be off-days.

"I spent the night with Flavio, so he knows," Kyler said. "And he sent mindspeech to Merrill, so he and Adam know, too," she smiled.

"Is that wily vampire good in bed?" I asked innocently.

"You know it. And stop digging, or I'll ask how Kifirin is."

"I have no complaints," I said and sat up. "Roff, we have to haul our asses out of bed." Roff smiled at me and sat up, getting one last kiss before sliding off the other side of the bed and padding off to the bathroom.

"It's nice just to get snuggled, sometimes," I said, as Kyler watched Roff walk away. Roff had gotten his bite when we'd gone to bed the night before; it was the second monthly bite he was allowed.

"I think those two Falchani women have discovered vampires," Kyler's dimple was showing.

"Oh, you're kidding?" I watched her face. She wasn't.

"Baxter and Dmitri," she snickered.

"The Enforcers?"

"Yeah. Gavin and Tony had them up here for palace security. Those two women went to them like moths to a light bulb."

"Well, they might not want to go back to Falchan now," I said.

"I think that was a given the minute they showed up. Drake and Drew have had them up to the light side, so they could get some sun. We should consider sunlamps for the humanoid contingent," Kyler said. "I can fold away, but not everybody can."

"True," I agreed. "Let me get cleaned up so I can get to breakfast at a decent hour and we'll talk about that."

"Our application was approved, we'll be the next gambling planet," I said over breakfast later. I wasn't completely happy with the news, but the others certainly were.

"I have a stack of applicants for the brothels which are currently being built—the Belipharan vampires are well-versed on building things. Everything is going up quickly, once Adam, Merrill and the others got the supplies and building materials in." Gabron was in his element, now.

"And what do the applicants for the brothels put under experience?" I raised an eyebrow at my Refizani vampire.

"They don't describe their abilities in detail, if that's what you mean," Gabron sighed. He and I just wouldn't see eye to eye on this. "I would appreciate your talents in weeding out the unsuitable ones, however." He was going to make me look at those damned applications.

"Fine. Drake and Drew can stand outside my office and fall on the floor laughing," I muttered. They were having a hard time keeping the laughter back even now.

"Are you going to hang signs up that say *No Compulsion Allowed?*" Drake couldn't hold back a snicker any longer.

"Compulsion should not be needed," Gabron huffed. He was frowning as the twins laughed helplessly.

"Well, meals around here are certainly never boring," I dipped into my oatmeal.

"Lissy, it'll be all right," Tony said. He was sitting next to me now. Well, it was his night, then. I was missing Karzac, though. A lot.

Karzac, I miss you, I sent. I didn't get a reply. I had a forever of days like this to look forward to.

Fucking lovely.

~

I was depending on whether my skin itched or not while making decisions on the stacks of applicants. If it itched even slightly when I put my hand on the paper, it went into the "No" pile. Everything else went into the possible pile. Gabron could choose whom to interview from that stack. I sighed.

"Lissa, you placed two of my former employees in the wrong stack." Gabron was pulling those applications out and putting them in the other stack. I was too weary to argue with him over it.

Nearly a thousand applications had been tested—and that was after the boring meeting, lunch, and then more boring meetings. There would likely be more applicants—on a daily basis, if I guessed correctly. I wanted to bury my face in my hands and moan.

How had Le-Ath Veronis come to this? I had envisioned a tranquil and idyllic environment where the comesuli worked, played and raised their children while the vampires watched over them.

I hadn't counted on those vampires wanting some of the things they'd enjoyed during their lives on other planets. They were bored, so of course something had to be done about that. We were building whorehouses. And casinos. *Fuck.* I moaned and misted away before Gabron could stop me.

~

It would have been too easy to find me sitting on the roof of my own palace. I'd folded my mist to the High Demons' world and sat on top of their palace, instead. The newly arrived humanoids were doing their best to clean away the evidence of the previous occupants from Veshtul's streets. These looked as if they knew what they were doing. I hoped so—I was feeling guilty enough over the whole debacle already.

"Lissa." Garde came to sit beside me.

"How did you know I was here?" I grumbled.

"Glinda has wards up. She knew the moment you touched the roof. Otherwise, she'd never have felt you. You're sort of untraceable, you know."

"Lucky me," I said. I was depressed. Even I realized it. My chin was on my knees as I stared out at the world named after Kifirin.

"What's wrong?" His hand was on the back of my neck, moving the hair aside so he could rub my nape.

"Le-Ath Veronis is about to turn into the biggest, commercialized piece of crap," I muttered. "There'll be neon everywhere, advertising whorehouses and gambling dens. People will walk the streets drinking and carousing. The noise will be continuous, Garde. They're already talking about the types of vehicles they want to import to provide transportation, which means navigable streets have to be built. You won't believe how many want to set up souvenir shops. Want a shirt that says, my friends went to Le-Ath Veronis and all I got was this lousy top?" I asked. "Pictures of my palace are going to be printed on coffee mugs. I wanted to build a university. I'm getting casinos, instead."

"And brothels," Garde nodded beside me.

"And brothels," I echoed. His fingers felt good on my neck.

"My claiming marks go here, just below Kifirin's." He was breathing on my neck.

"Uh-uh. Roff told me that you guys do that and make the woman sick for days. Nope, not going there. It was bad enough when Kifirin stuck his teeth in my neck. That hurt, but at least I wasn't ill afterward." Garde's hand had stilled on my neck.

"It is only the once, avilepha. I will be gentle and I will find healers for the illness if it comes."

"Hmmph."

"Glindarok loves my brother very much and he was far from gentle when he placed his marks upon her. He was angry at the time. She has forgiven him."

"And how long did that take?" I asked. His fingers were moving again.

"A while. Perhaps a month or two. But then Glinda knew beforehand what was coming and she endured it."

"Sounds like fun."

"You are being sarcastic."

"Duh."

"I was hoping you would find me worth the pain."

Oh, Lord. He was putting that on me? "Do you know how many males guilt their dates into sex by saying *you don't love me?* Do you?"

"I can see that was a foolish statement." Garde was still rubbing my neck.

"There's no other way with you people?" I asked. Did they ever forego that unpleasant little ritual?

"Not with the one chosen by our Thifilathi. We have to change at least once a month to keep it under control at other times. Mine howls for you when I change. I have to be far away when that happens, otherwise it might be persuaded to hunt you down."

"And yet I cooked for you for nearly two months and there was nothing."

"That is not completely true—I thought I was going mad, lusting after a comesula. That had never happened before and they have no way of having sex anyway—not in any conventional sense."

"Garde, why is my life complicated? I have a mate that I am terrified to have sex with. Another mate who prefers males in this particular cycle of his existence. One of my mates insists on building brothels on my planet. Plus, and I know this, because I *Looked*, that he used to train most of his employees. Tell me how to deal with that?"

"I don't know what to tell you," Garde was back to breathing on my neck. Yeah, I wouldn't mind going to bed with him—if it could be normal sex. It might be, after a bite that made me sick. "Glindarok had a harder time with Jaydevik, because she was virgin for the sex later," Garde offered.

"Oh, Lord." I echoed my previous sentiment.

"We can do this now—I will take you to my bed and ask Jayd to place a guard so we will not be disturbed."

"Honey, I think I'll only consent to this if you knock me out first," I said, leaning away from him.

"I will do that for you, since Gardevik does not have the talent." Kifirin was there suddenly, placing fingers against my forehead. I only remember blackness after that.

~

"Be as gentle as you can," Kifirin instructed. Garde held the sleeping Lissa in his arms—Kifirin had folded Garde and Lissa into Garde's suite.

Kifirin watched as Garde placed Lissa on his bed and pulled her blouse away, exposing her nape. The Thifilathi was already threatening—he was blowing smoke from his nostrils as he leaned down to nuzzle bare flesh. He turned her onto her belly, allowing his smaller Thifilathi to manifest. Kifirin folded away. Garde's darkened skin made a sharp contrast against Lissa's lighter flesh as he sank his lengthened fangs into her neck.

~

"Lissa, avilepha, please wake." Those were the first words I heard and I ached. All over. My neck, though, felt as if it were on fire.

"Shhh, we will take care of this." I think I was moaning and crying at the same time, grasping sheets in hands that had grown claws, ripping them and possibly the mattress underneath, I was in so much pain.

"Lissa, pull your claws back or we will not come close." Karzac was issuing an order.

"Get the hell away," I hissed between my teeth. "Fuck, this hurts." I realized quickly that I was half-naked as I forced my eyes open. I was lying on my stomach on a bed—Garde's by the scent of it.

I struggled to sit up; I had to pull in my claws to do it. Punctures covered the sheets and mattress. The fucker was going to have to get a new bed, at least. A trail of blood dripped over my collarbone and then farther down, nearly to my left nipple. My neck was on fire and Garde's Thifilathi had made me bleed.

"Lissa, we're here to take care of this," Karzac stood beside the bed with Frank, Shane and Tomas right behind him.

Fuck cubed. Wasn't it lovely that they were all here to witness this? Garde stood right behind them, a huge look of guilt on his face. Well, he needed to look guilty. He and Kifirin, both.

"Since when do you respond to mindspeech?" I snapped at Karzac and got myself off the bed. I could barely move but I wasn't about to let them know that. "Where the fuck is my shirt?" I felt feverish as I jerked it off the floor where it had been tossed and misted away.

"That went well," Shane sighed.

"You will not find her now," Karzac said and sat down on the side of the bed. "When did she send mindspeech?" He had to go *Looking* to find the answer. "Ah," was all he said.

Earth

"I don't care how much it costs; I just need a room with a spa tub in it." Yeah, I looked like crap and the desk clerk at the five-star hotel was giving me shit, questioning me about whether I wouldn't be happier at the three-star hotel down the street.

I was in New York and just about to jerk the dickhead over the desk and give him compulsion he would never forget. He took my credit chip that still hung on a chain around my neck, gulped when he saw the rating after scanning it on his computer and gave me a room double quick. I got my chip back, took the key and got the hell away from him as fast as I could.

Soaking in the jetted tub helped a little, but I had trouble getting in and out of it. Garde's bite had made me stiff and achy everywhere and I wondered briefly if aspirin would help. I ended up abandoning that idea—vampires tended to be impervious to drugs.

~

Le-Ath Veronis

"Where is she?" Tony demanded. Garde had gone to Le-Ath Veronis, hoping Lissa had come home.

"I don't know," Garde sat down heavily at the dinner table. Giff was having a meltdown, as was Roff, although he was attempting to calm his oldest child. Gabron was cursing under his breath and Gavin refused to leave his suite.

"Come, my friend, you cannot do this." Erland folded into Gavin's suite.

"She doesn't like this whole thing," Gavin muttered. "The brothels, the casinos, all of it. We are pushing her and she is consenting to it, to please the rest of us."

"She knows the planet is more than just her," Erland sat next to Gavin on Gavin's sofa.

"But shouldn't a part of it be about her? If she were not here, there would be no Le-Ath Veronis. Tell me this is not so."

"So we are going forward with this and not including her, is that what you mean?"

"I believe so. All of this is quite exciting to the vampires, but we failed to look at it from one perspective, and perhaps two. How do the comesuli see this? We have not given them a vote."

"Why are you bringing this up now?" Erland was puzzled.

"I overheard the kitchen staff talking this afternoon—I went there for something to eat after Lissa left abruptly and I heard them long before they knew I was approaching. Many of them are frightened that we will treat them as the High Demons treated them—working for those who will come, with little or no compensation. They are satisfied with what they are earning now and the Queen is making sure they are paid, but with the influx of visitors that many of the vampires are talking of, they expect to be treated once again as second-class citizens or worse. It made me wonder just how it is they will be treated. I had taken no thought for this before."

"But I thought many of the vampires were forging relationships with them."

"Some of them have their favorites, but it is not the same as full sex, as you know. That was something else they were discussing—that the pleasure houses will take their vampires away because the women and men will offer their vampires more than the comesuli can provide. They worry that they will only provide a warm meal, now and then and mean nothing more to the vampires." Gavin had been spending the evening thinking about this, Erland could tell.

"Under normal circumstances, the comesuli would have been the vampire's family—their children, cousins and future vampires. That connection will come in time, but is not in place as yet." Erland was thinking this through for himself. "We have not yet hammered out the amount of taxes to be collected for the crown from this venture. I currently pay the San Gerxons a full twenty-five percent and still make a good profit. Lissa will not demand anything close to that, but it will be necessary to maintain Le-Ath Veronis."

"I heard that Gabron paid fifteen percent to the Refizani government—it was a luxury tax as decreed by the Reth Alliance, because he did not provide what is considered a vital service. Only the businesses providing basic needs were taxed less—food, housing, clothing and medical care."

"Yes, and the Alliance will be expecting their percentage—for membership," Erland agreed. "It was two percent, the last I heard."

"It is two and a half," Gavin replied. "To maintain the Alliance army and things of that nature. I asked Wlodek about this already."

"We are still no closer to finding a solution for Lissa and the comesuli," Erland observed.

"I know," Gavin acknowledged.

❧

Earth

The vid screen covered an entire wall in my hotel room and I was watching something that made no sense at all. I muted the sound; I no longer wanted to hear it. It was something to distract me and nothing more. I hurt. So much so that I contemplated calling for Karzac anyway. I don't know who had called him to begin with, but at least he had come.

"Lissa, I do not know if you want me here, but I wanted to come."

Reemagar was suddenly there in my hotel room, sitting on the end of my bed. I was huddled against the padded headboard, dressed only in the robe the hotel provided for its guests.

"I'm not good company right now. I don't feel so good," I muttered.

"I know this," he folded next to me and placed large blue hands on my body, taking the pain away easily and trilling to me while he did so. "Lissa Beth, I've missed you so," he soothed, in between trilling. His words made me go still, and then I shivered. "I only wanted to hold you again," he whispered. "You don't have to take me back if you don't want to."

Why hadn't I seen it before? Connegar had been René once. Now I had my first love back, as a Larentii. Don deserved that if anyone did.

"Did someone want to give me the best gift ever?" I asked, nearly sobbing.

"Shhh, don't cry, my love," my tears were wiped away by large blue thumbs. "See, I am better at this, now," he was trying to smile at me.

"I missed you so much," I almost threw myself into his arms. He cradled me against him and trilled again. Light formed around him and I knew he was healing my body while he held me. His eyes were closed in bliss while he did this. I felt so good and so free I could have flown afterward.

CHAPTER 8

$\mathcal{L}$e-Ath Veronis

There was quite a stir in the meeting when Reemagar and I showed up together the following morning. He'd stayed the night with me in the hotel room. I'd *Pulled* clothing in to dress, after he enlarged the spa tub and let me lean against him while the water bubbled around us.

Connegar had folded in and smiled at both of us. He'd known, the little devil. Well, not so little, since he was nine and a half feet tall. He'd sat on the edge of the tub and trilled for Reemagar and me. Yeah, I loved my Larentii.

"Lissa, where have you been?" Gabron was upset, I could tell. Well, so was I. And Gardevik, the slime, who knew where he was?

"Before we get started today," I announced, "I want to make a proclamation. The palace will be moved when the casinos and brothels open. I will move it myself, if I have no volunteers to help."

That caused a stillness throughout the room.

"Lissa, what are you saying?" Gabron didn't want to dress me down in front of the Council.

"I'm saying I don't want to be anywhere near this," I said. "I have no desire to see the comesuli treated like slaves or children. I have no desire to see pictures of my palace on T-shirts and coffee mugs. Go ahead and turn my planet into a circus if you want, I just don't want to see it on my front doorstep when I wake up in the morning."

"Lissa, that is not our intention." Adam and Merrill showed up in a flash of light. Flavio must have sent them mindspeech.

"That's easy for you to say, you don't live here," I pointed out. "Imagine a casino in your front yard, Merrill. Tell me how the comesuli will be treated. The tourists will be coming to see vampires. The comesuli are my family. I will not have them mistreated. They are already frightened by the brothels being built, thinking the pleasure workers will entice their vampires away. How will you calm their fears, Gabron?" I turned to my Refizani vampire mate. "Who will be training the pleasure workers, Gabron?" He knew I knew, when his eyes met mine.

"We can control the visitors into the capital city," Adam offered. "We will make it so they must apply for a permit to visit. The casino city will be ten miles west of Lissia and we can offer day passes to those who wish to visit. You may reject any of those, if you wish."

"Adam, I have no desire to sit at my desk and go over hundreds of requests daily," I said. "Select one day a week when tours may be arranged. I will most likely be out of town on that day."

"What has precipitated this?" Gabron asked. He wanted to tell me I was acting foolishly—I could see it in his face.

"Am I Queen of Le-Ath Veronis or not?" I asked. "Am I Queen of all its inhabitants and not just the vampires? When you build this, tell me that I will not become a laughing stock—Queen of the casinos and brothels. A figurehead only, while all of you make the decisions. I will not be put on display while tourists snap photographs of me to transmit to their colleagues at home."

Jeral stood near the back of the room. "I do not believe it was our intention to upset the Queen," he said. "The Belipharan vampires are grateful for the comesuli who live among us, now. They have become like family in such a short amount of time. I cannot imagine that we would treat them as less, even if we do seek the pleasure houses."

"I thought you were moving into the palace," I said.

"Davan and I are making arrangements with help from our brother, my Queen. We are working with my associates to ensure a smooth transition." He sat down again.

"My Queen," another vampire stood, near the middle of the room. "You will never be a figurehead to me. When two others and I came to you three months ago, we were not turned away at the door as we expected to be. We were ushered directly into your study and we discussed vacation time for the workers. You told me then that you had already considered it and showed us several plans. You also informed us that the Reth Alliance planets might be possible destinations if we desired to travel off world. Then you took my two colleagues and me to visit the space station, which was being built. I was shocked that the Queen would take time to do this for us."

"Don't you think you deserve it?" I asked.

"Perhaps. But deserving and receiving are generally two different things," he bowed. "The four weeks of vacation that you insisted on went over very well with the workers at the blood substitute manufacturing plant."

"Well, since we don't have to pay for Social Security or health insurance," I said. He laughed and sat down.

"Lissa, we've had offers to buy either the formula for the blood substitute or to buy the bottled product itself," Merrill said, attempting to calm me down by changing the subject. He was probably wise to do so, my fangs were pricking my lower lip and my eyes were probably a shade away from red.

"Well, you guys came up with that, you can do whatever you want with it."

"Lissa, you're not being selfish enough over this," he informed me. "The plant is sitting on property owned by the crown. You own a piece of this. What do you want to do?"

"How big is the market?" I asked. "Do we have the facilities to manufacture enough to meet the demand? If so, then let's do it from here. If not, then sell the formula. That's simple enough."

"I think we can manufacture here," Adam said. "If we triple the size of the plant, which can be done soon. I'll have a feasibility study on your desk by next week."

"Sounds good," I nodded.

"Will you consider leaving the palace where it is if we build you a home on the ocean for your one day retreat per week?" Wlodek had been sitting in the back all along.

"I'll consider it, but the first time somebody drags tourists into this palace without my permission is the day I move it."

We got down to business after that. I was tired and yawning when it was all over. "Lissa, you have to appear at dinner, the others are about to become more upset than they already are," Gabron informed me as we walked out of the Council Chamber.

That was just what I needed. I figured Gavin was going to give me an earful, whether it was over dinner or later. Gabron wasn't high on my list at the moment either. "Lissa, I never said I wasn't going to have sex with other women," Gabron said, as we walked down the lengthy hall toward my suite. I almost stopped in my tracks but forced myself to keep going. I wasn't about to be a hypocrite.

"I know that," I sighed. "But I was hoping it would be somebody you actually cared for, if you did. Just do me a favor and don't come home smelling like one of them." I misted away.

"I am in the dog house, I think the phrase is," Gabron sighed as he sat down to dinner. They were waiting on Lissa again. He knew that she might not come and he knew he'd be the reason.

"In your case, I think the phrase might be cathouse," Drake snickered.

"What did you do?" Garde had come for dinner, hoping he could speak to Lissa afterward.

"She knows I trained most of my employees," Gabron replied. "I told her I never said I would not have sex with other women. She told me she was aware of that, but hoped it would be someone I cared for if I did. Then she told me not to come home smelling like one of them."

"I think that is a reasonable request; Lissa's nose is the most sensitive I have ever encountered," Wlodek observed. He, Adam and Merrill had stayed for dinner.

"She may not come to dinner, I have upset her," Gabron sighed.

"I will go get her," Garde offered.

"Karzac told me about last night. She may not be happy to see you, either," Drew said.

"I have to apologize to her and I wish to see my claiming marks," Garde sighed. He rose from his seat. "I will return." He walked out of the dining hall.

I sat on the vanity bench in my dressing room, staring at my image in the mirror. I'd lost my appetite after the tiff with Gabron. "Lissa?" That was Garde's voice. I'd heard the door to my suite open, but thought it might be Giff or Roff.

"What do you want, Gardevik?" I used his formal name. Yeah, I was pissed at him, too.

"Lissa, you know I want to apologize to you, on my knees if it will make any difference. And I wish to kiss my claiming marks." He came up behind me and moved my hair aside. I'd left it loose; his marks still looked red and angry, which reflected my mood at the moment. I'd checked them myself only a few minutes before. My neck ached, still, although Reemagar had healed it as much as he could. The rest of me ached too, and I wasn't in any mood to have sex for a few days.

"Avilepha," he breathed on my neck and placed his mouth on my nape carefully. "They are beautiful, my love. So beautiful. Like my Queen." He scooted me over and sat next to me, putting his arms around me. "I will never hurt my love again that way; my Thifilathi is quite satisfied. He shouted from the roof last night, howling out his joy. You do not know how long I waited for you."

"Yeah, I'll bet," I grumped.

"I am your second oldest mate," Garde nuzzled my collarbone, planting kisses there and down my neck. I watched him in the mirror; his dark hair thick and curling slightly, his eyes closed in pleasure as he placed careful kisses on my nape. "Only Kifirin is older than I." That made me sit up straighter.

"How old are you?" I asked.

"I do not recall the exact number of years. My brother Jaydevik is more than nine hundred thousand years old and he is younger than I. I am something over one million and eldest of the House of Rath. Many Larentii, even, are younger than I, avilepha." He lifted his head and I watched his dark eyes in the mirror; they were watching mine in exchange, begging me silently to forgive the pain his Thifilathi had brought.

"Holy crap," I muttered. I couldn't gauge High Demon ages very well since I didn't have a reference point. I did, now. Glinda, I knew, was quite a bit younger than Jayd and Garde. A lot younger. Less than fifteen hundred, I think.

"I look forward to the day when I may make love to you and form the linking."

"Well, I still ache all over, thank you very much, so nobody's getting any for several days."

"I am sorry. I remember how soft and perfect your body was; my Thifilathi was holding your hands in his afterward, marveling at how small and beautiful they were. He was careful with his claws and made sure not to mark you in that way."

"You make it sound as if it's a separate entity," I said.

"It seems that way, most of the time—he is more primal and attuned to the natural world. Come now; let me take you to dinner. You must eat." He nuzzled my neck again.

"I'm not hungry."

"I know you feel this way. Come with me, avilepha. You will lose your strength if you do not eat properly." He lifted one of my hands to his lips and placed a gentle kiss. "For me?" he coaxed. I walked out of my suite with him.

Roff got to spend the night in my bed. He let me sleep in his arms. Somebody must have gotten all my mates to back off for my off-days; Drake and Drew sat in the hot tub with me the following day. They teased me a little but knew not to ask for sex.

Tony came and let me lean on him while I read afterward. I fell asleep that way, too, while he kissed my forehead and stroked my hair. I went to bed alone that night, but woke up held tightly by Karzac.

"Did you think I would abandon you?" He nuzzled the tender spot behind an ear.

"What about Gracie?" I watched his hazel eyes as he smiled at me, the corner of his mouth quirking nicely. I traced the attractive crease with a finger.

"I am not her only mate. Dragon and Crane are taking very good care of her," Karzac murmured. Well, he was a savvy healer. He got what the others weren't getting. He was careful about it and did a little healing afterward.

I slept late and nobody forced me to get up and go to breakfast. Giff brought in a tray for Karzac and me. Karzac left after we ate, so I showered and dressed lazily, then decided to see what I could get into.

"Bryan?" He'd seen me walking down the street—he'd been out trimming some sort of shrubbery that grew in his front yard. The vampire belt—where the light was constantly in twilight, still supported plant life—a few things had adapted to the weak light available.

Even certain types of flowers grew and Bryan, it seems, was taking full advantage. He'd already planted a very nice garden in his yard. Bryan Riley, former assistant to the night director for one of the local news channels in London was now trotting happily in my direction.

"Lissa!" He gave me a huge hug.

"Are you doing all right?" I smiled at him when he let me go.

"Great. But I wanted to come and talk to you about our media, or lack thereof," he grinned.

"Ah. Well, we probably need it, don't we? I can imagine that those vampires are just starving for news and weather reports."

"Flavio says he'll set me up, if I want to manage the whole thing."

"Well, I can't think of anyone I'd rather have in charge," I said. "Would you like to walk with me for a bit?"

"Absolutely!" He was quite happy with that idea. We talked about where we could build the station and he mentioned public access for the Council meetings, which was a good idea. I agreed with him on that.

We both agreed that some meetings would remain private, and most of those dealt with trials and (when we needed them) executions. He and I also talked about communication satellites, where we could get them and the cost.

"You might want to talk to Joey and Shadow," I said. "Since they're engineering geniuses or something." As we walked along, we gathered more vampires. One of them was painfully shy, but he managed to speak up after a while.

"Queen Lissa, I can't get the toiletries and laundry soap I like," he mumbled.

"What?" I stopped right there in the street, causing everybody else to stop, too. "Why can't you get those things?"

"We don't get shipments from Earth—we have to deal with what comes from the Alliance worlds," someone else spoke up.

"Let me see what I can do about that," I said, wondering if Radomir, Russell and Will might want to go into the grocery/pharmacy business.

I think Brock and Stephan were considering my proposal to open sporting goods stores and clothing chains. Vampires weren't much on groceries, but the tourists would be. Somebody had to sell snacks. And shoes and books—my gosh, how had I forgotten books?

"Who likes to read, here?" I asked. Several hands went up. "Good. I'm looking to open a library and maybe some bookstores. Come to the palace tomorrow and we'll see what we can do."

We ended up at somebody's house, about forty or so of us, and we talked about all sorts of things. Bottles of blood substitute and wine were passed around, if anybody wanted it. I had a glass of red wine and enjoyed the company.

By the end of the week we had books, both paper and electronic, on order, a news channel in its infancy and Radomir, Russell and Will were going together to put up stores offering a variety of toiletry needs. My shy vampire got what he wanted—I folded to Earth and got him a case of everything.

His name was Grant and I decided he would make a very good personal assistant. He already knew his way around Alliance hand-held computers, could file like the wind and was overjoyed when I offered him the position.

He moved right into the palace (cases of toiletries and all), and Roff, Giff and little Toff liked him very much. Actually, Toff loved Grant and would squeal and laugh if Grant held him. Grant had a cubicle just outside my large, private study and started making sense out of all the paper that was piling up, in addition to pointing me toward the important electronic messages I was now getting from the Reth Alliance.

We were also coming along with the rules and laws concerning the vampires and comesuli, and then we had to hammer out the rules and laws concerning the gambling guests who were already lining up to come for a visit, cameras in hand, no doubt.

Bryan got his network set up and running smoothly, which meant that vid screens were ordered by the thousands. One of the Reth Alliance worlds made a lot of money on the sale of giant vid-screens and I think it might have been Refizan.

Gabron, no doubt, had connections. He and I still weren't talking much. Two months later, the brothels were in place and the pleasure workers were arriving. I hoped they all didn't expect a personal greeting from the Queen when they walked off the ship—that wasn't going to happen.

~

"He's married to her?" Shala stared at Elthine. They'd worked for Gabron on Refizan and leapt at the opportunity to come to Le-Ath Veronis. They enjoyed the climax they received whenever a vampire had bitten them before and often begged for it. Gabron had frequently satisfied them himself. They were now discussing the Queen, whom they hadn't seen.

"Seems to be. He wears a ring he never had before." Elthine had noticed that right away, when Gabron had shown them their new home.

"She can't compete with us," Shala snorted, making Elthine laugh.

Campiaa

"I applied for this under your name," Arvil San Gerxon handed the ticket to his assistant. Theos stared at the official document—it bore the crown of claws on the front, which was the Queen of Le-Ath Veronis' royal seal.

"You want me to go?" Theos squeaked, reading the acceptance card in surprise.

"I do. I want information," Arvil snapped. "I have all the hype the media are releasing, but I want someone there on the ground. You will send me regular updates; you're scheduled for a two-week visit."

Theos knew what concerned Arvil the most. Erland Morphis and the A&M Consortium had pulled all their employees away from Campiaa, closed down their casinos the previous week and Arvil had wakened the following morning to find both casinos razed to the ground.

Arvil had yet to determine how that had been accomplished. Of course, there were rumors that Erland was Karathian, which might explain things. Some of the other casino owners were allegedly negotiating with Le-Ath Veronis to open casinos there.

Arvil was considering breaking his own laws and building on the now vacant lots still owned by Erland Morphis and A&M

Consortium. That would increase the San Gerxon holdings and their profits.

"Get my contractor on the phone," Arvil barked, breaking Theos out of his stupor. He'd been staring at the ticket Arvil placed in his hand. Theos rushed to obey.

~

Space Freighter T'Armuun

"I will consider almost anything, if the money is sufficient," Gart examined his fingernails. A Karathian Warlock by birth, Gart had been on Wylend Arden's most wanted list of rogues for a very long time. He nodded to his newest client, who'd identified himself as Felix. "How many do you have and where would you like them transported?"

"Beliphar is ripe for a takeover," Felix smiled. "You'll get your money."

"Tell me what I am transporting, for curiosity's sake," Gart feigned indifference.

"A new race. A little faster, a little better than your average humanoid," Felix replied. He didn't add that they were capable of reproducing themselves by sharing a bit of DNA. All it took was a simple kiss or a bite and the victim was immediately infected—one of the unexpected but useful advantages of the Ra'Ak DNA that had been spliced into cast-off Elemaiya. They'd purposely bred quarter and eighth blood children, just to achieve these results.

The Elemaiyan races were no more, but these children had been hidden away at the suggestion of the Khos'Mirai. The Bright Elemaiyan Queen regretted her decision regarding the Khos'Mirai, but that could not be changed, now. She no longer existed, either. Not in her former capacity, anyway.

Felix, a quarter-blood and enhanced like the others, was quite happy with this turn of events. The gates had been closed against them, but there were other ways of getting from one place to another.

Le-Ath Veronis

"Stand still, love. They'll think you're a servant." Garde was teasing me about my clothing—I was wearing jeans and a silk top—not the outfit one might expect a Queen to wear as the first tourists and gamblers came through the Alliance-required customs stations.

No weapons were allowed—coming or going. Vampires manned those stations; they were trained to pick up any scent of gunpowder, but those weapons would be archaic. Laser tasers were now the weapon of choice and could kill if aimed at the proper part of the body. A zap to the heart was all it took for most humanoids. Vampires operated the machines that would detect those and any other weapons visitors thought to bring with them.

Shadow had also come to see this for himself and was giving me his best grin as we watched the new arrivals drag their luggage toward waiting public transportation. Some—the wealthy or those who'd purchased an upgraded package, had vampire chauffeurs waiting with private transportation. Their bags were carried by vampire valets, too. I'd hate to be some of those tourists if they tried to treat the vampires carrying their luggage in a less than respectful manner.

"Can you help me?" A woman walked right up to me with a brochure in her hands. "How do I sign up for the tour to the palace? It says here that it only happens once a week and I don't want to miss it." Shadow almost bent double, trying to hold back his laughter. I kicked him unobtrusively.

"You can sign up for the tour at the hotel desk when you check in," I answered her question. "Be sure to fill out the form completely. You'll be notified if your application to go on the tour is approved."

"But why does it have to be approved? Shouldn't it be open to the public?" The woman demanded. She looked to be in her late forties and wore a bright fuchsia top and cream slacks.

"Because the Queen is a reclusive bitch who enjoys her privacy," I replied, causing Shadow to guffaw. Garde snickered.

"Should you be speaking of your Queen that way?" The woman

asked. "From the moment I read that she was taking over and rebuilding the vampire planet, I've wanted to meet her." She seemed a little annoyed.

"I can speak about the Queen any way I want," I said. The woman frowned at me. "What's your name?" I asked.

"Galene," she replied huffily.

"And the hotel you're visiting?"

"The Chessman." Well, she was uptown, then. Adam had lent his family name to his premier hotel and casino.

"I believe that Mr. Chessman is actually there today, to greet some of his guests." I took the brochure from her hands and *Pulled* in a pen. "Tell him I approved your application personally for the tour." I was busily writing the same message on her brochure for Adam—he'd know it was authentic—and then signed my name. Galene stared in fascination as the pen materialized in my hand and then watched as I signed my name.

"See, I really can talk about the Queen any way I want," I smiled and handed her brochure back.

"Should I bow or curtsy?" Galene got her voice back after a few seconds.

"Please don't. I don't require it of anyone else," I said. "You should go before you miss your bus. Do you need help with your luggage?" She had a roller bag sitting next to her.

"Maybe," she said.

"I'll get it." I lifted the bag easily and walked toward one of the waiting buses.

"Lissa, what the hell are you doing?" Flavio demanded. He'd come to make sure everything was flowing smoothly.

"Helping Galene with her bag," I replied, handing said bag off to a vampire, who was loading things into the luggage compartment. "This is Galene," I introduced Flavio to the woman. "Flavio is Head of the Vampire Council from Earth and one of my trusted advisors. Also the third most beautiful man I've ever met."

Galene thought so, too—she was staring at Flavio with an expression of complete worship on her face.

"You," I motioned a vampire over; he was making sure the passengers were loaded safely.

"Yes, my Queen?" he smiled at me.

"Will you see that Galene gets a good seat?" I pointed the woman toward the vampire.

"Are you a vampire, too?"

"Yes, Madame. Most certainly a vampire. Eight hundred years a vampire, from Refizan." He led her away.

"That poor woman is so stunned she is nearly immobile," Flavio commented dryly.

"Well, she got her wish, right off the bat. It's all downhill from here," I said. Flavio winked at me. I could hear Shadow and Garde still laughing where I'd left them.

We were getting the newsfeeds; Alliance news crews were everywhere and there was Galene, talking to one of the reporters. "Oh, no," I slapped a hand over my face. A vid screen had been brought in so we could all watch during dinner.

"The Queen approved my application to visit the palace personally and then helped me with my bag." Galene was still in heaven.

"What did you think of the Queen?" The reporter asked.

"Quite lovely. The photographs don't do her justice—her skin is beautiful. She was shorter than I imagined, but you can never tell from those magazine pictures anyway."

"She approved your application personally, you say?"

"She wrote a note to the owner of the Chessman, telling him so. A lovely man," Galene gushed.

"And there you have the truth," the reporter took over. "A guest gets the royal treatment while the news crews are held at arm's length. This is Rowan Alder, for News Nine."

"He's named after two trees?" I couldn't believe it.

"And he just sent a bullet your way, since you insisted that the media not be allowed inside the palace," Tony was eating spaghetti we'd been served for dinner. It was good—Cheedas used my recipe for meatballs.

"I have no desire to have those people crawling all over my home," I grumped. "Grant will faint from the stress and pressure." Grant was sitting nearby and nodding at my assessment.

"Grant is a vampire," Gavin pointed out. "He will survive." Well, Grant wasn't about to argue with Gavin. Gavin scared the bejeezus out of him.

"You want me to do this?" I couldn't believe it.

"If it will keep them from taking shots at you in the future."

"Now see, this is the flaw," I pointed my fork at Gavin.

"We will be with you, if you choose to give an interview," Connegar and Reemagar folded in and sat down at the table. After enlarging the chairs, of course.

"As yourselves?" Larentii seldom placed themselves on display like that.

"Of course. There is no reason to alter our appearance. The Reth Alliance knows we exist. We visit their worlds often."

"But you don't talk to anybody," Shadow pointed out.

"Talking means we have less time to observe," Connegar defended himself. "So we ignore any overtures."

"Well, you're welcome to be with me during my interview," I said. "When can we set this up? The sooner I get it over with, the better I'll like it."

"I will go now to select your dress," Giff rose from the table. Little Toff was sitting in a high chair between Giff and Roff, eating spaghetti. Roff was doing his best to teach his youngest to eat with a fork, but it wasn't working very well. Toff could get more in his mouth using chubby little fists.

"I'll set this up before she changes her mind," Flavio whipped out his communicator. I was set up for a mass interview in two hours. Eighteen news crews were on the planet at the moment and they were all coming, including tree guy.

I was dressed and primped, my hair piled up and wearing my dressier gold band with the Tiralian crystal solitaire (six carats) in the center. Both my tall, blue Larentii were sitting on either side of me when the news crews were ushered into one of the larger meeting rooms.

Photographers were already snapping photographs that were transmitted instantly and the 3-D digital cameras were recording. I wore a blue gown trimmed in jeweled lace that complimented my Larentii quite well. If nothing else went right, at least we were color-coordinated.

Flavio, Wlodek, Adam and Merrill had come; Drake, Drew, Gavin and Tony were providing security. I saw Hart and Nima standing discreetly in a corner, helping the others. Roff was attempting to keep Grant from hyperventilating—they stood near the door in case Grant did faint.

"When did you become vampire?" That was the first question? I thought they wanted to talk about the casinos.

Wlodek had to supply the information; I couldn't remember. Thankfully, it was sent mentally. Now I knew why he and the others were all here.

"Three hundred four years ago," I replied, doing my best to look queenly and regal. No sense in explaining that three hundred of those years I'd skipped over, with a little help from dear old Dad.

"How old were you when you were made vampire?" someone else asked.

"Forty-seven," I replied.

"What were you dying of?" Oh, Lord, here it came.

"I wasn't."

"But it is my understanding that the Reth Alliance requires that all vampires be near death before they may be turned." That was tree man.

"That is true for nearly all vampires, not just the ones from the Reth Alliance," I replied. "I came from a world that did not belong to the Reth Alliance. The vampire who made me broke the law. He was punished for his crime."

"Did you love him? Is that why he turned you?" Tree man wasn't giving up.

"You—come," I crooked my finger at him. He gulped nervously but came forward anyway. All the cameras were trained on him and then on both of us as he stood before me.

"The vampire who turned me," I wanted to hiss, but held it back, "was making a bet with another vampire over how long it would take me to turn. No love was involved; I was a stranger to them. Someone they found in a bar. I was there because my husband died only a few hours earlier and I wanted to numb the pain. When I turned against their expectations, they attempted to hunt me down and kill me. Now, do you still think there was love involved?" I made a shooing motion with my hand. He scuttled back to his spot.

"How did you become Queen?" someone else asked.

"Do you know what makes a Queen Vampire?" I asked.

"I heard that a Queen was stronger than the others," one of the reporters offered.

"Not necessarily," I replied. "A Queen is not susceptible to the compulsion that an older vampire can place. Which leaves her in a dangerous position. If she is not duty-bound to uphold the laws and justice for her race, she has to be destroyed."

"I see you're still alive," one of the reporters joked.

"I stand before you now as a strong proponent of justice," I nodded slightly at all of them.

"What will you do if a vampire attacks a guest?" Tree man was back at it again. *Watch him*, I sent to Drake, Drew, Gavin and Tony.

"You all have copies of the new laws, do you not?" They should, I had to get them ratified by the Alliance Council. They were nodding.

"The law will be enforced," I replied, "if the vampire is found guilty."

Garde, can Jayd come? I sent. Garde was in a far corner, watching everything closely.

"And how will you determine whether the vampire is telling the truth?" Tree man, again.

"Are you familiar at all with High Demons?" I asked sweetly.

"I have studied their race, since their planet is now applying for Alliance membership."

"Are you familiar with the Guli—the Truthsayer for the High Demon race?"

"Yes, I found that fascinating," he replied. "They know when anyone is telling the truth or giving you a lie."

"Very good," I said. Jayd folded into the room, wearing a carved gold band on his head and looking like the king he was. "This is Jaydevik Rath, King of the High Demons and a Guli. Say something to him. He will tell you if it is true."

All cameras turned to Jayd, who had as good a non-expression on his face as any vampire I'd ever seen.

"I have been married twice," tree man declared.

"Lie," Jayd proclaimed. I was enjoying this—I'd never seen Jayd work.

"I have been married four times," tree man went on.

"Lie," Jayd said, crossing arms over his wide chest and glaring at tree man. I just hoped Jayd could keep his Thifilathi in check—if he started blowing smoke, we might all have to leave.

"I have been married six times."

"Truth."

"It really does work," tree man was obviously impressed. "And you're not worried that the vampire will use this compulsion on him?"

"No spell or compulsion works on High Demons," Jayd answered. "We were made that way. We will have the truth from any criminal."

"Ask him why he's here." I nodded toward tree man. Tree man backed up and swallowed hard. He hadn't expected things to turn in his direction.

"Why are you here?" Jayd smiled nastily. He smelled it, just as I did. The guests had to undergo rigorous screening to come to Le-Ath Veronis. The media didn't.

"I am here for the same reasons the others are," tree man pointed around him.

"Lie," Jayd pronounced. "Why are you here?"

"I don't have to answer that," tree man whined. Now all cameras were on him, including those of his crew.

"I think it would be wise if you did." Gavin was there quickly, standing before tree man. Drake and Drew were backing him up.

"I took the money—it seemed harmless enough," tree man quavered.

"Truth," Jayd said. "What money and from whom?"

"They didn't tell me, they said it was a secret society that wanted to learn about the vampires."

"Partial truth," Jayd proclaimed. "You have a guess. What is that guess?" Damn—Jayd was good at this. Well, he was nearly a million years old. He ought to be.

"I think Solar Red is reforming," the man whimpered.

"Fuck," I muttered. All the cameras turned back to me. "Detain him and ship him to the Reth Alliance," I said. Solar Red was supposed to be out of business. The Reth Alliance had outlawed them two hundred years ago, according to Gabron. Anyone having information on the sect was held for questioning. If they practiced the religion, they could be imprisoned for participating in or condoning human sacrifice. Gavin, Drake and Drew hauled the reporter from the room.

"Thank you, Jayd," I said. He gave me a regal nod and skipped away.

"This is the most exciting interview I've ever done," a reporter chortled.

We were back to business after that, with normal questions pertaining to the new gambling district. Until we arrived at a tricky area.

"Have you seen the casinos on the light side of the planet?" A female reporter asked.

"Yes," I replied, without thinking.

"You can walk in daylight?" She sounded incredulous.

"Her Larentii mates may supply a shield for her, if it is needed," Connegar replied stiffly. He wasn't lying, he could do that—he just didn't have to.

"Oh my, we have a Larentii speaking during an interview," another reporter sighed in bliss.

"You have Larentii mates?" Someone else asked.

"I have two," I said.

"These two, here?"

"Yes."

"How many mates do you have?"

"Thirteen, I think," I said. That got chuckles. Reth Alliance worlds recognized multiple mates.

"Are the other eleven vampires?"

"No. Only three are vampires," I said. "The others, well, one is Kifirin—I assume you recognize that name?" They nodded—they'd seen the tapes of my coronation, I'm sure. "Two Larentii, two Falchani, one Karathian warlock, one High Demon, one Grey House wizard, one Refizani and one comesula."

"Can you get us a discount with Grey House?" Someone joked.

"I don't have any influence on the pricing structure for Grey House," I said. That got another laugh. The interview was over shortly after. I shooed the reporters and their crews into the state dining room, where food and drinks would be served.

I had to go, too, unfortunately; it was a reception, after all, and the crews were still filming while the rest of us mingled. Wlodek, Adam and Merrill were talking business with one reporter, who wrote for a gambling vid-magazine.

"Your husband died on the same day you were turned? These are delicious," the reporter was eating an oxberry tart. A specialty of Cheedas'.

"Yes and yes," I said. "My comesula cook loves to make those for my non-vampire residents." He made them for some of the vampire residents as well, but we weren't going to let that cat out of the bag.

"Raona, Reemagar said you were thirsty before he left." Roff was at my side, handing me a bottle of blood substitute. I took it and smiled at him. He leaned down to give me a quick peck. Well, that was going to be plastered all over the news immediately.

"How does that taste?" The reporter asked, curious.

"Like blood," I said. "It's the best substitute I've ever had." I drank from my bottle. Also something that would be plastered on the news.

"May I try some?" Well, he was an adventurous soul. I nodded to

Roff, who motioned for someone to bring another bottle. These were room temperature—better if you liked blood. Worse if you didn't.

"Yes, it tastes the same as when I cut myself," the reporter grimaced and handed the bottle back to the comesula waiter.

"Thanks," I told the comesula. He smiled at me and took the bottle away.

"These are the next wave of vampires?" The reporter meant the comesuli.

"Yes. They normally live a life span of six hundred years, barring accidents. If they are worthy when they are dying, the turn is attempted. Not all will be turned."

"Have any been turned since Le-Ath Veronis became inhabited again?"

"Not yet, but we are watching some of the older ones closely. When the time comes, we will act." I drank more of my blood substitute. I thought briefly about calling it BS before reconsidering.

"If they don't want the turn?"

"We will honor their wishes." That was a flat and final answer.

"What about humanoids wanting the turn?"

"Highly unlikely, at this point. I won't say impossible, because very little is impossible. I will not entertain applications for vampirism. Those will be returned unopened," I replied. "Female humanoid vampires are very rare. The mere attempt at turning a female humanoid almost always results in her death. It is suicide to attempt it."

"What do you think the success rate is?"

I had to call Wlodek over to get an answer. The reporter repeated his question. "Perhaps one female in twenty-five thousand attempts will make it," Wlodek replied smoothly, his dark eyes betraying no emotion. If anybody would know, he would. There had been few females on Earth and none on Refizan or Beliphar. The other six worlds whose vampires now lived on Le-Ath Veronis had maybe a handful between them.

"And the success rate for turning male humanoids?"

"Nine out of ten are successful," Wlodek knew that answer right away.

"That's a huge discrepancy," the reporter whistled. "What do you think is the cause?"

"I have spent three thousand years attempting to find an answer and have personally reached no verifiable conclusions," Wlodek replied enigmatically.

"Gabron, stay with us for a little while," Shala coaxed. She and Elthine had wandered around the brothel naked, taken several clients and now they were off the clock.

Shala had the tip of a nail under Gabron's chin, smiling at him. She was slightly taller than he was and rubbed her body suggestively against his. Elthine, not to be outdone, was at Gabron's shoulder. "We will make your day worthwhile," she kissed his cheek. Gabron nodded and they led him toward a room.

CHAPTER 9

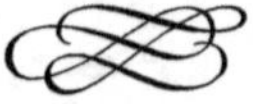

*C*ampiaa

Arvil San Gerxon paced. Sat down, angrily rearranged items on his desk and rose to pace again. The vampire planet was all over the news networks. The first week's take had far exceeded every projection.

Customers were coming away from the place happy. There were winners and losers as always, but this was completely unexpected. He'd walked through his own casinos, listening carefully while his customers discussed Le-Ath Veronis even as they gambled on Campiaa.

Many of his high rollers were discussing trips to the vampire planet—they'd already applied for tickets and were waiting to hear if their applications had been accepted. The hidden deals that might be brokered on Campiaa could be brokered anywhere—they didn't need Arvil's casinos for that. Gambling payouts were regulated and certainly better on Le-Ath Veronis—those were mandated by Reth Alliance laws.

Arvil was not willing to accept this—it could certainly affect his business concerns and cut into his profits. Theos was scheduled to return to Campiaa in two days. Arvil had gotten information daily from his employee, as requested.

Theos was a good servant and completely under his thumb. As quickly as he could review the information provided, Arvil planned to get his management and security teams together to see if it could be exploited in any way.

Arvil sighed. The interview with the Queen of Le-Ath Veronis had received more airtime than it deserved. Who cared that she'd caught a criminal during the interview—the man had accepted a bribe to pass information over to some archaic religious sect.

Arvil snorted. More than likely, it had all been set up for the public's entertainment. He could do the same, if he wanted. Perhaps he should consider it. The Larentii, though, that was a stroke of genius.

Who could have imagined that any of the blue giants could be bought or convinced in some way to pose there with the Vampire Queen? Unheard of. If they were Larentii. Perhaps she'd hired two warlocks to present themselves as Larentii. A possibility to look into.

Arvil had begun building casinos on the property abandoned by Erland Morphis and A&M Consortium. He would not be losing business over this. He'd still draw the criminal element; they always had money, but the regular, wealthy customers? They might all be lured away and it was never wise to cheat the non-Alliance criminals that came to Campiaa to gamble. He always made sure they won frequently.

Theos and the information that he would provide upon his return —information that couldn't be sent through normal channels—was what Arvil waited for. His eyes gleamed at the prospect. This was a challenge and Arvil was more than up for it. If he could damage Le-Ath Veronis and its bitch Queen, he would—in any way possible.

Le-Ath Veronis

"Why am I buried in fan mail?" I had everything from scented paper notes to electronic messages. Grant was doing his best to coordinate everything and had drafted form letters that could be personalized and sent back.

He also pulled out the ones that sounded threatening and turned those over to Gavin and Tony (which could be a mistake) and the special ones he held out for a personal reply.

Erland had arrived two days after the interview, saying that my fan clubs (I had them and didn't know) were having parties just to watch the footage. People were dressing up as one of my mates or me and having themed balls.

"It won't do a bit of good to do another interview," Erland laughed at me. "They're not interested in finding something better to do, even if you tell them that. Somebody already tried it. It didn't work."

"And we have the requests for personal meetings," Grant handed a stack of papers and a comp-vid to me.

"Oh, Lord, what next?" I muttered.

"Did you address me?" Erland laughed. Yeah, he was Lord Erland Morphis, but he wasn't the one I meant. I thought a good elbow in his ribs might shut him up.

I leafed through the requests. I was about to hand all of them back to Grant when something made my hand tingle. I went back through the stack slowly, until I got to the tingly one again and pulled it out. Someone named Theos Wimple had asked for an audience.

"Bring this one in," I handed it to Grant. "As quickly as possible."

"Want me to stand guard with you?" Erland offered a blindingly beautiful smile and then took a chance and kissed me. The kiss was nice. He seemed surprised that I didn't hit him afterward. "We'll work on more of that later."

"Uh-huh. How are your guarding skills?"

"I can create a gate and send them somewhere they never expected to go," Erland grinned.

"Good enough." I watched as Grant contacted Theos Wimple on the communicator and told him we'd have a car sent for him right away.

He was in my office in less than an hour and Drake and Drew had come along to back Erland up. Erland recognized Theos right away; Theos cringed and whimpered when he saw Erland.

"This whelp works for Arvil San Gerxon," Erland snarled and Drake and Drew were just about to haul him out the door. Theos was short and slight of build, with no strength to tussle with two strong Falchani, even if they weren't Spawn Hunters for the Saa Thalarr.

"I want to beg for asylum!" Theos wept, his heels dragging on my expensive rug. "I hate Arvil San Gerxon. If I leave him, though, he'll have me killed—I know too much!"

That was how Theos ended up in my study, under compulsion by Merrill, Adam and Gavin, answering all sorts of questions. Merrill asked Theos what Arvil San Gerxon was doing with the vacant lots he, Adam and Erland had left behind. Theos explained that Arvil was already building on the property.

"We don't have much in the options department, since Campiaa isn't an Alliance world. This is why we razed the casinos to begin with," Adam raked a hand through his dark-brown hair. I could tell he was frustrated at the information.

"I'd like to send this one back as a spy, but that could get him killed and not in a nice way," Merrill glanced at me, piercing blue eyes asking a nonverbal question.

"We can't send him back." I was sure of that. Merrill nodded—that was the answer he wanted as well.

"We need more employees on the light side," Erland suggested.

"Fine," I shrugged. "But how are we going to pass the news along to Arvil San Gerxon? He'll put a contract on Theos. Theos," I turned to him; he was sipping his second Scotch and soda. He needed it; he was shaking. He lifted his eyebrows at me. "Do you have any family or loved ones that Arvil can threaten?"

"No," Theos' gaze dropped to the floor. "He already killed everybody I know."

"Christ," Adam muttered.

"Find him a place to stay on the light side; we'll figure this out," I sighed. "And don't put him to work for a week—he needs some time."

"Thank you," Theos was about to cry again, I think, when he was led from my office.

"How do we get a message to Arvil San Gerxon?" I asked Erland, who was still there. Grant was, too, and he'd watched the entire incident with openmouthed astonishment.

"I can get a message to him; what are we going to say?"

"I have an idea," Grant volunteered.

"We caught your spy," Gavin snarled into the camera while Theos, cuffed and chained, sat in a chair behind Gavin looking terrified. Well, he probably was; Gavin's eyes were red and he was showing fang. "He will be detained indefinitely."

"That's a wrap!" Bryan Riley was getting a high five from Brock and Grace, who also had experience in this sort of thing. I didn't know that Brock and Grace had once been award-winning documentary filmmakers. Who knew?

"We'll have this put together as an electronic message in no time," Brock was having a blast. Gavin went back to normal; Theos breathed an understandable sigh of relief as Drake and Drew removed the chains and cuffs.

"Do you want to come to the kitchens and have something to eat?" I practically pulled Theos from his chair. He went with me and Cheedas found something for Theos to snack on.

"Do you do this all the time? I thought the Queen would be inaccessible," Theos said over his roast-beef sandwich.

"She comes to my kitchen often," Cheedas nodded. "We talk. If I need anything, I tell the Raona. Things get done after that."

"I can see how things get done," Theos nodded. "Yesterday, I was a slave to Arvil San Gerxon. Today I feel like a free man."

"You are. As long as you're honest with us, we'll protect you as well as we can." I was having half a sandwich with Theos—dinner had gone right past me, causing quite a bit of grumbling among the mate department.

～

Campiaa

"What the hell happened?" Arvil's Chief of Security watched the video with Arvil.

"He got caught. Probably trying to record something he wasn't supposed to. No way to get him back—and he wasn't that important anyway. We'll just have to find someone else to send. Look through the applicants and see who might qualify."

"Will Theos provide sensitive information?"

"Nothing Erland Morphis didn't already know," Arvil snorted. "I kept him out of the important things."

"I'll find someone else for you," the Chief promised.

～

Beliphar

"You all know what to do." Gart had dropped Felix and twelve thousand troops in the plowed fields on Beliphar. Now, Felix was handing orders to his troops. Spring had arrived and planting was about to begin. Farming had been done by vampires before they'd all disappeared—during the night since they could see just as well then as anyone else might during the day. Now, Beliphar was missing its slave labor.

Most of the population had wakened one morning to find empty cuffs lying everywhere. Most of the cuffs were near piles of ash, but many were clean. The authorities were now scrambling to place humanoids in vampire positions and laying blame while they did it.

Felix's second and third in command nodded to their leader as he stood in the soft soil of the tilled field. All they had to do was pass their saliva or blood to any one of the Belipharan population and they would be infected.

It took roughly a month for the symptoms to manifest and about twenty percent of the population would die—the very young and the older ones, mostly; their bodies wouldn't adapt. The rest would become soldiers, like them.

Felix had already made plans to get off world—Beliphar still had starships. Granted they were aging and hadn't been used in a very long while, but that shouldn't matter. They'd get where they were going, one way or another.

Felix had lost touch with the contingent on Falchan and didn't know what that meant. It could be something as simple as a broken communicator, since Falchan didn't have that technology, supplies or equipment to facilitate repairs. Felix would consider that problem later. For now, he had a planet to take.

~

Le-Ath Veronis

"He left his ring." Shala held the gold ring in her hand. Gabron had removed everything when they'd gotten into the hot tub with him. "Look, it has the royal crest on it." Elthine pointed out the claw crown on the round signet ring.

"I think I know what to do with this," Shala giggled.

~

Kifirin

"Roff, how did you do this?" I picked oxberries at lightning speed alongside Roff and twenty other comesuli on the High Demon planet. Giff had come, too, after leaving Toff with Grant.

Grant loved to babysit and found a sling to carry Toff while he worked. He didn't even mind feeding Toff. I'd ordered a new wardrobe for Grant, since his current one was stained with Toff's lunch selections.

The sun shone warm and bright over our heads as we picked berries. Garde had come when we'd gotten started, laughed at my straw hat and then went to do Prime Minister things for Jayd.

"It just takes determination and experience, Raona," Roff grinned

158

at me and kept picking. We were piling baskets of oxberries off to the side and Franklin, Shane and Tomas were folding them to Roff's new winery on Le-Ath Veronis faster than we could pick them.

The thorns on oxberry vines weren't much of a treat, either, and my hands were already scratched up. I figured I wasn't feeling as much of the pain as the others had to be; I imagined Frank and the others would have patients lined up when we finished for the day.

Hands were stained with purple juice, too; if we brushed our hair back or wiped sweat from our faces, those were getting stained as well. It made me wonder what would remove berry juice stains from skin.

It was supposed to be off-day, but the fall crop on the Southern Continent wasn't waiting. We had to get these picked before the rainy season began on Kifirin's Southern Hemisphere.

Roff explained that the conditions were right and oxberries were so hardy that they would yield twice in most years this far south. Therefore, we were picking as quickly as we could.

Just before sunset, we picked the last of the berries. I straightened up and stretched my back, listening to it pop. We were all exhausted and I was thankful Roff had a crew at the winery that would take care of things in his absence.

Oxberry wine had become a big hit with the tourists and gamblers and we could sell a bottle for quite a bit, since it was an exclusive item.

"Ready to go home?" I glanced at Roff. If I looked like he did, we might scare people. We needed to head straight for the bath in my suite and not come out until we were scrubbed clean.

Actually, the scrubbing might wait a while—I was so tired that a soak in the tub sounded good. I'd get to the scrubbing when I got a bit of energy back. Roff offered me a weary smile and nodded when I made the suggestion.

"Come on, then. Let's go." We folded home; I landed us into the kitchens for a quick glass of water before Roff and I took the back way toward my suite. We'd almost reached it, slipping into the main hallway to arrive at the double doors leading into the family wing, when someone spoke. I didn't know the woman, but I recognized what she held in her hand.

"Gabron left it at the pleasure house two days ago," she held it out to me. The woman seemed nervous, but I was exhausted and attributed it to her being afraid to approach the Queen. If my skin itched, I was too tired to separate that from the scratches and scrapes I'd gotten while picking berries. She was humanoid—the scent told me that.

"I'll take it," I said, moving forward and holding out my hand. This meant one thing—Gabron had removed everything he was wearing, including his ring. I wasn't sure how I felt about that. Truly, I just wanted to lie in a hot tub of water with Roff until we recharged.

I was almost in front of the woman, prepared to accept the ring as weary, filthy and covered in dust and berry juice as I was, when two things happened. Roff realized before I did what the woman intended. He leapt in front of me, which meant the sharp stake went through his chest instead of mine.

I'm not sure what she expected to happen after she's done her misdeed, but she was thrown against the opposite wall so hard and fast I think I heard her skull crack. I was weeping and shouting mentally and vocally for help in the next second—Roff was dying in my arms.

"Don't leave me, Roff," I begged, but his eyes were already glazing over. Griffin appeared and knelt in the floor beside me.

"I have him in stasis, baby," he said as light formed around his fingers. Blood stopped pouring from the wound as Griffin placed his hands against Roff's chest.

Many people appeared after that. The one who knelt beside Roff's body and did the only thing left for us to do was Flavio. He opened his wrist with a claw and held it over Roff's mouth.

"Drink, honey," I wept. Flavio repeated my words—he was commanding Roff to drink. Roff was swallowing blood while Griffin timed it. Four of the longest minutes of my life ticked by. Roff's breath and heart stopped the moment Griffin called time.

Flavio pulled his wrist away.

"Please don't let him die." I sobbed. I'd forgotten the bitch that had done this to my Roff. Griffin reached in, then, and removed the crudely fashioned stake from Roff's chest. It left a gaping hole in Roff's body. If the turn was successful, the wound would heal. If not, it wouldn't matter anyway.

"Lissa, sweetheart, we've done what we can for him—we have to wait, now." Flavio lifted Roff and carried him into my bedroom.

"Is this the one who stabbed Roff?" Tony, Drake and Drew were standing over the woman.

I rose stiffly from the floor and turned to the three who'd shown up. "Yes. Is she dead?"

"She's still breathing, but I think her skull is fractured and her neck may be broken," Drew knelt beside her to check.

"What's this?" Gabron walked up. "What have you done to Shala?" he demanded. It was all I could do not to slam him into a wall, too.

"She had your ring," I wiped tears away. I looked awful, covered in dust and berry juice, but right then I didn't care. "She was holding the ring out to me, saying you'd left it behind earlier. When I went to take it, she tried to stab me with a stake. Roff stepped in front of me and she hit him instead. I'm sorry if I damaged your fucking employee when I threw her against the wall."

"Where is Roff?" Gabron's gaze now focused on me.

"Flavio is attempting the turn. If he doesn't live, well." I didn't finish my sentence. Karzac appeared and Merrill's son Jeff and Selkirk Grey were right behind him. They moved Gabron and me aside so they could examine Shala.

"Patch her up," I jerked my head in Shala's direction. "I want her nice and whole when we put her on trial."

~

"His body isn't deteriorating; that's a good sign." Merrill, Wlodek and Flavio were all watching with me through the night. Merrill said the first two nights were critical and if the turning wasn't going to take, we'd probably know in that amount of time.

I was numb. Giff had been weeping uncontrollably. Grant was helping the comesula babysitters deal with Toff. Toff screamed for his father and there wasn't anything we could do for him. Karzac had to put Giff under eventually and the baby finally went to sleep. Gabron had melted from the palace like snow on a warm, spring day.

Garde had come and he, Drake and Drew cleaned me up and dressed me in pajamas; I was still crying off and on the whole time. Jeff and Selkirk had gotten Roff cleaned up but his face was so pale and still, he looked dead to me.

That frightened me more than I can say and I felt as if someone had kicked me in the stomach. Reemagar and Connegar came in three hours before dawn and took me to Reemagar's suite. The bed was huge, they put me between them and I was out like a light the moment Connegar placed fingers against my forehead.

"Do not fear, I will keep watch." Jeral nodded to Griffin and the others. Jeral had done so many turns in his long life. Wlodek, Merrill and the others all needed sleep; they'd been up all night. The Larentii had come and taken Lissa away, forcing her to sleep. It would kill her if Roff died.

Shala had been imprisoned in the palace dungeon—and she had someone else in the cell next to hers. Another pleasure worker—Elthine. Shala admitted under compulsion that she and Elthine devised their plan carefully, with Shala sneaking into the palace with the scheduled tour and then separating herself from it, waiting for the Queen to return.

Garde had gone to the dungeons and paced before their cells in full Thifilathi, blowing smoke and frightening both women. Neither had seen Gabron since they'd been incarcerated.

Merrill and Wlodek performed the initial questioning with Drake, Drew, Tony and Gavin looking on. The two women hoped that with Lissa out of the way, the rule would be shared among her mates, giving Gabron more importance. They'd intended to convince

Gabron to make them his concubines so they might live in the palace with him. Gavin had snorted in disbelief at their plan.

"And just how did you think you might get away with this?" he demanded. Shala shrank from his anger. Gavin wanted to execute her immediately but Lissa forbade it, choosing to wait and see whether Roff accepted the turn.

❧

Gabron sat and drank at a bar in one of the casinos. In the beginning, Lissa had set both Shala and Elthine's applications in the pile not to be considered. Like a fool he'd pulled their applications back and hired them anyway.

They'd tried to kill Lissa. Instead, Roff had protected her. Gabron was a very old vampire and he'd allowed two scheming women and his own lust to bring him down.

"Drinking generally doesn't solve anything." Erland settled on the stool next to Gabron's and ordered a drink.

"She will ask for her ring back and dissolve the union." Gabron fingered the ring in his pocket. He hadn't worn it since the night he'd taken it off and foolishly left it behind at the brothel.

"You can't say that for sure." Erland sipped his bourbon.

"The odds are very good, my friend." Gabron wiped the condensation off one side of his glass with a finger.

"She loves you. You can't just turn that on and off," Erland offered.

"But she will do it," Gabron sighed. "I remember the night I first saw her, walking along a street in Ordinandis, more than three hundred years ago. I caught the scent of a female vampire and was drawn like a magnet. She was beautiful. The rarest of jewels, had I but known it at the time. We talked and she seemed unafraid of me. I gave her my card and she came to find me the following evening. She almost left me when she discovered what kind of business I ran. I allowed two women, the most selfish and conniving I have known, to bring me down. If they'd managed to kill Lissa, where would we be at this moment?"

"Without a home," Kifirin folded in and sat on the empty stool next to Erland. "This world exists because of Lissa. I would have allowed the comesuli to stay, but all others would have been forced away. You might be living again on Refizan. Lissa may forgive you, vampire, but I may not."

The bartender set a glass of wine in front of Kifirin without a blink. Kifirin had placed his order mentally and the bartender automatically complied. "I do not know yet if Roff will survive and Lissa loves Roff very much. What do you think that will do to her, if he dies?"

"My ability to end my life by walking into the sun has been negated. What do you wish me to do?"

"Make amends with Lissa, if you can. Or walk away from her, if that is her desire. How much do you love her, vampire? Of all her mates, your love is the weakest, I think."

"I kept telling myself that I could have sex any time I wished, whenever I was not in her bed," Gabron held up his empty glass. The bartender went to make another drink for him. "That is what I was used to. I had my pick of any of my girls and they enjoyed the bite. Some even said they loved me. I shored myself up with that. Kept myself alive with that. It wasn't love, though, was it?"

"You weren't willing to give yourself in return," Kifirin replied. "How many of those girls did you love? Did you tell them so? And if you told them, did you mean it?"

"If I did, I didn't mean it. My heart has been cold and still for a very long time."

"You do not love Lissa?"

"Lissa makes me ache. She makes me ashamed, that I cannot be as warm and loving as she."

"She asked for nothing more from you than what you gave."

"Except for her disagreement with me over my brothels." Gabron snorted.

"Even though she feels no jealousy, that made her feel inadequate," Erland said. "Those girls are trained to give pleasure. She cannot compete with that. Before she was turned, she only had one lover during her lifetime. I learned this from Gavin. Did you miss your trained girls when you were in bed with her, Gabron?"

"No. All I could think about when we were together was pleasing her. And pleasing her pleased me. It made me feel warm, to bed her."

"Because she gave love in addition to sex." Kifirin drained his glass. "Those girls you hire and train may give you the exotic and the unusual, but they will not give you love. They take your money and go to the next customer. Tell me this is not so."

"Are you telling me to never bed another woman?"

"Lissa herself did not tell you that, so who are we to gainsay it? We have immortality facing us, my friend. Boredom can become a very real malady. Lissa told you that she was hoping you cared for whomever you took to your bed."

"The truth is that I almost got her killed." Gabron was back to the crux of the matter. "And she will dissolve our union. Those things matter not from this point."

CHAPTER 10

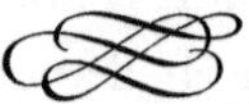

*L*e-Ath Veronis

I sat with Roff the entire second night. The minutes and hours passed in tiny, ticking eternities. There was no change.

No change.

No change.

I talked to Roff after a while. Told him I loved him, even though Griffin was there. Or Merrill or Flavio. What if Roff's warm brown eyes never opened to me again? That pain was too hard to bear. I concentrated on the clock.

I'd asked Wlodek earlier for the signs that the turning was not successful. He hadn't wanted to tell me, but he did anyway. "The skin will become gray and then turn to ash," he replied. "Lissa, this was not your fault. Roff would have died with you, if you had been the one hit. Do not second-guess yourself or his actions in this matter. Accept the gift from Roff. This is what he desires."

I hadn't been to the dungeon to see Roff's attacker, either. She'd had an accomplice, but Shala had been the one to put the stake in Roff's chest. I was afraid that if I did go see her, I wouldn't be able to control myself and she would die.

According to our laws, she must be judged by the Heads of all the

City Councils. Those laws had been devised for a reason and I had no right to circumvent them, even though I wanted to.

Kifirin was the only one not bound by the laws of Le-Ath Veronis and I didn't expect him to weigh in on this. Justice would come, eventually. Gabron had not come forward to apologize or to check on Roff. He was receding farther and farther away from me. It seems he'd made a choice and that choice had not been me.

"Granddaughter." Wylend Arden had come. Griffin had probably told him about Roff—father and son were becoming close. Except for the day I'd discovered he was my grandfather, Wylend and I hadn't spent much time together.

"Em-pah." I borrowed Kyler and Cleo's term and hugged him when he sat beside me. Roff lay on my bed, as still as death, though his body was still intact.

"My father explained to me once why Karathian witches and warlocks have no power over death," Wylend settled more comfortably in his chair after I let him go.

I turned to look at my grandfather's face when he spoke. His eyes were slightly unfocused, though they didn't change as I'd seen Griffin's do. "Death is not the evil that many believe it to be," my grandfather said. "So many of us do whatever we can to avoid it as long as possible."

He drew in a breath before continuing, as if he were carefully choosing his words. "We even grasp at straws, sometimes, to keep death away from us," he said. "But death is not the enemy. It takes us when our bodies are no longer prepared to carry on in our current lives. Brings us peace and freedom from pain. It is life that is often the enemy. The siren that convinces us to hold onto it as long as we can, even though we are filled with pain or have lived long past our usefulness. My father always said that we should let our life leave us when it is time and do it gladly, instead of with sorrow and bitterness. Something else awaits us and when we arrive, we will wonder what it was that held us back from it so long."

"Em-pah, right now might not be the best time for that lecture," I wiped tears away. I was surprised I had any left.

"I know," he lifted me from my chair as easily as any vampire might and settled me on his lap. "I didn't get the chance to hold you when you were small. Or kiss your scraped elbows or skinned knees. So many things are owed to us, Granddaughter. I hope your little comesula lives, because I do not wish to see my granddaughter's heart broken."

He sat quietly with me for the rest of the night. I had hope when the night ended, although there was no dawn and never would be where my palace lay. Roff's body was still intact, albeit pale and still. It could take as few as three days and as many as seventeen, in Wlodek's experience, to make a full turn. My hopes had risen the barest of fractions when my Larentii put me to bed.

I'd been sleeping in Reemagar's suite, but they'd put me in with Drake the night before. I woke with a very amorous Falchani beside me. Drake took care of me and took care of business. I was clean and dressed, too, when I went to sit with Roff.

"Why is Roff lying on his stomach?" Flavio was waiting when I walked into my suite and asked the question as I settled on a chair beside him.

"Kifirin came and said we had to do this, to allow his wings to grow if he lives and thrives." Flavio looked tired as I explained what I knew. I recognized that weariness.

"Lissa, you must call me if he begins to wake at any time. A sire must be there—it is not only the law, but for the welfare of the new vampire. They feel the connection with a sire and I must feed him the first time—it establishes the bond. Do you understand?"

I thought I did, although nobody had been there for me when I woke the first time. There were no reassurances for me when my eyes had opened in an unfamiliar place. A frigid cellar had greeted me, along with a signed cocktail napkin lying on a desk, indicating my status as the source of a bet between two vampires.

"Lissa, don't go down that path." Flavio watched as those emotions played across my face. "My vampire father has wished many times that he might have been there to welcome you when you rose the first time. Many of us would have given much to watch your eyes open. That was not to be, my Queen. I beg you not to regret your turning. It has become a blessing to all of us."

It didn't feel like a blessing at the moment as I gazed at Roff's nude body, now lying face down on my bed. "Flavio, you look exhausted. Go eat something and get some rest. I promise to send for you if he shows any signs of waking. I want Roff to have the best of care."

"I will, little sister. I will answer your call immediately if you send mindspeech."

I nodded to him and he folded away. Kyler had done this for him—given him that ability plus mindspeech and a few other things, although he was still mostly vampire. I sat down to keep watch over Roff.

Giff came in after a while with a breakfast tray. Toff had not been allowed inside the room, lest he reach for his father. I understood that feeling all too well; I wanted to reach for his father as well. I'd been told it was better not to disturb the body. I did talk to him once in a while; they hadn't told me I couldn't.

Giff and I sat and ate breakfast, though neither of us was hungry. It was something to do—a distraction. I warmed our tea several times using the power that I had, though I seldom used it.

Meetings with the Council had been canceled. Thank goodness, another tour of the palace would not be coming through for a few more days. Drake and Drew had guards arranged to check every tourist that came to the palace from this point forward.

We'd learned that Shala had rubbed herself against the tour bus driver, promising him who knew what, and was allowed on the bus. The driver now faced charges and sat in an underground cell, wearing the cuffs that could control a vampire.

Yes, a vampire had aided my would-be murderer, for the promise of sex. The whole thing sickened me. I was afraid to turn my thoughts to Gabron. I still wore his ring but thought many times of flinging it away or sending it back to him, wherever he was. I thought about shouting at him and telling him we were done. Yet there the ring was, still on my finger. I sighed.

Giff left me after a while—Rolfe had come for her. He lifted her in his arms and carried her from the room. Grant crept in with papers for me to sign and other things that desperately needed my attention.

We spoke quietly together, I signed and read and dispensed the Queen's words and wisdom. *Wisdom.* What a useless word to me at the moment. I didn't have any wisdom. It had floated away from me the moment I saw the light beginning to die in Roff's eyes.

"Grant, who turned you?" I looked at him. He was one of the hundred thousand or so from Earth and I had never met his sire. Grant was more than nine hundred years old—that's all I knew about him.

"Sarita turned me," he sighed. "I was barely twenty and dying of an infection. I was really sick. I think she hoped I would be the child she couldn't have. I was a disappointment to her, when I woke. She walked into the sun a week later."

"Who helped you after that?" Grant now had my full attention.

"Someone named Victor. You won't know him; he gave up his life when I was two hundred years old. Victor was old, Lissa. Really old. But he knew so much. Sometimes I thought that if I stared into his eyes long enough, I could see the origins of everything."

I sent mindspeech to Merrill, who was there in a blink. "You never told me Sarita sired a child," I looked up at him. Perhaps it was the Saa Thalarr blood in him that had confused the scent, since he'd be Grant's grandparent, after all. I hadn't known until I'd gone sniffing for it after Grant told me. It was so faint it almost wasn't there but I found it, once I knew what I was looking for.

"She didn't," Merrill started to deny and then went *Looking.* I saw the confusion on his face after a moment. "She got away from us, there at the end. Wanted time alone, she said. Barely a month later, she gave herself to the sun. The aristocracy was only beginning to meet and come to agreement on the laws and such. The Council had yet to be. Child, Sarita was of my making." He smiled at Grant.

"Someone named Victor raised him," I offered.

"I knew Victor. He was ancient when I knew him. Tired of life after a while and gave it up." Merrill shrugged. "Child, if you need anything, all you have to do is come to me." Merrill nodded to Grant and folded away.

"That's your vampire grandfather," I patted Grant on the back. "He was my surrogate sire for a while. We're practically related."

~

Ten days it took. Ten long, worrisome, excruciating days. Roff's wings formed but they looked weak and small to me, pressed tightly against his back. They resembled a new butterfly's wings—soft and moist in appearance. They were a light brown as was his skin, now—almost a latte color.

He'd grown taller in the turn, too, but it was difficult to gauge his height as he lay on the bed. A soft moan escaped his lips and I was off my chair swiftly, calling mentally for Flavio and anyone else who could come. Wlodek, Merrill and Flavio answered my call and the worst thing in the world happened. Flavio went to Roff and I was hauled from the room by Merrill and Wlodek.

"But I want to see Roff!" I struggled against their hold.

"Lissa, you cannot. Not for a while. You will confuse him when he does not need to be confused. He needs to focus on his sire and what his sire will be teaching him. You will not interfere with this." Wlodek was laying down the law, just as he'd always done before. Giff was crying in the hallway nearby—Adam and Gavin were holding her back. I started cursing.

"It's a fucking fine time for you to tell me this now!" I jerked out of their hands.

"Lissa, we did not want to upset you any more than you already were. We must take this argument out of Roff's hearing." I was folded into the kitchen and offered something to eat. I just stood and stared at Wlodek and Merrill.

"Fuck you. Fuck both of you." I didn't bother turning to mist. I went to energy—something I hadn't done for days, and went so far

171

away with that first angry thought it would have taken the fastest starship light-years to navigate back to Le-Ath Veronis.

~

"She has been gone four months. We should proceed with the trial." Kifirin had come to the private Council meeting. Only the Heads of the Councils were invited to these meetings and they were not broadcast over the news channel as the others were.

Kifirin had made brief appearances after Lissa's disappearance, assured the others that he knew where she was and refused to give further information. Gossip abounded that she was on retreat after the attempt on her life while other whispered rumors speculated she'd been staked and was now dead.

"I'm all for getting this over with," Flavio agreed. Roff had been left behind at Flavio's home; Kyler had come to keep the new vampire company. Not once had Roff asked after Lissa and Flavio knew that fact alone would have broken Lissa's heart.

Roff had no memories of her, his children or several others. Many more that he'd known were now only hazy memories in his mind. He was progressing very well, otherwise and Flavio was quite satisfied with his fourth and youngest vampire child.

"Then let us do this, while I am here. Bring the first prisoner forth," Kifirin commanded. Drake and Drew folded to the dungeons and brought the vampire bus driver in.

"I didn't know," the vampire begged Kifirin to understand. "I thought she was a tourist that couldn't get in otherwise."

"And yet you had compulsion available and failed to use it," Kifirin wasn't moved.

The vampire hung his head. "I realized this later. I wasn't thinking at the moment."

Kifirin lifted an eyebrow at the admission. "What do you think your punishment should be?" The vampire raised his head and gazed into Kifirin's dark eyes. Smoke curled from Kifirin's nostrils, making the vampire wonder what Kifirin truly was.

"Five years imprisonment," the vampire hung his head again.

"Two years. And something will be found to occupy your time." Kifirin pronounced judgment. There would be no debate in his court of law. The vampire was returned to the dungeon until something could be found for him to do. Elthine was led forward next.

Gabron was present, as Head of the Refizani Council. He'd returned to the palace after learning of Lissa's disappearance. Hardly anyone spoke to him the few times he came to dinner or breakfast.

Mostly he drank blood substitute and spent much time in his suite if he wasn't running his businesses. Those had proven to be wildly successful and he and the other Refizani investors were enjoying the boom the entire planet experienced, but it was a lifeless victory for him.

"You will speak only the truth while you stand before me," Kifirin addressed Elthine and she quailed before him. Stars appeared in Kifirin's eyes while smoke poured from his nostrils.

Elthine had no idea what he was, either, but power radiated from him and she was terrified. "Tell me your part in this," Kifirin demanded. Elthine wanted to fall at his feet and beg for her life. She was compelled to tell her story instead.

"We worked for Gabron, on Refizan," Elthine's voice quavered. "Shala and I, well, we liked the vampires. Very much. We became jaded with normal sex—even the more deviant types. We would often beg Gabron for the bite. He would give it to us in exchange for sex. Shala wanted this for herself, all the time. She wanted money. She wanted her own brothel. She even toyed with the idea of staking Gabron at times, but somehow knew she would not gain what she wanted with his death. She thought about going to him and asking if he would set her up and then backed away. She was afraid he would refuse."

"And you did not want these things for yourself?"

"Shala said I could be first assistant in her brothel. That appealed to me. I did not want to be in control. That is what Shala wanted. When we heard Gabron was here and looking for employees, Shala wanted to come more than anything. We had been without our vampires for months. This was our chance to be bitten again."

"So, you were anxious for the bite, is that it?" Smoke drifted from Kifirin's nostrils.

"Yes. Gabron hired us right away and we came with the first new employees. Shala wasted no time in enticing Gabron into our bed. We would both please him in exchange for the bite. Shala spoke of her old dream, too, from the beginning. She wanted her own place and a stable of vampires who would bite her whenever she wanted. Gabron would only bite once every two weeks or so. Of course, we convinced others to do this for us in between, although it was against house rules. When Gabron left his ring behind after going to bed with us, Shala fretted and complained, blaming her misfortunes on Gabron's mate—the Queen. She had his ring, however, and devised her plan with my help."

"What were your suggestions to her? Did you try to stop her at any time?"

"I did not try to stop her. I thought this would work out in my best interest as well. I was the one to suggest that she join the tour to the palace and then hide herself until she could get the Queen alone, if she could. Her plan was to offer the ring to the Queen so she would come close enough for the staking."

"You were eliminating a rival, is that it?"

"We thought so. The Queen was taking up much of Gabron's time and attention. We had to turn it back to us so he would perhaps offer us a position with him at the palace."

"Shala said before that you both wanted to be concubines to him."

"Or mates, perhaps, if he would agree. He would be mourning his Queen. We could offer comfort."

"All while living in her palace, which I built for her."

"You built this?" Elthine's lower lip trembled.

"I built every city that exists upon this planet, with the exception of the gambling city and the brothels, which others have built. I built it for the Queen. I did not build it for you or for Gabron or any other vampire that walks upon this world. Had you known what I truly am, you would never have allowed a thought of conspiracy to take root in your mind.

Gabron should have recognized the signs of bite addiction in you long ago, yet he did not. There are two known cures for bite addiction. The first is compulsion and then the recipient must never be bitten again. The second cure is death. You committed treason by conspiring against my Queen. What do you think your sentence is going to be?"

"B-bite addiction? I have never heard that."

"This happens when the humanoid is bitten too often by many vampires. How many times did you lie, just to get another bite? Anemia is the first sign, and then the vampire's saliva begins to work its way into the body's system. It is not the same as receiving vampire blood—that would have killed you in a matter of months. Normally, vampire saliva will heal the fang marks from a bite. Too many times too close together and from more than one vampire results in bite addiction. It affects your brain after a time. Inhibits reasoning. Damages normal thought processes. That is what bite addiction is. You are afflicted with this, as is your co-conspirator."

"Then we had no control—"

"I will not accept this as an excuse. You broke house rules long ago to get where you are at this moment. You will receive no sympathy from me, so do not expect it. Who wishes to carry out the death sentence?"

Flavio stood. Gavin stepped forward, Tony right beside him. "We have been given permission," Drake and Drew joined Gavin and Tony. Erland Morphis folded in with Wylend Arden. Reemagar and Connegar folded in. Gardevik came. Rolfe brought Giff in and set her down near the door. He joined Gavin and the others.

"Have mercy," Elthine wept and dropped to the floor.

"I will grant mercy, this time," Kifirin stood. "I will allow the Larentii to do this. I will not be merciful to the one who comes next." Kifirin nodded to Connegar and Reemagar.

Reemagar stepped forward and held out his hand. Light formed around it and Elthine's particles separated and floated peacefully away, the final, tiny motes of light winking out within seconds.

The High Council watched as this happened. If any of them had not known of the power of the Larentii, they were getting their first vision of it now.

"Bring the other," Kifirin commanded. Shala was brought forward —Drake and Drew had gone to get her.

"I have heard the testimony from the other two and have passed judgment. I grow weary of listening to irrationality," Kifirin growled at Shala.

"Gabron loves me. He will not allow me to die." Shala adjusted her plain cotton shift—she'd struggled in Drake and Drew's grip and was now setting herself to rights.

"Yet you considered staking him, did you not?" Kifirin's eyes narrowed. Shala patted her long blonde hair into place. She regretted that she hadn't been allowed a hairdresser or better clothing for this appearance.

"When he refused to give the bite," Shala pulled her shoulders back so her breasts would be more prominent.

"Your charms have no effect upon me," Kifirin glared at her.

"I can give you the best sex you have ever had," Shala boasted. She attempted to walk forward, to entice Kifirin. She hadn't failed to notice that he was the most attractive male she'd ever seen. An invisible shield prevented her from approaching Kifirin's seat at the front of the meeting hall. She stood still and pouted at him instead.

"I am done with this one. High Demon," Kifirin nodded toward Garde, "I give her to you."

"Ooh," Shala looked at the male approaching her. He was pretty enough. He would do nicely. Except that he changed. Grew taller. Darker. More demonic.

Gardevik Rath, in full Thifilathi, swept up the female in a huge, clawed hand before she could shriek and twisted her head from her body. Both parts were thrown violently and splattered against the wall where Gabron sat. The High Demon skipped from the room, leaving near-chaos behind.

～

"I swear I didn't realize they were bite-addicted." Gabron paced before Karzac. Karzac had deliberately stayed away from the trials—it was bad enough that Lissa was missing; Grace was now six months pregnant.

Women belonging to the Saa Thalarr couldn't use any power past the first trimester or they could lose or damage the child. Any pregnant Saa Thalarr was carefully watched and monitored.

Karzac had left Grace in the capable hands of Mack and Justin, two of her mates, so he could have this meeting with Gabron. He now studied the old vampire with a critical eye. Gabron was old as a vampire, but Karzac was older. Six thousand years older.

"And you failed to pay attention," Karzac sipped a cup of tea in the palace kitchen. He'd spent most of his time with Grace, watching over her while Lissa was gone. Kifirin said Lissa was fine—Karzac had to rely on that information, else he might have given way to his temper.

"I didn't fail to pay attention when Gardevik threw the body in my direction," Gabron sighed.

"Accept responsibility and go on," Karzac said.

"She won't take me back."

"Now we get to the truth," Karzac sighed. "How badly do you want her to take you back, or is this merely a point of pride?"

"I don't deserve to be taken back."

"Many certainly feel that way. I would wait for Lissa's opinion on the matter," Karzac emptied his teacup. "Meanwhile, I'd be thinking of ways that might convince her you're worth taking back." Karzac folded away.

Earth

The old myths that vampires can't walk on consecrated ground or into a church, or that they burn if holy water is dumped on them are exactly that—myths. Who came up with that, anyway? Somebody who wanted to convince themselves that there was a way to keep vampires away from them?

Granted, garlic was a little strong and offended a vampire's nose because it was so sensitive, but if a vampire was truly hungry, you might have to cover your whole body with the stuff to chase them away.

One of those little pamphlets they give away at funerals was pressed into my hand as I walked into the large, gothic-style church in Dallas. I'd bent time to get back to this point.

I studied the folded paper in my hand—a photograph of an older Winkler than the one I'd known stared back at me. I gently ran a thumb over his image.

An usher directed me to a pew at the back of the church and I sat. I was dressed in a black suit—I'd discovered that with power, many things are possible, including clothing yourself in the latest fashion wherever and whenever you might be.

I couldn't see Winkler's children from where I sat, though I craned my neck to find them. Someone played somber organ music and it made me wonder what Winkler might have thought about that. He liked jazz and classic rock and roll. He'd been one hundred forty-two when he'd died. Still young for a werewolf, if you weren't Packmaster. Winkler was gone fifty-three years after I'd seen him last.

The church was packed with werewolves, local celebrities, media and the curious. It made me wonder how many of those present had truly loved him. Winkler had been a powerful man—and an important one. Now he was gone. He'd given his position as Dallas Packmaster to one of his children in the only way he could.

The service was long, flowery and boring. Winkler would have hated it. Hated it with a capital H. The burial was supposed to be private, with only family and close friends. My interpretation of that was werewolves only. That's why I rode with the casket as mist.

A separate service was held graveside and I recognized the place when we arrived. Wilburn Ranch had changed little since I'd seen it last. Randall Wilburn was there but his human wife had died years earlier. Daryl Harper had come, as the current Grand Master instead of Weldon's Second. Weldon had disappeared to join the Saa Thalarr, leaving Daryl to fight for his right to hold the Grand Master's position.

I stood back from the others at the gravesite, shielding myself to keep them from seeing or scenting me. Several werewolves spoke, standing behind the casket—it lay next to the open grave, which was near two other tombstones.

Winkler's parents were buried there. Daryl, as the highest-ranking werewolf present, spoke last. He talked about Winkler's life and his contributions to both humans and werewolves. And then he talked about Winkler's exploits. Then the weirdest thing of all happened.

"Winkler once hired a vampire to work for him," Daryl began, as if pulling up a favorite memory. "A female vampire, and those are extremely rare. I won't go into the reasons why he hired her, but he did. She worked as a bodyguard for him and he even loaned her to my father once, to protect him during a spring summit. That vampire saved my father's life and held the peace between vampires and werewolves. You can thank William Winkler, now, for helping to preserve the peace you have with the vampires. The little vampire died, I'm sad to say, but my father made her a member of the Pack and that stands to this day. If she were here, I think she'd tell you that she loved Winkler.

"She is here and she did love Winkler." I walked through rows of standing werewolves as fast as I could. Daryl was shocked, I could tell, when I stood across from Winkler's grave, gazing steadily at him.

"Lissa?" That's all he managed to say.

CHAPTER 11

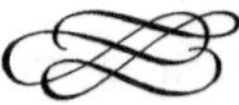

*E**arth*

    "You knew my dad." It was a statement and not a question. William Winkler, Jr. stood beside me as we stared at the wolf inside the open casket. Daryl managed to get all the others away for a private moment.

Winkler's daughter was still having a hard time with all this and hated her brother at the moment. She'd left with the others—they'd gone to Randall Wilburn's home to sit down and cool off. It was June in Texas and hot outside.

"I knew your dad." I reached out to stroke the fur around Winkler's ears. He'd died in wolf form—he wouldn't change back. "I've seen him fight. He was something to see." I struggled to come to grips with the fact that a few of the wolves remembered me when the vampires didn't. Maybe it didn't matter with them while it did with the vamps.

"I hope he didn't suffer," Winkler Jr. brushed tears away as he stared at his father's wolf.

"Honey, look at me." He looked a little like his father. Same dark eyes and black hair. Nearly as tall as his daddy, too. He turned those familiar, dark eyes to my face.

"Your dad struggled with this, too," I told him. "It ate at him the whole time—his father made him do the same thing so the Pack would come to him instead of going to the Second. Trust me, I knew Phil. Phil didn't need to be in charge of the Pack and he didn't need to be mated to your Aunt Whitney. Phil wasn't the best person in the world. Your grandfather forced Winkler to challenge and then pretty much threw the fight. Your dad gave this as a gift to you and as a gift to his Pack. Don't sully that gift by carrying this load of guilt around with you your whole life, like he did."

"I understand your words and I hope I can see things that way someday," he told me. "Right now, I feel like shit."

"Yeah. I know," I said. "But you have a Pack to run. Don't let this get in the way of doing your job. You're in charge, now. Your dad knew his job and he did it well. I hope he taught you what he knew." I brushed the fur on Winkler's face one last time before pulling my hand away.

"How are you here? Out in the sun, I mean," Winkler's son asked. "They call me Wayne, by the way, just so we wouldn't get confused." He closed the lid on the casket with a sigh.

"Strange things have happened since I was last here," I said. "And you wouldn't believe most of it if I told you."

Wayne raised his hand and two werewolves who'd waited patiently in the distance came forward. They'd be lowering the casket. Wayne took my arm and we walked toward the Wilburn's house on the hill.

"Lissa?" Whitney came forward when Wayne and I walked into the house. She was extremely pregnant, with Sam standing protectively beside her. I could see why she hadn't gone to the gravesite in the heat.

"Hi, baby. How are you?" I wasn't prepared for the crushing hug she gave me. She was wiping tears away when she let me go. Sam's hug wasn't quite so hard, but it was hard enough.

"Sam is Packmaster in Corpus, now," Whitney was proud of him, I could tell.

"From Shirley or somebody else?" I asked.

"Shirley," Sam nodded. Well, she'd always irritated me, when she hadn't lifted a finger to protect Weldon.

"I'm proud of you," I patted his shoulder.

"This is my twin sister, Wynter," Wayne brought his sister forward. She followed him reluctantly. "Will you tell her what you told me, earlier?"

I did. And I had a larger audience, before it was over. Daryl came to stand next to me as I explained the gift that Winkler had given to his children, and about their grandfather doing the same thing.

"Don't think to challenge Wayne, either. If he fights like his daddy, I don't have any hope for an opponent," I warned the others. Some of them laughed and nodded in agreement.

"Lissa, are you going to stay?" Daryl asked after a while. The guests had all gone and now it was just Daryl and Winkler's family.

"No, I've already stayed longer than I anticipated," I said. "It was good to see you, and even better that you remembered me."

"Lissa, tell me how you're here, now, instead of a pile of ash, somewhere," Daryl asked.

"That is a strange tale," I said, before changing the subject. "Have you ever heard of Harifa Edus?"

"No. What is that?"

"It was once the planet where the werewolves lived," I said. "All the werewolves. Harifa Edus means Hunter's Eyes. It had six moons, so the werewolves got to run six nights a month. And it wasn't far from Le-Ath Veronis, which means Heart of the Vampire."

"Are you making this up?" Daryl wore a crooked smile. He thought I was teasing him.

"Nope. On your father's furry ears I swear, I'm not making this up."

"That would be incredible—a planet with six moons. And only werewolves there, so we wouldn't have to hide."

"Yeah. A tale you can tell your grandkids," I said. "I have to go now. I'll tell your father hello." I turned to mist and folded away.

~

Harifa Edus
Everything crumbles to dust in a hundred thousand years. Stones still mapped out a few roads, but that was all. All was quiet

on Harifa Edus—only plant life existed now, with a few insects and fish.

Werewolves wouldn't be able to survive on fish. They needed game, not just to hunt but also to eat. I figured a few domesticated animals and fields of crops wouldn't go amiss, either.

I'd seen Winkler eat vegetables and salad. He seemed to enjoy it, too. I intended to do something about Harifa Edus, but there were other things demanding my attention first. I went to energy to attend to those things.

~

Beliphar

Beliphar was about to fall. Those who'd been shipped in were infecting the population quickly—the ones enhanced with Ra'Ak DNA were spreading their poison across the planet.

I ferreted out the plan—infect the planet and then send out those infected and transformed soldiers to infect others. Where was the end of all of this? Where had it started, even? I didn't have time to ponder that problem at the moment; if I were going to save any of these pitiful souls, it had to be now.

As energy, I surrounded the planet and pulled away what I could. The children and their parents, mostly—the ones who hadn't mistreated others. I carried them to the High Demons' world and left them, frightened and weeping, on the streets of Veshtul. I'd turned every starship on Beliphar to dust, too, before I left.

~

Kifirin

"They just showed up? With no word?" Jayd growled as smoke poured from his nostrils.

"Jayd, calm down—the current population is feeling sympathy for these people and are offering help. This helps them, too, you know—they've been in the same situation. They can prop each other up,"

Glinda reassured her High Demon mate. "You were saying yesterday that we needed to send people out to the other cities and towns, but we didn't have enough to send. Now we do."

"Fine. Where did they come from? How did they get here? Kyler and Kiarra said they didn't bring them."

"I think it might be Lissa," Glinda said quietly. She didn't want to say it too loudly; Garde had been like a lion with a sore paw for the past five months, since Lissa's disappearance.

"If it was Lissa, then we're okay," Jayd sighed. "She wouldn't bring anyone that had a criminal background."

"You can count on that," Glinda agreed.

Le-Ath Veronis

"Child, I will only allow you to go to the winery after we finish our lesson," Flavio informed Roff sternly.

"Father, this batch needs to be separated and bottled."

"I understand, but this is also important. I am going to teach you how to take blood properly. I have someone coming who will bite you so you will know how it is done. You may do this on your own afterward without harming your donor. A few comesuli have already approached me, offering their blood to the winged one."

"Who is coming to teach me, father? Do I know them?"

"You do not. You have not been introduced, child. That is why I asked him."

"What is his name?"

"Lucas."

"I do not recognize that name."

"As it should be. It is preferable that you do not know the one who bites you. This way, you have no expectations."

"He is here, father. I hear him at the door." Roff smiled. He enjoyed his enhanced abilities. His nose was so much better, now. Winemaking was easier, too—he could smell the stages of fermentation. Lucas was led into Flavio's private study.

"You must stand still, like so," Flavio placed Roff in the center of the floor. "Now, Lucas, take him through the steps."

"You must hold the back of the head or the neck, so that they cannot move—your fangs will damage fragile skin." Lucas wasn't as tall as Roff—Roff topped six feet after the turn. Lucas stood on tiptoe as he gripped the back of Roff's neck firmly. "Do not allow them to move, understand?"

Roff attempted to nod—Lucas' grip on his neck prevented it. "See, no moving, no nodding. Hold their body against yours, in case they fall or twist in your hold," Lucas pulled Roff against him. "Now, you may give a kiss, if you are so inclined," Lucas kissed Roff, causing Roff to blink in confusion. "You may also place a kiss over the artery," Lucas leaned in and kissed Roff's neck, nuzzling it lightly. Roff whimpered faintly.

"Then bite gently; your fangs are quite sharp and will pierce the skin easily," Lucas breathed on Roff's neck and then sank his fangs into the newly-turned vampire's throat. Roff was held tightly against Lucas as his body convulsed with the climax.

"What do you think of the bite?" Flavio asked after getting Roff settled into a chair and offering him a bottle of blood substitute. Lucas had left shortly after the lesson was over.

"The climax was pleasurable; the kiss was not." Roff drank from his bottle.

"I understand. You should have seen the one who bit me the first time," Flavio grimaced. "He was ancient and not so gentle. Father and I had an argument about it later, when I was older."

"May I go to the winery now?"

"I will come with you." Flavio smiled at his vampire child.

"But I was going to fly, Father, and you hate it when I take you flying."

"Child, it is frightening to be held aloft like that. I will take myself and meet you there."

"Good." Roff laughed at his sire and headed for the door.

❦

"Little girl, what are you doing here instead of going home? They are worried sick about you."

I'd found Weldon sitting in front of the home he shared with Fox, Wlodek and Fox's other mates. Most of them were elsewhere, thankfully.

"I just wanted to see you, that's all," I said. "And ask you a question."

Weldon blinked at me for a moment and then sighed. "I may know what you're going to ask, but go ahead."

"Why did some of the werewolves remember me?"

"I'm not sure, Lissa, but they remembered, even if the others didn't. Daryl and I mentioned you a time or two, but most had no recollection. Winkler was the one who argued your case hardest, but convincing the vampires was like talking to a block of concrete. He backed off after a while and never said your name again. The vamps thought you were dead in the beginning, and then the memories were stripped away. Come on, I have something to show you." Weldon heaved himself off the bench, the space between the bench and the table was a little tight for his large frame.

"Where are we going?" I asked.

"Probably right back where you came from," Weldon replied and folded me away.

"I didn't come here; I just went to Winkler's funeral." I was staring at Winkler's old mansion—it looked as if it had been rebuilt.

"I didn't bring you to see the house; I brought you to see what's next door." Weldon pointed me in the other direction.

"This is where the house was that Winkler bought for me," I whispered.

"Yes, and he razed it to the ground twenty-five years after he was told you were dead. He had this park put up instead." We walked through trees over the four-acre tract. I heard water splashing and when we walked past the outer ring of oaks and maples, I saw the fountain.

In the center of the fountain, up high, with the water dripping off it, was something that looked like the peak of a roof with someone sitting on top of it.

"It's you," Weldon said softly and led me to the edge of the fountain. It was me; doing my best roof sitting, my knees drawn up to my chest. The fountain had been designed so the water would run down the slope of the roof and drop into the pool below.

"I understand Winkler built this for the neighborhood kids and they'd come and play while he'd sit on a bench and watch them, right over there." Weldon put an arm around my shoulders and led me to the bench. We sat down.

"I miss him," I said, trying not to cry.

"I know. It's not the same, is it?"

"No." I shook my head, willing the tears not to fall. "And now Roff doesn't remember me."

"How did you find out about that? Have you sneaked back and then left again?"

"No. I can know things, too, Weldon, if I want to." I wiped away the tear that fell.

"Kiarra says that we don't fully understand what you are, Lissa. That now you help balance the worlds of light with the worlds of the Dark Realm. That the mix that you are is bringing everything back to what it should be."

"And it's forever, Weldon. I had to make that agreement, to be able to do what I did on the High Demons' world. I can't walk away from it or sleep for a hundred thousand years. If Shala had succeeded in staking me, my physical body may have died but my energy existence would have survived. I don't know how long I can do this without going crazy."

"We'll help you," Weldon put his arm around me.

"I know. Weldon, I miss my wolf. I never told him how much I really loved him, even if he did pick up strange women in bars or stupid Kellee on a night of the full moon. I was afraid to go to bed with him, because of Gavin. Now he's gone and I won't ever get him back."

"I know, baby," Weldon held me tighter.

"I'm thinking about going to look for a world where the conditions are primitive and there are plenty of werewolves," I attempted to straighten myself up. "I want to move them to Harifa Edus, if they want to go."

"Then I may have a suggestion," Weldon smiled at me.

~

Marrik

"You know, I always wondered at your unnatural fondness for flannel," I teased Weldon. He wore a flannel shirt but it was open, and he had a white T-shirt on under it.

"Come on, we have to go talk to some werewolves. There's no time to discuss my clothing habits." Weldon was pulling me along.

We were in the middle of nowhere. Definitely in the middle of a forest, but then what did I know? I followed Weldon, getting slapped in the face more often than not with stray tree limbs and low-hanging branches. When we came out of the trees, we found a clearing with plenty of log homes spaced close together. I imagined that they'd all been hastily built, their residents clustered together for protection. The smell of werewolf was everywhere. "What is it with you guys and log homes?" I hissed at Weldon.

"Shhh," Weldon said and kept going.

"Weldon?" A werewolf stepped out of his log home. He was dressed worse than Weldon, I noticed—his shirt was homespun and dyed in gaudier colors. He wore rough boots that looked as if they'd been made centuries ago and his hair was long and unevenly cut—as if he'd done the cutting himself. Everything about him spoke of a hard life.

"Mace, this is Lissa," Weldon brought me forward.

"I can't smell her, but she's not a werewolf. I'd know."

"No, not a werewolf," I shook my head.

"Lissa's here to make an offer," Weldon said. "But first you have to tell her why you'd like to live anywhere but here."

"I can show you easier," he said and cursed softly. Weldon and I followed him. Other werewolves were stepping warily from more log homes, some coming our way, others standing and watching. I figured they recognized Weldon but not me and they were wary.

"Here. The most recent that were killed by our King's royal hunt. They know we go out on the full moon. We've moved so many times I can no longer recall where we've lived. The king and his court, well, they enjoy their sport, you see."

I was looking at graves. Six of them.

"But how are they hunting you?" I asked. Werewolves were tough and nasty when they turned.

"ReaveHounds," Weldon muttered. "Three or four werewolves might be able to take one down. Maybe. They stand around six feet at the shoulder. You might be able to take them down, Lissa, but these here can't. The King's law protects humanoids, but on the days a werewolf becomes a wolf, they can be hunted. The King takes pleasure in it. Usually the ones killed are the younger ones and the females."

"Fuck," I whispered. "How many of you? How quickly can you gather? When is the next full moon?"

"We're all together now and the full moon is tonight. I figure the King and his hunters are not far away—they plan this ahead of time, you know. The ReaveHounds track us," Mace explained.

"Then let's go. Weldon, is there anything they might need on a regular basis that they can't supply for themselves? What about the game here, is it plentiful? And domesticated animals?"

"Well, let's see—they might need tools and food staples. They can raise domestic animals, but they've had to sell the animals they had—they can't move them as easily. Game is plentiful, that's how they feed themselves."

"Then we'll leave a little surprise for a King who likes to kill his subjects, one day a month," I said and raised my arms.

~

Harifa Edus

"Where are we?" Mace turned completely around. I'd moved

everything—houses, woodsheds, woodpiles, even the graves. I'd also cleaned out two-thirds of the game animals and half the king's domesticated herds.

Barrels of nails, stacks of boards and logs, hides to be scraped and tanned, a blacksmith's shop and many other things had found their way to Harifa Edus.

"This is Harifa Edus," I said. "It's yours, now. You have six moons, one of which will be full tonight. I will bring other werewolves when I can and perhaps Weldon will visit and bring supplies for you."

"I will, starting tomorrow," Weldon promised. "I'll bring seeds, farming equipment and other things you might need."

"How did you do this?" Mace was slowly joined by his neighbors.

I figured I was looking at two hundred werewolves, total. Only a few children and females peered at me from the crowd and silently I cursed a King who chose to hunt and kill them.

A frightened deer bounded past us, causing all of us to all jerk our heads up. The animal was confused at its new surroundings, just as the werewolves were.

"Remind me to go looking for abandoned worlds that still have wildlife," I told Weldon. "I'll see about moving them over."

"I'll help and so will Martin, Mack, Daniel and David. They'll want a hand in this." Weldon named off the werewolf members of the Saa Thalarr as he looked around him, more than satisfied with what he saw. "In fact, they may want to come tonight. It'll be the first hunt on Harifa Edus in a long, long, time."

"This world belonged to the werewolves, once," I said to Mace and the others gathered around us. "It is yours again. I decree it."

"How did you do this?" Mace repeated his question.

"Lissa is Queen of the Dark Realm, my friend," Weldon grinned and slapped Mace on the back.

"Either Weldon or I will return, to check on you and to bring others. Good luck." Weldon and I folded away.

"Little girl, where are you going now? Home, I hope?" Weldon asked when I dropped him off at his picnic table.

"I have other things to do," I told him vaguely.

"Those twins of yours are about to have a meltdown," he shouted after me as I disappeared.

~

Le-Ath Veronis

"Weldon saw Lissa today." Merrill interrupted dinner at Lissa's palace to pass on the news.

"And what was she doing?" Gavin was angry that she'd go to someone else and not come home.

"Worrying over the werewolf planet," Merrill sighed. "And moving a Pack of two hundred persecuted werewolves to Harifa Edus to repopulate the planet."

"Is she there, now?" Drake and Drew said at the same moment.

"No, she took Weldon home after they moved werewolves from Marrik. He asked her if she were going home. She said she had other things to do."

"She knows Roff doesn't remember her." Griffin folded in and sat down at the table. Griffin lowered his eyes at the admission.

"How's Amara?" Merrill asked.

"Five months pregnant and happy," Griffin was given a plate full of food by the comesula waiter. "Lissa hasn't been wasting her time. She moved some of the humanoids from Beliphar—the Ra'Ak-enhanced creatures are taking over, there. They intended to turn the entire population and then send them out using the aging fleet of starships still left on the planet. She picked up the decent ones that were left, took them to Kifirin and then destroyed the starships. If those creatures find a way off the planet, it'll have to be through other means."

"We could help her," Gavin grumbled.

"That may be true, but we have to wait this out, I think."

~

Marrik

"Where did they go? It's as if they disappeared completely." The King of Marrik sat his horse, talking to his master of the hounds and one of his knights. The ground where the primitive log structures stood was now bare. They couldn't have moved buildings such as those; there hadn't been enough time.

"Your Wizard warned you," another knight rode up beside the king and reined in his horse. "He said that you should stop hunting these creatures; that they were your subjects, same as any other."

"Is that why you came to me, tonight? To remind me of my Wizard's words?"

"No, I came to tell you that your Wizard has disappeared. Everything from his chambers is gone as well. Except this message that he left for you." The knight handed over the message, neatly rolled up and tied with a string.

"Justice is coming?" The king read the note aloud. "That is quite amusing, Warde. Take yourself back to the palace and track my Wizard. I'll determine his punishment when I return." Warde turned his horse and urged him into a run out of the clearing.

"They have to be here somewhere; this is a trick," the King stood in his stirrups and gazed about again.

"It's not a trick." I'd been listening to the schmuck for several minutes, now. I materialized right in front of his horse, allowing my shield to drop. The horse smelled the vampire about me and shied backward, his eyes rolling. The ReaveHounds, too, were backing away. They knew better than the King, who wrestled with his horse.

"You know where they are? Tell me or I'll have you killed," he threatened.

"You know, threatening me probably isn't the wisest thing you've ever done," I said calmly. This guy was a sadistic shithead, who liked killing female and young werewolves. He, his courtiers and knights skinned them and took the pelts. The whole thing sickened me. He knew they would turn back to humanoid after the full moon.

He knew.

"You have one last chance to tell me what you know, or you die."

"So, killing female and young werewolves isn't enough for you? You'll go after anybody?" I asked.

"You are disobeying your King. That is a death sentence."

"But you're not my King," I pointed out.

"You stand upon the soil of my kingdom," he snapped.

"Okay, you have me there," I said and levitated myself six inches off the ground.

"Kill her, she is a sorceress," the king shouted. A spear was thrown, and then another. I turned myself to mist and both weapons sailed right through, landing in the dirt behind me.

"Nice try, but you shouldn't do that again," I said after rematerializing.

"Kill her!" The King was now so angry that spittle flew from his mouth. That's always so attractive. Five more spears were thrown. I misted again and this time I didn't wait. Horses reared as heads were lopped off.

The ReaveHounds, which were abominations created by dark spells, well, they died, too. There wasn't a thing left alive inside that clearing when I was done—the horses had all run away. I shook blood off my claws afterward and got a good look at my clothing. It was a bloody mess.

"He who lives by the sword, dies by the claw," I toed the king's body—his head was about two yards away. Marrik would have to find a new King. Well, couldn't be any worse than the old one. I folded away.

~

Karathia

"Hello, Grandfather. I'm sorry I look such a mess." Wylend Arden, King of Karathia, was sitting in front of a fire in his bedchamber, looking over accounts. He appeared as young as I did. Or Griffin, for that matter. At least he and Griffin looked to be related. I favored my mother's side of the family.

"Granddaughter, where have you been?" Wylend was out of his chair and staring curiously at my bloodied clothing.

"It's not mine—the blood, that is," I waved off his concern. "Do you know someone named Gart?"

"Yes. A Rogue warlock and high on my wanted list, is our Gart. Why do you ask?"

"Because he transported twelve thousand Ra'Ak-enhanced humanoids to Beliphar. They've pretty much taken over, now."

"You're sure of this?" Wylend was staring at my face instead of my bloody clothing.

"Yes. The leader of the twelve thousand—somebody named Felix, put five million Alliance credits together and paid Gart for the favor."

"That is interesting news, Granddaughter. May I offer you the use of my bath and perhaps some clean clothing?" Wylend kept his hazel eyes glued to my face. I realized then that Wylend wasn't used to people just showing up in his private study, dressed mostly in blood and the occasional piece of trachea. Again—none of it mine.

"That might be nice," I said, absently picking a stray bit of flesh off my shirt.

"Come this way." He led me through a sitting room and past a library, then into a huge bath beyond. This bathroom was larger than most people's houses. Everything was trimmed in gold and the tiles had gold and silver veins running through them.

The tub was immaculate and large enough for a few Olympic events. I didn't see a shower anywhere. Well, it might not hurt to soak for a little while.

"Go ahead and run your bath, I'll send someone after clothing." My Karathian Grandfather smiled at me. He might have looked proud, even. I had no idea why. I turned the taps and water poured into the tub.

I sat in warm water up to my chin, cleaning blood and bits of this and that out of my hair when my clothing arrived, via Erland Morphis. I should have known.

"I got these from your closet inside the palace and never set off the alarm," Erland was quite proud of himself. He laid everything on a dressing table nearby and sat on the wide edge of the marble tub.

"Now, what sort of trouble have you gotten yourself into?" He folded arms over his chest. I gaped at the second most beautiful man I'd ever met, realizing that I cared about him. He wasn't yelling, either, which was a real plus. His question (and tone) had been a conversational one.

"Where do you want to start?" I asked with a shrug.

"Start with why you came in covered in blood and guts and go from there," he suggested.

"I wiped out the King of Marrik and his asshole entourage."

"And the reason you wiped out the King of Marrik and his entourage?" Erland was withholding judgment until he had the full story. I was caring more about him as time went on. Gavin's shouting and cursing would have sent echoes through my grandfather's palace if he'd been present.

"They threw spears at me." I ducked under the water and rinsed my hair.

"Here," Erland handed a small towel to me to get the soap and water out of my eyes.

"Thanks," I said and wiped my face. He took the towel when I was finished.

"They threw spears at you because?"

"I went to tell them that I'd taken their werewolves to Harifa Edus —they were only hunting them down and killing them anyway, so I thought it would be polite if I informed the king about what I'd done. He and his guards got a little testy with me and threw spears. Twice."

"Then you are completely justified, although it isn't very attractive to have blood and bits of flesh in your hair and on your clothing. I took the liberty of turning all of your clothing to ash for you, by the way."

"Thanks," I said. "I wasn't sure what to do with it." I finished washing myself, even the naughty bits, although it might have been a little uncomfortable having Erland watch. He wasn't budging and I was too tired to make him move. "How about a towel," I said, when I finished with my bath.

"Step out and I'll wrap you up," he said.

"Erland," I whined.

"Lissa," he whined back.

"Fine," I muttered sarcastically and pulled myself out of the tub. Erland had a big, fluffy towel in no time and he did wrap me up before drying my hair. He was picking it out with his fingers afterward before setting me on the dressing bench and going through it carefully with a comb.

"There, that looks better." He was still going through my hair with his fingers, drying it with some sort of spell. It was curling in his hands. "Do you know how much women pay to get hair this color?" He was smiling at me as he worked.

"No," I said, leaning my head against his shoulder. His fingers were doing something to me. Relaxing me.

Soothing me.

Making me sleep.

CHAPTER 12

*K*arathia

The air was cool, the covers warm and the arms around me even warmer. Someone was nuzzling my neck and then the sensitive spot behind my ear, gently moving my hair away to brush gentle kisses there.

I was struggling to get my brain engaged so my sense of smell would tell me who was doing this to me. Treating me so gently, as if he knew every sensitive spot on my body. "I know where they all are, because they are the same for me, every other hundred years," Erland murmured against my ear.

"Erland, what are we doing in bed together?" I slapped a hand over my face.

"What I've wanted to do for a very long time, my love. I want to love you. I want to fuck you. And then fuck you again, more than likely." He moved my hand, flashed me a beautiful smile and then leaned in to kiss me. Yeah, he hadn't bothered to dress me the night before. I should have known he was weaving some sort of warlocky spell. I'd fallen asleep while he worked on my hair and I'd slept right through his getting me into bed.

"Erland, what is poking," I reached down to—oh, Lord.

"Lissa, I told you I wanted you. You count me among your mates yet you keep putting me off. Tell me why that is?" He was back to nuzzling, stroking and rubbing insistent parts of his body against me. I reached up to run a hand through thick, black hair. He smiled against my mouth and pulled the sheet away from my breasts.

I suppose that if you were male but went through a female phase every other hundred years; you probably would know what to do. Erland sure as hell did. Top to bottom, he knew.

He was gentle in all the places that required it and vigorous in all the places that needed it. I hadn't had sex in more than five months and he took full advantage of that fact. He was quite proud that he made me come twice before doing so himself.

"Erland, you look smugly satisfied." Wylend observed as a servant poured fresh orange juice for him at the breakfast table. Erland had herded me off to breakfast as soon as I was cleaned up and dressed.

I should have known my grandfather would know all about what was going on. I wanted to slap a hand over my face but that would be an all-out admission of guilt. Erland got me seated at the table, then sat down on Wylend's other side. There was no way to misinterpret the huge smile he was wearing.

We got breakfast before Wylend gave us his news. "I had Gart brought in late last night," he beamed over that fact. "And he conveniently admitted to everything." Erland wasn't the only one smugly satisfied this morning.

I listened in fascination; I wanted to hear everything Wylend had to say. "We were able to track his path from Beliphar," Wylend chuckled. "It was an easy capture." Wylend busied himself with breakfast for a moment.

"So knowing where he'd been made it easy?" I asked.

"It's a simple spell, if we know where they've been in the past few months. Longer than that and the spell scent dissipates," Erland nodded.

"And we were very motivated. It's a serious violation of Karathian law to have anything to do with the Ra'Ak, or any of their spawn." Wylend grinned. "In any form," he added.

"Wylend has been itching to take Gart down for a very long time," Erland explained, buttering a croissant. I didn't tell him the thing was loaded with butter already. "We've suspected his hand in so many things, but couldn't catch him in the act, as you might say."

"But now you have him." I was biting into my own croissant, without the extra butter.

"He'll be sentenced next week, during the Council meeting," Wylend sounded gleeful.

"You've found him guilty already?"

"Commanded admission," Erland grinned. "But before we can do that, we have to know exactly what they're guilty of. It can't be suspicion only. We wrap the facts with power and slam it into them. The truth pops right out." Erland stuffed half a buttered croissant into his mouth.

"That sounds sort of cool," I said, admiringly.

"What was really cool, as you put it, was getting the initial information from my granddaughter," Wylend gave me a wonderful smile.

"And the sex was even better," Erland remarked casually. "Fantastic. Orgasmic. Incredible."

"Another croissant, honey?" I held one out to him on the tip of a lengthy claw.

"Absolutely." He pulled the roll off the end of my claw and laughed.

∾

Belen's Temporary Quarters

"Who knows how many there are?" Belen spoke with Kiarra in his office. It wasn't really an office—not in the traditional sense, anyway. It was a floor, one wall, a bookshelf, a desk and two chairs, all floating amidst fluffy, white clouds.

"How did this get past us, all this time?" Kiarra shook her head, perplexed over the news.

"I wouldn't object, normally, since they keep their humanoid shape —the transferred DNA increases speed and endurance." Belen heaved a sigh. "But the sad truth is, once they're infected, they can no longer reproduce in the traditional sense. They can only turn others; they will have no young after the turning. They die sooner, too, after the turn. I estimate forty years is the longest that any of them will survive. This has built-in obsolescence for all the humanoid races, if it is allowed to spread unchecked. Lissa can scent them, and the rest of you must create an alternative method of finding them. The wolves and vampires may be able to track them by scent as well."

"I already sent Kyler to destroy everything left on Beliphar," Kiarra nodded, pacing. "Lissa was wise to pick up the uninfected ones and then destroy the starships so the others couldn't get off-world."

"Yes, she was, but this cancer is spreading elsewhere among the worlds of light. The Saa Thalarr must pull together and go out searching for these creatures. It is my command. The Larentii Liaisons have been recalled and they will assist with this. I am asking you to coordinate, Kiarra." Belen wanted to pace while in corporeal form. "Since Grace is pregnant, I may choose a temporary replacement for her."

"Any help will be appreciated," Kiarra agreed.

Harifa Edus

"This should get them through the next six months; they can begin to plant their own crops by that time." Weldon and I had bought necessities for the werewolves on Harifa Edus; shoes, jeans, coats, hats —plus all sorts of supplies, including flour, sugar, oats, dried meats, canned vegetables and manual can openers.

Daniel, Mack, David and Martin were all there with us. Erland wanted to come but Wylend asked him to do a few things for him instead, so he'd stayed on Karathia.

"We have to do this quickly; Kiarra wants to have a big pow-wow when we get back," Weldon sighed. He folded the supplies and the rest of us to Harifa Edus. We unloaded everything, talked about the canned goods and supplies and told the werewolves we'd check on them again soon. They'd already butchered some game, so things were going as well as could be expected.

"Where are you going now, little girl?" Weldon flipped my braid.

"Home, I guess," I sighed. "I'll go face the music. I figure Gavin is going to start shouting and cursing the moment I get back."

"Well, it's been six months."

"I know. Grace and Amara should be ready to pop soon," I muttered.

"Lissa, we don't always get what we want. Do we?" Weldon pulled me against him and kissed the top of my head.

"Yeah. You're right," I nodded against him and folded away.

~

"That's the only vampire I ever called Pack," Weldon sighed when Lissa folded away.

"I remember—I signed her certificate," Martin grinned. "Come on; let's go see what the big news is about."

~

Le-Ath Veronis

I'd been going about during daylight for the past six months. Landing on the central dome of the palace on Le-Ath Veronis was a bit of a shock—it was twilight there constantly. I was still mist when I caught the movement, not far from where I'd landed. I would have gasped, if I could have. He was more than beautiful. I'd said long ago that Roff would be a winged vampire and that I wanted to see it for myself. I was seeing it for myself. His wingspan was at least twelve feet, stretched out.

I could also see how the rumor had gotten started of vampires becoming bats—his wings resembled those of a huge bat, only they were beautiful—the color of soft brown leather. Roff's skin was darker, too, and his black hair was slightly longer than he'd kept it before.

He was now more than six feet tall, incredible to look upon and didn't remember a thing about me. I didn't materialize until he leapt away from the roof, allowing his wings to lift him in an updraft. He glided away for a long while, flapping lazily as if he enjoyed his flight. I sighed at the beauty he'd become and sighed again for myself, because he was no longer mine.

～

"I'm going out looking for her." Gavin cut into his steak so viciously I was surprised his knife didn't go right through the plate. His claws certainly would have, if he'd used those. I'd misted into the dining room, just as dinner was being served.

"And where are you going to look?" Shadow asked. He didn't sound happy either. Drake and Drew weren't saying anything—they were eating and not talking, which was out of character for them. Tony was prepared to go with Gavin, I could tell. Gabron was missing. I had no idea where he might be and I was still upset with him anyway.

"You don't have to go anywhere, Gavin. I'm right here," I said, materializing at my place at the head of the table.

Gavin handed me a dark look. "Lissa, it will be in your best interest if you sit down right now and eat. If we ask you questions, I would appreciate answers."

Drake or Drew must have sent mindspeech to Garde and Karzac, because they were both there in a blink. I wanted to tell Karzac to go back to Grace, but I didn't. I sat down, just as Gavin said, and food was brought.

"Where have you been?" Gavin growled.

"Earth, Harifa Edus, Earth, Beliphar, Earth, Karathia, Harifa Edus, Kifirin," I was trying to remember if I'd left anything out.

"Lissa, I am extremely angry at this moment," Gavin said, stabbing his fork into a chunk of steak.

"I know that," I said, staring at my plate. I wasn't hungry anymore. I guess it was too much to ask for them to be glad to see me, and I was depressed about seeing Roff and knowing he wouldn't recognize me.

"Baby, eat," Tony urged.

"Lissa, just a word or mindspeech once in a while would have gone a long way," Karzac weighed in.

"I know."

"Lissa, we were imagining that you were dead or someplace terrible, needing our help and we were helpless to find you."

"I know."

"Lissa, please do not do that to us again. I don't think we can survive that."

"I know."

"Lissa, you have wounded me."

"I know."

"Lissa!" Grant came into the room at a run, lifted me from my chair and spun me around, hugging me and laughing. Well, at least somebody was glad to see me.

"I missed you so much," Grant beamed as he set me down.

"I missed you, too, hon," I patted his face. "Is there a stack of fan mail a mile high?"

"You wouldn't believe what I have piled up. You have to come see it."

"Lissa will come see it later," Gavin snarled. Grant gave me a frightened look and left the dining room quietly. "Lissa, what do you have to say for yourself?" Gavin broke open a crusty roll.

"Well, I don't have much to say for myself. I didn't mean to make you suffer and I sure didn't mean to make you angry. That's always such a pleasant experience for me. I might have come back sooner, but I learned that Roff doesn't have any idea who I am. Doesn't remember me in the tiniest bit. How do you think that makes me feel, Gavin? I still have a mate out there somewhere, I assume, whose employee thought I'd look a lot better with a stake through my heart.

Have I gotten an apology over that? Has Roff? Because he stood in front of me and took that blow—for me. And somebody let that witch into my palace to begin with. Explain that to me, Gavin. Who dropped that ball? If she could get in, then anybody can just waltz right in here and do me in, or anybody else, for that matter. I was promised that those tours were foolproof. Except they weren't. Were they?" I slapped my napkin on the table.

"I'm not hungry," I snapped and walked out.

"That's been building for a while," Tony said softly.

"Six months," Drake agreed.

"We failed to do our job." Gavin stood. "Where do you suppose she is, now?"

"I hope she is in her suite. I'll take food and try to get her to eat if she is." Shadow stood and went to pull Lissa's plate off the table.

"I'll come with you." Karzac rose from his seat.

"We're coming." Drake and Drew stood.

"You're not leaving me behind," Garde said.

"Lissa, we brought your food." The door to my suite opened and nearly all my mates trooped inside. I was sitting on my bed, my knees to my chest. Yes, I was sulking. I was fine, flying through the universes, but the moment I got home things went straight to hell in a hurry.

"Lissy, we missed you. A lot. We should have been checking those tours before. We are, now." Tony was attempting to set things right. Shadow held my plate in his hands and he brought my bed tray over, setting my plate on top of it.

"You need to eat, love," was all he said.

"She's back?" Gabron looked up at his vampire assistant.

"The word just came down from the palace. She'll be at the meeting this afternoon."

"Thank you, Heathe." Gabron dismissed him. Heathe left Gabron's office, closing the door softly behind him.

"I'll take him with me to the meeting this afternoon, but it will likely do no good at all. He was extremely curious about his new genitalia and asked me why he woke with an erection after sleeping. I took him to one of the brothels—not one run by Gabron, by the way."

Flavio was having lunch with Wlodek and Merrill. Roff had been allowed to go to the winery by himself—Flavio knew he wouldn't stray from there—he loved his business. The earnings were placed in an interest-bearing account for him.

"How did he react?" Merrill asked.

"He refused to allow any of the women to put their hands on him. The whole thing distressed him greatly." Flavio sipped his glass of wine.

"He prefers men?" Wlodek asked.

"I called Lucas back in and he offered. Roff backed away from him faster than he did the women." Flavio shook his head. He didn't understand any of this.

"So, now what?" Merrill said.

"Lucas showed him how to masturbate—you know that vampire has absolutely no shame or shyness about him. Roff now handles things himself, every morning," Flavio didn't bother to hide the smile.

"You may want to keep him near the back, in case there's trouble with Lissa at the Council meeting," Merrill suggested. "It might not be a good idea to let the cameras find her bursting into tears when Roff doesn't recognize her."

"He doesn't recognize Giff or Toff, either; we've tried that already," Wlodek shrugged. "That I find unusual. Karzac thinks it is some sort of Systematized Amnesia—where he's lost all memories of the ones closest to him. He vaguely recalls Gavin, Tony and some of the others, but not all. He also can't remember anything about the stabbing, or at least he hasn't brought it up. Karzac thinks his memories may return eventually, but where will we be in the meantime?"

"Lissa is fragile enough at the moment. Karzac tells me that she blew up last night, after she returned home. She knows Roff doesn't remember and she was upset that Gabron hasn't come forward and offered an apology or an explanation." Flavio was angry enough about that, on Roff's behalf.

"Griffin has gone *Looking* and he says that Lissa placed Shala and Elthine's applications in the pile not to be considered. Gabron pulled them out and hired those girls anyway. Lissa knew, according to Griffin, that they were unsuitable with that talent she has to recognize such things. Gabron overrode her decision." Merrill had talked at length with Griffin over the entire thing. Griffin refused to tell Merrill what the outcome was likely to be.

"I must go pull my youngest away from the winery," Flavio rose from the table. Flavio owned a grand mansion in Lissia, as did many other vampires who'd paid for upgrades. There was plenty of space and Flavio had plenty of money.

"We'll see you at the Council meeting; we're going, just in case," Wlodek nodded.

"Giff, I don't know why your father doesn't remember us." I wanted to cry again, but I had a meeting with the full Council and a few guests in less than an hour so I was doing my best to hold the dam up. Grant had Toff in the usual sling, but the baby was already trying to walk—or in Toff's case—run.

Grant was up to that challenge, though—no normal baby was going to outrun a vampire. Toff smiled and laughed at me as I made faces at him. He'd sat in my lap during breakfast and I'd fed him off my plate. He loves ham.

Giff was the one in tears, now. She didn't understand what had happened to her parent. Well, I didn't understand, either.

Giff talked and wept while she'd gotten me dressed in a plum silk tunic and pants, the tunic glittering at neck, cuffs and hem with jewel dust. Yeah, I don't know how they get it to stick, either.

She'd done my hair next and placed my coronet carefully afterward. I might look like a Queen in the mirror, but I wanted to curl up somewhere and feel sorry for myself. I wanted Roff back and it didn't look like that was going to happen.

Drake and Drew were acting as guards today, even though they were my military and not my palace guards. Maybe they won a bet with Gavin, but I didn't really see that happening.

Both were dressed in full leathers and had twin blades strapped to their backs. Four more vampire guards joined us as we neared the Council Chambers. The media had arrived in full force and was crowding the main hall, all of them attempting to record images of me. Somebody, it seems, had failed to tell me that my return to palace life was going to be plastered across vid screens everywhere.

I saw Tony and Gavin off in the distance, holding the news crews back behind a barrier. Reporters were shouting questions; I ignored them as I was herded to the left and down the hall leading to the Council Chamber.

I thought I was getting there early, but I was wrong. Everybody was already there and the place was packed. They all rose as I entered the room.

Kyler was there as well, calling out the topics of discussion for the day, which was what to do with the excess profits from the casinos, brothels and other business taxes. The floor was open to suggestion.

Someone wanted wider streets to handle increasing traffic. There was a call for more solar energy farms to be put up on the light side to supply the demands of Casino City. There was a consensus on that item, so it was put to a vote and passed.

That only accounted for a fraction of the funds. Someone else stood—someone I didn't recognize. He was the newly elected Head of the Council for a city of vampires pouring in from Alliance worlds.

Someone else in my absence had made decisions on those applications.

"I have been approached by exclusive clothing designers, shoe designers and jewelry designers," he began. "They are all willing to pay for the opportunity to open shops here and sell their work to tourists and residents alike. I propose that we clear ground on the eastern edge of Casino City and build those shops between there and Lissia."

I didn't like that idea at all—they wanted to build inside the buffer space I'd demanded between Lissia and Casino City. It would continue to creep in this direction; I just knew it, until the two became one. Plus, it was more retail, on top of that. I wasn't opposed to fancy dresses, shoes, or jewelry, but I wanted a public library and a university, too.

"I was hoping to spend some of the money on a public library and a university," I said, causing everybody to go quiet.

"My Queen, those things should be discussed in time, but the designers may lose interest if we do not act on this quickly." The vampire was pushing his agenda. It seemed that most of the crowd was behind him on this.

"Call for the vote on whether we should consider this proposal, or go on to other things," I snapped. Kyler called for the vote and (no surprise) sixty percent wanted designer clothes and jewelry.

I wanted to walk out of the meeting right then and there, but I sat there instead while a list of retail shops was discussed and a letter was drafted, inviting interested parties to submit applications to open shops here.

"I do not want those shops between Lissia and Casino City," I said, when we got to the part on where to put them. "I was very specific on my requirements when the proposal for Casino City was discussed. I required a buffer zone and I wish to keep it. I do not want tourists wandering into my city, without permission."

"My Queen," the vampire was standing and talking again, "we all realize that you have experienced trauma, but you cannot keep the visitors out of the city forever. They are paying taxes to support you and your palace. You cannot deny them access."

"What is your name?" I stood up as I asked.

"Xandus, my Queen. From Villius, an Alliance world."

"Kyler, how much of the taxes brought in from Casino City are going toward supporting me and the palace?"

Kyler *Pulled* a handheld electronic device into her hand and searched the records. "That would be nothing, Raona. In fact, the mining concerns you have set up under the ice cap are paying for the public vid screens that have been installed throughout Casino City, as well as paying for the water treatment and desalination plant that supplies water to Casino City and her sister city on the light side. Those funds also pay for repairs to the electrical lines that run from the solar energy generators on the light side."

"Now, Xandus, what did you say again about the taxes supporting me and my palace?" I was so angry by that time that I wanted to mist right in front of him and make him bleed. Xandus gulped; I think he was getting that idea, too.

"Please pardon me, my Queen, I was misinformed."

"If you will hand over the source of your misinformation, I will be pleased to set them straight."

"Raona, I wish to propose that the crown cease paying for all those items mentioned earlier—I had not guessed that anything provided to Casino City was being subsidized by the crown." Merrill stood near the back of the room.

"The invoices came to me, Merrill, what did you suggest I do with them? You all seemed oblivious to the fact that they existed at all."

"That will be rectified quickly, Raona." Merrill nodded and sat down.

"What do the taxes go toward, that come to the city?" Another vampire stood.

"Flavio is in charge of the Lissia city government; I suggest you ask him," I replied as coolly as I could. I was afraid my fangs would slip out and my eyes would go red. Since this was being recorded and fed to the public, that probably wasn't a good thing.

"Those records are available and open to the public," Flavio stood. I could tell he was angry as well, simply by the stiffness in his body. "We recycle as much as possible, which is near one-hundred percent, but we have to pay employees to accomplish this, as well as repair and maintain the water and sewer lines, the water treatment facility, pay for the expenses of getting information out to the citizens, street maintenance and repair; the list is quite long," Flavio huffed. "How long have you been involved in government, or was your election merely a popularity contest? Many of us here have acted in public office for the vampire race for a very long time. If you have complaints, I suggest you go through the proper channels instead of tossing them into the Queen's lap, when you haven't even begun to exercise your options."

"My apologies, I am new to governing, as you say," the vampire bowed stiffly and sat down.

"How many here now have been involved in governing for less than one year?" I asked. I was still standing and scanning the crowd. About fifty or sixty hands went up. "The crown will pay for courses to be offered to those members of this Council. I suggest strongly that you attend those courses. Are there any questions?"

"I will be happy to provide instruction, Raona." Wlodek stood. He'd been seated next to Merrill.

"Perfect. Set them up and put the word out. I want those courses taken and passed. I have no patience for foolishness right now."

Xandus was standing again although he looked pale, if that were possible for a vampire. "My Queen, we still have not decided where to put the new shops."

"We can put them on the north side, just west of the buffer zone," Gabron now stood. "There is empty ground there and it would be ideal for the shops in question."

Gabron's suggestion was put to the vote and passed. I refused to look at him the entire time.

"I want all the applications for the designer houses to come to me," I said after the location had been approved.

"But my Queen," Xandus was on his feet again. "These are my contacts. I have been working on this already."

"How much have they promised you in return, if their application is approved?" I asked. If Xandus could have deflated, he would have. "Kyler, have Xandus' accounts investigated," I sighed. Kyler made a note on her microcomputer. Xandus shrank into his seat.

Have him watched, I sent to Drake and Drew.

Already there, they chorused in my head.

"Did you think that I would be easily fooled?" I asked. "Is that what you thought? That I was some provincial, backwater monarch who might be fooled by your superior intelligence? Is that what you thought?" I walked toward Xandus, who was cowering, now.

"I can tell by your scent that you are five hundred years of age," I went on. "And there is a slight taint about you. Why is that? I am sorry I was not here to reject your application, because I surely would have rejected it. There is a lie in you somewhere, Xandus. What is it?"

∾

"Now they see what a Queen can do," Flavio muttered. Roff, sitting beside his sire, glanced briefly at Flavio before turning back to the drama unfolding inside the Council Chamber.

∾

"Let me see his application," I said. Kyler handed her computer over. I studied the records she'd pulled up. "It says here you are seven hundred years of age," I was reading the application form. "Why the discrepancy, Xandus? Wait—that isn't your real name, is it?" I stopped right in front of him.

"My Queen, I beg you to have mercy. I did take another's identity, because I wanted to come here very badly."

"I will see him questioned, Raona." Gavin was at my side quickly, closely followed by Tony. They hauled Xandus from the Council Chamber.

The meeting was over shortly after that and I was glad—I was drained and the media was still waiting in the hall outside the Council

Chamber. Drake and Drew flanked me as I strode toward the waiting reporters. All cameras turned to me immediately.

"Raona, was that for real in there? That wasn't a plant?" The reporter had his tiny microphone held across the barrier as far as it would go.

"Let's see, you're about thirty-seven and you had fish for lunch," I said.

"My credentials say thirty, but well, you're right," he muttered.

I could tell them you had sex within the last three hours, too, but that might be too embarrassing, don't you think? I sent to him. He jerked visibly when he received my mindspeech.

"What did I have for lunch?" The female reporter beside him asked.

"You smell like lasagna, with chocolate cake for dessert," I said. *And you had sex with the man next to you afterward*, I added mentally. She turned a light shade of pink.

"I'm convinced," the woman said. "Do you have anything against designer clothing or jewelry?"

"Obviously not," I tugged at the hem of my tunic. "I prefer Revili, since he designs this sort of thing." I dropped the hem.

"Who designed your earrings?" Another reporter asked.

"These are Tiralian crystal, designed by Grey House," I replied. They were a gift from Shadow—he'd given them to me that morning.

"Those alone could run her palace for five years," another reporter joked.

"They're protection jewels, so it would be ten years," Shadow came forward.

"Where have you been for the past six months?"

"Many places. I am not prepared to discuss my journeys at this time."

"Were you in an asylum or undergoing psychiatric treatment?"

"No. I am sorry to disappoint you, but no treatment facilities were on my list of places to visit or things to do."

"Tell us at least one thing you did while you were gone."

"I went to the funeral of a friend. That's all I have for now." I turned away, even as more questions were shouted at my back.

"Father, where are we going?" Flavio guided Roff down a hallway.

"We're going to visit a friend," Flavio replied. Flavio walked quickly, following Lissa and the guards that surrounded her. She was heading toward her suite while the media cleared out behind them. There would be no reception tonight.

Roff's wings were tucked tightly against his body—Flavio had hired tailors to make shirts that fit around his wings. Roff was also dressed in tailored slacks, although he insisted on wearing sandals. Flavio made sure they were tasteful and went well with the rest of Roff's clothing.

"I woke in this room." Roff gazed about him. Lissa's suite was getting crowded—Drake and Drew had come inside, Merrill and Wlodek had folded in, Shadow had arrived and Reemagar and Connegar had come. Lissa was inside her spacious bath, the door closed.

"Yes, child, this is where you woke as vampire. Do you remember anything else?"

"No, Father. Only the waking."

"Would you like to sit, Roff?"

"No, Father. I want to stretch—those seats inside the Council were not very comfortable."

"I agree," Flavio smiled. "I also wish to stand."

"Giff, let's just get the coronet off for now," I sighed. I was exhausted. I was beginning to hate the media. More so than usual, anyway. Giff gently lifted the band off my forehead, careful not to mess up my hair.

"I believe you have visitors," Giff said, setting the coronet on its velvet stand.

"I know." I rubbed my forehead where the pale line showed from wearing the ornate gold band. "People waiting on me and I have hat lines."

Giff and I walked out of the bath together and she shrank against me when she saw Roff standing next to Flavio.

"It's okay," I said, hugging her against me.

"Lissa, whose funeral did you attend?" Wlodek asked. "Or was that a lie?"

"Wlodek, do not make me call you an old goat," I grumped. "I went to Winkler's funeral, if you must know."

"I should have known," he said and settled on the edge of my bed.

"You're co-mates with Weldon—he knew," I went on. Giff was hugged up against me as tightly as she could get. "He's not going to bite," I said soothingly.

"Why is she frightened of me?" Roff asked, puzzled. His voice was deeper, now. It was a nice voice.

"Roff, I don't think fear is the real motivator, here," I said. "I think sadness is. How do you like being vampire, now? Your wings are amazing."

"I like flying," he replied. I watched his handsome face carefully. There wasn't a bit of my old Roff hiding behind those beautiful, honey-brown eyes.

CHAPTER 13

*L*e-Ath Veronis

"They're recalling all the Saa Thalarr and Demon hunters," Merrill explained over dinner. Wlodek had let the initial bomb drop inside my suite, when he announced that Drake and Drew had to go back—Kiarra was coordinating hunting parties to search for and destroy Ra'Ak-enhanced humanoids. They'd been planted everywhere and the Saa Thalarr would be stretched to their limits to find them. That sucked.

"How about hiring High Demons?" I asked, when Merrill said they'd be short-handed, with all the worlds that had to be searched. "They could probably take those guys out with no trouble."

"That's an idea," Merrill said. "We'll look into that."

"We really need to find where they're from," Wlodek added. "They had to originate somewhere. Nobody is able to find any particular location. They're being shielded, somehow."

My eyes strayed to Roff more often than I wanted as I listened to the conversation. He sat quietly next to Flavio, drinking a bottle of blood substitute and listening attentively to everything we were discussing.

"We have to go back now?" Drake asked. I knew what he wanted—
to spend the night in my bed before they had to go.

"Kiarra wants you there in the morning, ready to go," Merrill
replied.

"We'll be there in the morning," Drew promised.

"We'll bring in more vampire guards," Gavin said. I nodded. I had
to replace my Falchani at the palace. That sucked, too.

❧

"We'll be back. Soon, I hope," Drake kissed me first and then Drew
took over. I was trying not to cry. Both kissed me again before folding
away. I cursed a little and threw pillows around. At least I didn't break
anything.

❧

"Drugs," Tony said after he and Gavin finished questioning Xandus.
"He had some friends using their business as a front to sell," Tony
went on. "We've already contacted the Alliance—they have records on
him and they'll be here in two days to pick him up."

"Good. I want him out of here." I looked at Xandus through the
bars of his cell—he wore the cuffs to keep him subdued. They'd have
to bring a lightproof box or bag to keep him from frying when they
picked him up—he was safe on Le-Ath Veronis but he wouldn't be
where he was going.

"I didn't believe it," he said, before I walked away. "I thought it was
all hype and lies." I turned back to stare at him.

"There weren't any Queen Vampires. That was a myth. I was
taught that by my maker. He said the only females he'd ever seen were
mostly playthings that someone accidentally turned. He said if I
wanted sex to find a humanoid female. At least they were good for a
meal with the sex."

"Did he teach you the drug trade, too?" I asked.

"Yes, but I was a dealer when I was turned. The drugs didn't work afterward."

"So, do you still believe there aren't any Queens?"

"There is only one Queen, now." Kifirin had come to weigh in on the situation.

"Hi, honey," I said. Xandus jerked in surprise when Kifirin appeared.

"You're the King?" Xandus had seen the footage of my coronation, I'm sure.

"I am Lord of the Dark Realm," Kifirin blew smoke, indicating his annoyance.

"If I serve my time, will you consider allowing me to come back?" Xandus asked.

"I'll consider it," I said. "As long as you straighten up."

"Avilepha, come," Kifirin said and away we went.

I hadn't gone to energy in a couple of days, so Kifirin forced the issue. We passed over several worlds. I felt it on a few of them—the Ra'Ak-enhanced. I sent mindspeech to Kiarra, who in turn sent mindspeech to the others. She told me she would send someone out quickly. I thanked her and Kifirin and I continued our journey.

Earth

"When she's energy, she can sense them when she passes the worlds they've invaded," Kiarra sighed. Merrill had his arms around her, nuzzling her neck. "She would have been the ultimate weapon, as Saa Thalarr."

"True." Merrill continued his seduction.

"Out of our reach, now." Kiarra was relenting to Merrill's attention.

"True."

"Yet you had her in your care, once. Had a M'Fiyah with her, once."

"Fucked that up. Beyond repair." Merrill was kissing and nipping, now.

"True," Kiarra agreed.

Campiaa

"Now I know how Theos was taken." Arvil San Gerxon cursed at the current turn of events. He'd watched the news vids of the Council meeting. The Queen had sensed the wrongness in one of her Council members and he'd been investigated and imprisoned.

Arvil's Chief of Security had made several suggestions on whom to send to Le-Ath Veronis as a spy, but they'd held off until the Queen had returned to the planet. Now, the Chief brought in what he considered the perfect employee to send to Le-Ath Veronis, but Arvil had his doubts.

His gambling dens were still getting business from the ones who couldn't get permission to visit the casinos on the vampire planet, but many of his regular customers had deserted Campiaa in favor of Le-Ath Veronis. He was still making money, but his profits had been cut in half. Arvil wanted to damage Le-Ath Veronis. He wanted to hurt its Queen, too. His hands clenched in anger.

"We will send in one more and see how that goes," Arvil snapped. "After that, we try other measures. Have we gotten approval for this one to travel?"

"Yes. We have the ticket already," the Chief replied. Arvil walked around the woman. She was quite lovely.

Just the thing to seduce any vampire.

"This will work," Arvil was convincing himself as much as anyone else.

Le-Ath Veronis

I was making a habit of going to energy early in the day, before breakfast. I made a point to cover different worlds so I could send information to Kiarra. It was my own brand of spying and if it got my Falchani back to me sooner, so much the better.

Today was off-day, so I toyed with the idea of taking Giff with me and going to do some shopping. She was depressed, though Rolfe was doing his best to bring her out of it. She missed her parent and was weighed down with Toff's care.

The other thing I knew, even if she barely knew herself, was that she was going to become a parent herself. Perhaps she'd ignored the tiny knob growing on her left side but I knew—her scent had changed.

I was going to order some of those carry sacks the comesuli wore to support their baby pouch so it wouldn't be dead weight on her left side through the pregnancy. Giff didn't need to be worrying so much about Toff when hers came.

I'd talked to Grant about it and he was more than willing to help, but he was so busy it was frightening. I needed to hire a second assistant, I just didn't know where to find one I liked and trusted.

Charles had gone off with the others—he was a Spawn Hunter, just as Drake and Drew were. Glinda hadn't been called out since her children were so small and Grace wasn't going either, since she was scheduled to have her baby soon, as was Amara.

I went to the roof of the palace, just so I could think things over. Roff flew overhead, his winery the likely destination. I was very surprised when he circled around and came back to settle on the dome five feet away from me. It was fascinating to watch him fold his wings. He sat down and looked over at me.

"You fly, too?"

"I don't have wings—I have to turn to mist. I can fly that way."

"Why didn't I know you before?" He was watching me carefully.

"Roff," I sighed his name while my shoulders drooped. "We did know each other." I wondered what had happened to the ring I'd given him—it wouldn't fit now, but he'd had it on when he was staked. It had disappeared sometime in all the commotion and nobody had brought it back to me.

"I don't remember everything," he gave a slight shrug.

"I know. How are your lessons coming?"

"I hated the one on eating."

"I hated that one, too. I got sick."

Roff moved closer, until he was two feet away. "The one I fed from first was very drunk. Then Flavio made me eat a meal at one of the casino restaurants. I felt very bad after that."

"I know. Merrill wouldn't let me get rid of it for more than an hour. That's what made me sick."

"I was nearly so. Flavio made me wait until we got home before he would allow me to rid myself of it. It smelled terrible."

"Yeah. That's really awful. I like the way you dress, now. Flavio has really good taste."

"He said that I must look fine from now on, since I might be going out with him to check on the casino that he owns or dealing with some of his business associates or friends. Sometimes I go with him and Kyler, when they meet with Cleo and her husband Harvel."

"Harvel is a Grey House Wizard, like Shadow," I said.

"I want to visit Grey House someday—but Flavio says I have to ask you for that favor."

"Then I'll take you sometime, if you want to go," I said. "Shadow is Glendes' Grandson. Glendes is Eldest of Grey House. We have to get his permission, first."

"Harvel and Cleo explained that to me. Cleo and Kyler are Glendes' daughters."

"Yes they are," I smiled. "And they are my nieces—did they tell you that? That their mother was my sister?"

"No. They did not tell me that. What was she like?"

"I don't know; she died before I was born. I wanted to meet her, though. I just never got the chance."

"People stare at my wings when I go out," Roff said.

"Because you're the first of your kind to come along in a long time," I said. Roff lowered his honey-brown eyes and studied his hands for a moment. It bothered him, I could tell, that he was the only winged vampire. "A few others are like you and they'll have wings when they're made vampire too."

"So I won't be alone?" He lifted his head, his eyes searching mine for the truth of that statement.

"No, you won't be alone. Other winged vampires will come. It just may take some time. As of now, the oldest winged comesula is only four hundred years old. Unless he is involved in an accident, it may be two hundred years before he is turned."

"How many are there?" That was something that Roff could have told me himself, before things changed.

"Eighteen comesuli exist who will become winged vampires, but there may be a nineteenth sometime soon—I think Giff will have a child within the next year and many of the others have not had a first or second child, yet. There could be many, eventually."

"Flavio says that Gavin and Tony will come to me soon to teach me how to fight."

"Well, that's a good skill to have," I agreed. "Every vampire should know how to fight. All the vampires I know fight very well."

"Do you fight, Raona?"

"I do." I nodded. "When I have to."

"I should go; they are expecting me at the winery." Roff stood and shook out his wings.

"It was nice talking to you," I said. I felt like weeping when he leapt off the dome and flew away.

∾

"Father, something strange happened today."

"What is that, child?" Flavio looked up from the reports he was going through on his microcomputer.

"I found the Raona sitting on top of the large dome of the palace as I was flying over, so I stopped and spoke with her. She was very nice."

"There's nothing strange about that—Lissa is nice most of the time."

"But Father, I got an erection while I spoke with her and I was worried that she would learn of it."

"Child, getting an erection near a lovely woman is quite natural—there is nothing wrong with that. It merely means you might like to bed her. It can be controlled, as you most likely discovered."

"Yes, but it was somewhat uncomfortable."

"Your clothing is sometimes restricting and it is quite rude to make adjustments in public."

"You explained that to me before, but it was never necessary until now."

~

"I am fully trained."

"No. No employee of mine is fully trained unless I say so. Come. When you please me, then I will consider your training complete." Gabron held the door open to one of the pleasure rooms. The new pleasure worker shook her hair and stalked past Gabron, heading for the bed. Gabron closed and locked the door behind him.

~

Harifa Edus

I went to check on the werewolves on Harifa Edus on my second off-day. They seemed to be doing well. I'd brought them soap and other toiletries—most everything available was safe for the environment. They were happy to get the supplies and the airtight containers I'd purchased for flour and other staples. I thought insects might be a problem.

Afterward, I went hunting the Ra'Ak-enhanced again. When I sent mindspeech to Kiarra, however, she told me that everyone she had was engaged. *Not to worry*, I said and went to get them myself.

It took hours, in energy form, to cover the entire planet and rid it of more than fifteen thousand infected humanoids, burying them in mass graves in uninhabited lands. I felt sorry for the ones who would be missing family members, but these were no longer the loved ones they knew. They were programmed, somehow, to pass on the DNA. Their family wasn't safe from infection.

Nobody was.

I cleaned out the nest, I sent to Kiarra. She sent a thank-you in return.

Another five days went by, filled with dull and dreary meetings as the rainy season started on Le-Ath Veronis. I didn't know Le-Ath Veronis had a rainy season, but it did. Kifirin came to explain it to me while the newly hired meteorologist was explaining it to the rest of the population.

It didn't stop the gamblers, the shoppers, or the visitors to the brothels. I still hadn't heard from Gabron and I was at a loss as to what to do about that, so I went to visit my grandfather.

"Granddaughter," Wylend smiled at me and invited me to have a drink with him in his private quarters. Of course, Erland showed up, beaming a beautiful smile and sitting down with us to share a glass of wine. I wondered where he'd been but didn't ask.

"Em-pah, I came to ask for advice," I said.

"That makes me feel loved," Wylend said, handing Erland a glass of wine. Erland accepted and sat next to me. He put an arm around me, too, pulling me against him on Wylend's sofa. "What advice can I give?" Wylend asked. Erland kissed my temple and his breath against my ear was comforting.

I twisted Gabron's ring on my finger. That was the only clue I needed to give to my grandfather.

"He has not come to you, or offered an apology, has he?"

"No, Em-pah."

"And you find this unacceptable."

"Yeah. There's a chasm between us now and I no longer want to build a bridge across it."

"He has no respect for my granddaughter, or her position as Queen," Wylend huffed. "Imagine how I might feel if I had a mate who insisted to me that her brothels were legitimate businesses, and then insisted that her training of all her employees was purely business. While that might be true on the surface of things, it makes you seem less in others' eyes that you accept it because you are desperate to keep his love and affection. If my mate did this to me, I would end our relationship, Granddaughter. I will not have my subjects laughing at me behind my back, because my mate does this to me in such a public fashion."

"Em-pah, I don't think the public is laughing at me."

"No, Granddaughter? You have not been watching the vids on other worlds. You only pay attention to what is produced on Le-Ath Veronis and the ones who run your news network care for you too much to publish what others are running away with."

"Erland, what is he talking about?" I turned to my Karathian Warlock for an explanation.

"Lissa, I can show you, but it will be painful." Erland's beautiful face was set in a frown. That statement had me drawing in a breath and closing my eyes. I nodded. Wylend had a vid screen hidden in a table inside his library, where we sat. It rose when he flicked his hand —who needed a remote control when you had that kind of power?

"I learned of this one's presence a short while ago—I still keep spies on Campiaa to watch Arvil San Gerxon," Erland said as Wylend flicked his hand again, causing the vid screen to display images.

"She works in San Gerxon's private stable of call girls that he hands out to his best gamblers. She came to Le-Ath Veronis three weeks ago, to work in one of Gabron's pleasure houses."

Erland took my chin in his fingers and turned it toward the screen. I watched in shock and horror as Gabron taught this woman how to put her mouth on a man. He was shouting at her when she didn't do it to his satisfaction. Somehow, a hidden camera had recorded this for the universe to see.

"There are other images too—images of his training her in other ways. These images are now being shown all across the Alliance. This spy for Arvil San Gerxon is seeing to that. She has managed to record these lessons and now your name is being sullied and ridiculed, because Gabron remains mated to you." Erland flicked his fingers, stopping the images. His dark eyes held a great deal of anger. On my behalf.

Stunned was too small and meaningless a word. I had no idea this had been happening and I couldn't even cry, I was so numb. Wylend flicked his fingers again and other images were displayed on the screen.

I remembered the gossipmongers from the television programs

three hundred years earlier. Those people had nothing on what was happening now. These so-called journalists ripped into me, calling me stupid, oblivious and desperate, all while showing clips of Gabron and his training sessions.

I couldn't believe this. I'd trusted him, once. Fought alongside him and helped save his home planet. Accepted his proposal and his ring. One of his employees had tried to kill me and almost killed Roff. Now, Roff was without his memories of me. Gabron had not attempted to apologize.

"Em-pah, what do I do?" I moaned.

~

"This letter came for you," Heathe handed the heavy cream envelope to Gabron. It bore the claw crown—Lissa's royal seal. Gabron glanced up at his assistant.

"Do you know what this is?" he asked.

"No, sir. It came just a few moments ago and I was instructed to bring it directly to you."

Gabron broke the seal on the envelope and lifted out the note.

Raona Lissa requests your presence, tonight at eight of the evening. Dress is casual. Gabron reread the message aloud so Heathe would know.

"What do you think she wants?" Heathe asked.

"I think I may be a single vampire, after tonight," Gabron replied stiffly.

Heathe watched his employer. He'd wondered, over the past several months, why Gabron had not gone to the palace to speak with Lissa. That was the proper thing to do. He dared not argue with Gabron, however.

"Would you like for me to lay clothing out for you?" Heathe asked instead.

"One of my black suits, Heathe."

"Of course."

~

"Lissa, this will be over quickly." Gavin attempted to reassure me. Every one of my available mates was there, including Connegar and Reemagar. Connegar waited to place a healing sleep afterward, if things went badly.

I had to get through this. I had to. Griffin and Wylend had come and both looked so angry they could have chewed nails into tacks, I think. Flavio had also come, accompanied by Kyler. Kyler wanted to strangle someone, I think.

Gavin had gone into a cold fury when he'd seen the footage that Wylend brought. They'd all seen it; all my mates had. Erland was now watching me pace inside my library. The vid screen on the wall there was huge—Gabron would see all of it—his secretly recorded sessions and then what the Alliance media said about me as a result.

I planned to have a talk with Bryan in the next few days. I intended to ask him to expand the media on Le-Ath Veronis to include feeds from the entire Alliance. I never wanted something like this to happen again.

Gabron arrived a few seconds later, nodding to everyone present. "Lissa, why did you ask me here tonight?" he inquired.

"Sit down, Gabron. Would you like a drink?" I asked as politely as I could.

"No, thank you," he refused. Just as well, I didn't want to give him another thing.

"You have an employee named Desire working for you?" I asked.

"I do—she needed instruction when I hired her, but things are better with her now." His answer was stiff—as was his body. He suspected. He just didn't know what it was he suspected. I doubted he'd watched any vids, just as I hadn't.

He'd carefully groomed himself and dressed formally for this occasion; he'd armed himself as well as he could. Well, he should have dressed in steel for what was coming his way.

"That's what I wanted to talk to you about, Gabron. She's a spy for Arvil San Gerxon. Did you know that?"

I stood before him, my arms crossed over my chest to keep my hands from shaking. I didn't want him to see how upset I was. Gabron sat on a sofa, blinking up at me. "I was not aware," Gabron replied tautly. "Are you sure this is not a product of your overactive imagination, Lissa? I know how you feel about my girls."

I wanted to shout at him, then. Tell him what kind of fool he was and what kind of fool he'd made of me. I didn't. Wylend did his little trick and the vid screen powered up. Gabron sat and watched image after image of his instruction of Desire.

Then, other articles were shown. Gossipmonger after gossipmonger. Laughing at me while the vids of Gabron and Desire played behind them. Calling me all sorts of unkind things.

One even pointed out that the camera angle could have been better, but he wasn't going to complain—Desire could do that for him, any day. He then went on to say that I must have been cold and unimaginative in bed and deserved all the mud being slung in my direction.

"Your ring, Gabron," I handed the envelope to him when Wylend cut off the images after a while. "Desire is in a cell in my dungeon. You have passage booked to Refizan tomorrow, and a note of deposit will be handed over to you when you leave. The amount has been increased to cover the fair price for all your brothels. You may take any or all of the workers with you." I stalked out of the room.

"You have made my granddaughter a laughingstock across the Alliance," Wylend stared at Gabron. "Whether this was your intention or not, I do not know. This will follow her for years, vampire. I very much want to kill you, but she forbids it. What have you to say for yourself?"

Gabron folded the envelope carefully in his fingers. "Tell her I am sorry," he said and rose from his seat. Tony and Gavin followed him, to make sure he left the palace. Additional guards fell into place as Gabron walked away.

Campiaa

Arvil San Gerxon strode into his study the following morning, reading a few messages on his microcomputer. Therefore, he was unprepared for what he found sitting behind his desk.

Desire, the spy he'd sent to Le-Ath Veronis, sat naked in his chair, her wrists and feet bound and tape across her mouth. A sign hung around her neck. *Try this again, it read, and your death will be swift.*

Gabron boarded the starship docked at the space station orbiting Le-Ath Veronis. A private compartment had been reserved for him, with enough space for twenty more people. He was alone. A valise had been handed to him when he'd arrived and he didn't bother to check the contents.

Sitting heavily on one of the well-padded seats, he stared at the vid screen mounted on the wall before him. Images of Lissia were being shown from a Refizani news feed. A statue of Lissa, erected in the main square of the capital city had been defiled. *Whore Queen* had been painted across the base in tall, white letters. Other graffiti ridiculing Lissa marred the bronze surface.

"She is not the whore," Gabron whispered softly. "I am."

Flavio wanted to speak to every Council member before the meeting, but knew he couldn't. There wasn't any way to protect Lissa. None at all. The media had also arrived in great numbers.

Lissa said to open the wound and let it bleed. She was suffering and there wasn't a damn thing anybody could do about it. The Larentii had to place her in a healing sleep at night. She wasn't allowing any of her mates into her bed and Karzac threatened to administer transfusions if she continued to refuse meals. She disappeared for two hours after waking every day and none knew where she went.

The meeting went quietly for the most part and then Lissa, flanked by Gavin and Tony, went out to speak with the media.

~

"Are you angry? I thought vampires killed over things like this." A tiny microrecorder was shoved in my face.

"Our laws prevent that kind of indiscriminate killing," I replied. I felt weary. Bone tired. It probably showed in my face. I no longer looked at my image in the mirror; I allowed Giff to have her way with my hair and clothes and ignored it all.

"Didn't you want him dead? Where is he now?"

"I didn't want him dead and he was sent home."

"Where is home?"

"I will not reveal that; he has a right to privacy." Gabron's right to privacy had been violated in the ugliest possible way. No, I wasn't going to take him back. He'd had a chance—a good one—at making amends.

He hadn't taken it by failing to come see me, talk to me or offer an apology after Roff was attacked. Instead, he'd chosen the brothels over me. Not surprising; that's all he'd known for thousands of years. I was the upstart. The latecomer. I snorted at the thought. Whatever I was to him, I hadn't been important enough.

"How does this make you feel?" The reporter stood behind those pressing against the barrier and had to stretch to make himself visible.

"You want to know how I feel?" I snapped. He swallowed uncomfortably and nodded. "I feel betrayed by a man I loved," I said. "That's how I feel. I feel as if I've been punched in the stomach and then kicked a few times. I can't sleep and I can't eat. That's how I feel. A former mate is splashed across all your vid screens while he's screwing one of his employees and you call me the whore. You laugh at me because I was foolish enough to trust him. To believe in him. To think that he cared about me. Well, as you all have so eloquently put it, too many times to mention, in fact, I was gullible. That's how I feel. Gullible. Dumb enough to love somebody. And stupid enough to stand there while he threw it back in my face. That's all for today." I turned and walked away from all of them.

~

"They're reappearing on many of the worlds we've cleaned out already." Kiarra wanted to tug her hair out by the roots. "Where are they coming from? How are they getting there? This is driving me insane."

~

"Roff, shouldn't you be at home?" I was sitting on the domed roof of the palace, too tired to get off. He'd flown past and then circled around to land and sit near me.

"Flavio says you are harming yourself." His honey-brown eyes displayed concern.

"Flavio means well, I know. But there's no way I can act differently right now."

"What would make this stop for you?"

"Unless you can turn back time for three hundred years or so, I don't think there's anything."

"I can fly you down, if you'd like. Perhaps you will consent to have a bottle of blood substitute with me. There is a lounge nearby, owned by my sire."

"A lounge?"

"Flavio calls it that. It is a place vampires go to socialize while having their evening meal. Or they go there if they need more blood. They stock blood substitute, warm or chilled. They also serve food there, if some of the comesuli come with their vampires. You may even order blood substitute mixed with alcohol if you want, but Flavio says I cannot do that unless he is present."

"What do they call this place?" I smiled for the first time in a long time. Flavio had owned El Diablo on Earth and it was pretty much the same thing. This was a good idea, I think.

"He calls it New Fangled."

That made me laugh. Leave it to Flavio to come up with something like that. "If you feel up to flying me there, then I'll go," I agreed, still smiling. Roff gripped my arms tightly as he lifted off the roof.

It wasn't like flying as mist; Roff's wings lifted and lowered us as he flapped along through wind currents. He set us down right outside New Fangled just as rain sprinkles came.

New Fangled was spelled out in red and purple neon across the building's facade and the business was quite tastefully constructed. The interior was even nicer, with tables in the center or more private, circular booths lining the walls. The place was nearly full and there were comesuli there, accompanied by vampires. They were eating and talking with the vampires while the vampires drank bottles of blood substitute.

"This is my favorite seat," Roff led me to a booth near the kitchen door. Comesuli were inside the kitchen, chattering away while they filled food orders or made drinks. "I like to listen in," he grinned and jerked his head toward the kitchen door.

A vampire waiter sidled up discreetly to take our order. We asked for bottles of blood substitute.

"Are you just enjoying the conversation or are you listening for anything in particular?" I asked.

"I just like to listen," Roff said. "I learn many things that way. The comesuli are all cursing someone named Gabron."

"Well, they're not alone," I sighed.

~

Refizan

"You know I have no problem with your business, or with your attraction to some of your girls, Gabron. What I have a problem with is your treatment of Lissa. What your normal practices have cost her. I was the one who brought this to my king's attention, because it involved many things, some of which concern him. My spies found out about Desire nearly three weeks ago—shortly after you hired her.

You did not allow Lissa to review the application, did you?" Erland's arms were crossed over his chest. Gabron had been a friend and he was doing this out of respect for the old vampire.

"Lissa was not speaking to me."

"Lissa would have spoken to you if you had asked. If you had bothered to apologize. Yet you did not. Why is that?"

"I am old as a vampire—you know this. I allowed my pride to hold me back. I generally know more than most—the experience is there. I have only dealt with the females who worked for me all this time. I have forgotten that not all women are meant to bow or be subservient to my every whim. I certainly had no experience with a Queen Vampire. It went right past me that she ruled Le-Ath Veronis instead of me. I am used to being in charge, Lord Morphis. Much of Refizan has been under my influence for a very long time."

"Could you not have loosened that grip, just a bit, for the Queen?"

"I did not think so. I threw it all away, as you see."

"What do you intend to do now?"

"I do not know. Perhaps I will turn my interests in another direction. In the meantime, I have paid to clear away the graffiti from her statue. I still have some connections, after all. It was the least I could do."

"There were unkind things painted there," Erland agreed.

"I saw the interview she gave two days ago."

"Disturbing, wouldn't you say?" Erland examined his fingernails.

"She looks frail."

"She does. We are at a loss as to what to do about it. She has lost two mates, after all."

"Two?"

"You know Roff doesn't have a memory left in his head concerning her. Or his children. Some effect of the near-death, I assume."

"I know. At least she doesn't despise him, now."

"You have a choice to make, Gabron. Work to forget her, or work to get her back." Erland folded away.

～

Flavio had placed a piano in New Fangled, but nobody was playing. I'd gotten through half my bottle of blood substitute and Roff had ceased talking, choosing to listen to the kitchen conversation instead. He didn't notice when I left my seat and walked toward the piano.

I played and performed *Follow Me*, an old John Denver song. I got a round of applause when I was done, so I followed that with another John Denver song, *Seasons of the Heart*. Abba's *I Have a Dream* finished it off.

"I'm going home," I told Roff when I went back to our booth.

"I did not know you could do that," he nodded toward the piano.

"Now you do," I said and turned to mist in front of him. It would have been too heartbreaking to stay.

"Lissy, come to dinner with me." I was cleaning up in the huge walk-in shower in my suite, which meant that Tony could walk right in. The spray from my shower hid the tears that had fallen.

Tony had stripped down to his underwear, but that came off quickly, all it took was a quick rip-through with his claws. Tony doesn't ever have to bite to make me come. He knew me. Up, down and sideways.

He knew to cushion my back with his hands against the shower wall. He knew I didn't like the spray in my face. He knew just the right pace to go to make me crazy. He knew to urge me on when the climax started and he liked it if I squealed a little.

Dinner was roast beef and I ate. More than I had recently, anyway. We settled in the library after the meal, having coffee or drinks. Shadow had come—he was splitting as much time between Grey House and Le-Ath Veronis as he could.

It was becoming a habit to watch the vid screen in the library to see what new crap was being spouted about me or Le-Ath Veronis. No, gambling hadn't slacked off—the applications were increasing.

They all wanted to be near the scandal, I guess. Another vampire had paid the crown to take over Gabron's brothels and they'd become a tourist attraction. Figures. I made sure I was far away when the tours came through the palace.

News travels fast, too, I learned, as footage of me singing inside New Fangled was splashed across the screen during the news. Somehow, either a vampire or a sneaky reporter had recorded all of it.

Then the program switched to their version of breaking news. An Alliance world was displayed and an entire city there was on fire after an explosion had destroyed more than half of it. Then the camera turned to show all of us something I hadn't ever expected to see again. My mates were shouting at me as I folded away in a blink.

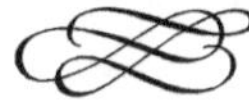

CHAPTER 14

*P*hericia

Ra'Ak. Copper Ra'Ak—three of them, blasting everything about them with barely a thought. There were no High Demons here to neutralize their power. I figured the attacking Ra'Ak had already eaten as many of the population as they could hold, there on Phericia.

They were now toying with what was left, killing, exploding, destroying. Where had these come from? I'd forced all living Ra'Ak back to their original forms on Kifirin, as well as taking power away from the Elemaiya.

Now I was looking at three of the Copper bastards. Well, I knew how to take care of that. They exploded in quick succession. Since the attack on the city was being recorded, too, the deaths of the Ra'Ak were shown in live vid feeds across the Alliance.

After I eliminated them, I went looking for any spawn or Ra'Ak-enhanced humanoids. They'd taken over an entire island and were preparing to ship out to other parts of Phericia. They died. I went to energy and just blasted them. I was filthy when I got back to the palace. Gavin didn't say a word; he just plucked me from the floor and took off toward my suite.

"Cara, you frighten me more than I can say," he muttered as he scrubbed me. My clothing had gone straight into the garbage.

"Gavin, I know you love me," I put my hands on either side of his face, keeping him from talking for just a moment. "I love you too, in case you haven't heard those words from me for a while. More than I can say. Let it go for now, all right? Just let this moment be good. As perfect as we can make it. You know by now that this is what I am. If vampires could have exploding aneurysms, you would have had one long ago."

"Cara, I only do this because the idea of losing you is so frightening to me. Perhaps that is why I took so long to remember you—I think they had to give me an extra dose of forgetfulness to begin with."

"It would take an extra dose for you, honey."

"Yes, it most certainly would." He finished cleaning me up and then took me straight to bed.

～

Taakus

"Our baby took care of business." Drake gave Drew a high five as they watched the vid screen in the bar. They'd been hunting down and clearing out the Ra'Ak-enhanced as quickly as they could, but they'd stopped to eat at a local pub and watched as three Ra'Ak exploded, one right after the other, surrounded by a burning city that the Ra'Ak had done all they could to demolish.

"You know something about that?" The bartender pointed to the screen.

"Not a lot," Drew hedged. He couldn't lie, and that wasn't a lie. They just knew Lissa had done the deed, that's all they knew.

"Hell of a thing," the bartended said, placing a fresh beer in front of the twins. "The Alliance troops are still trying to figure out how they died. Nothing else was getting through to those things. The city was on fire because the troops started throwing everything they had against those snakes."

"They're pretty nasty," Drake agreed and went back to his food and beer.

~

Le-Ath Veronis

"Father, I think I upset the Raona."

"How did you do that, child?" Flavio studied Roff, who seemed distressed. Roff's wings rustled in agitation; Flavio had no hope of controlling Roff's emotions in that way. He'd never turned a winged vampire.

"I took her to New Fangled to get a bottle of blood substitute, but I had to ignore her after a while, to keep my body under control." Roff's golden-brown eyes begged for Flavio's help.

"What did she do?"

"She left the table to play the piano you brought in and she sang, too. It was lovely, but then she came back, said she was leaving and disappeared right in front of me."

"Child, I have erred and not taught you the proper way to date a woman," Flavio sighed. "You must never ignore your date. If you had told Lissa the truth, I think she would have made you happy. Very happy."

~

"Lissa, wake up, avilepha."

"Hmmm?" It was three hours before I was scheduled to rise; I could feel it. Yet here Kifirin was, waking me up in the middle of, well, it was always night on this part of Le-Ath Veronis.

"Shhh, do not wake Gavin. You must come with me, m'hala. Now." I opened my eyes and looked into Kifirin's angel face. He was so beautiful.

"Avilepha, it pleases me greatly that you find me appealing, but you must come. There are things you must do, my love and quickly, before the universes are torn asunder."

"What's wrong?" I was coming off the bed in a fraction of a second.

"I was hoping you would search for the source of the Ra'Ak-enhanced before the Ra'Ak themselves began to appear. Too many other difficulties have distracted you instead. I will visit one of those distractions shortly. Meanwhile, you must rise, dress, have a cup of tea with me and reason this out swiftly. Time is very short."

I was flinging clothes on as I walked down the hall leading away from my suite. Gavin continued to sleep peacefully in my bed—Kifirin must have muted the noise I made. The guards posted outside my suite nodded to Kifirin and me as we walked away from them. Comesuli were already in the kitchen, preparing dough to rise and getting things ready for the day. A cup of tea was handed to me with a smile. I kissed Cheedas on the cheek and he grinned at me.

"Now, avilepha, think. Where are these things coming from? And bear in mind that many of the worlds that have already been cleared are now infected again."

Somehow, Kifirin couldn't help me with this. I didn't know why, but I knew things had suddenly gone critical. Kifirin and I wandered down the lengthy main hall through my palace as we talked.

"This started with the Khos'Mirai, I think," I told him. "Dragon said he was involved. He must have said or done something to make the Ra'Ak aware that they could combine their DNA with the Dark Elemaiya."

Kifirin nodded enthusiastically at my assessment. Yeah, I wasn't at my best, trying to think this early. I hoped the tea was helping. "And," I went on, "The Bright Elemaiya sure wanted to get their hands on the Ka-Mirai, because they wanted to change something awfully bad. But we never found out what that was, did we?" I drank more tea, begging my brain to wake.

"Who would know?" he asked.

"Let's go back to the kitchen," I glanced at Kifirin. His dark eyes looked as if they held stars in their depths, at times. I pulled myself away from that and headed to the kitchen almost at a run.

"Cheedas, can you pack a basket of goodies, like for a picnic?"

"I can, Raona, but it is raining outside. Not the best of times for something like that," he informed me as he packed food into a hand basket pulled hastily from the pantry.

"We're not staying here for the picnic," I said, patting Cheedas on the shoulder. I grabbed the basket and folded Kifirin to Evensun.

∼

Evensun

"Grandmother, I brought food for you if you will answer my questions," I told her. Narissa's hair was matted and she was filthy. She smelled, too.

My murderous grandmother sat outside a poorly constructed lean-to, covered in limbs and wide leaves. It probably leaked like a sieve when it rained. She hadn't done much to help herself—that was evident.

The Bright Elemaiya, once so pristine, had fallen completely. They were all as filthy and unkempt as Narissa. She glared angrily at me and if she hadn't been hungry, I would never have gotten anything from her.

"What do you want, hateful child?" She spat at me.

"Why did the Bright Elemaiya want the Ka-Mirai so badly?" I asked. "If you tell me, this food is yours. Refuse and I take it with me."

"Stupid girl," Narissa wasn't finished hurling insults. She cursed me in the Elemaiyan language, calling me names I would never use against even the worst offenders.

Well, she didn't have much room to talk—as far as her insults went. Kifirin stood nearby, blowing smoke. I didn't know whether Narissa realized how much danger Kifirin presented.

I swung the basket a little, enticing her. She knew she would never be faster than I was—she was mortal and I had vampire speed. "We all voted, after the proposal was made," Narissa grumbled. "We were offered money and an entire city was taken by the Ra'Ak for us in which to spend the winter. They killed all the humans, leaving everything they owned behind. We had food, warm beds, stores of goods and fuel and it was warmer there than where we've been forced to winter, most times."

"What did they ask for, in return?" I said. Narissa was taking the slow way toward the destination.

"The Dark Mirror—the Khos'Mirai, was sold to the Ra'Ak long ago by our Dark cousins. We could not find the Ka'Mirai, so we set about taking him back for ourselves. We should have ended his life immediately when he was brought to our Queen. He could do nothing for us—his ability was reserved for the Dark Elemaiya only. Instead of killing him, Friesianna let him live. The Ra'Ak came to us after a time and made an offer. Our Queen placed a geis on the Khos'Mirai so he could never harm us. That was our fear with the Khos'Mirai—that unless he was carefully supervised, he would bring about the destruction of the Bright race. We sold him back to the Ra'Ak for one winter's comfort. We should have asked for more."

"Old woman, I pity you at times," I said and handed the basket over. This was the worst of news—the Ra'Ak had gotten their hands on the Khos'Mirai a second time. He was still alive. Now, terrible things were happening and if what Kifirin said was correct, everything was about to collapse.

❧

Earth

"I'm sorry to barge in like this, but I have rotten news," I said. Kiarra sat at her kitchen island having breakfast with Joey, Bearcat and Norton, Erland's other honey-loves. I wondered briefly if they knew about the male-female cycles.

"What do you have?" Kiarra offered Kifirin and me a place at the island.

"Do you know that the Khos'Mirai was sold to the Ra'Ak by the Dark Elemaiya, and then somebody managed to get him away and turn him over to the Bright Elemaiya?" I asked, accepting the glass of orange juice she poured for me. Kifirin got one, too. I noticed Joey and the others were now staring at Kifirin. Yep, definitely the most beautiful man I'd ever seen.

"Yes. The Ra'Ak were using him to cause terrible things to happen," she nodded.

"Well, those fools that called themselves Bright Elemaiya turned around and sold him right back to the Ra'Ak, after their queen put a geis on him not to destroy their race."

Kiarra's fork clattered onto her plate. "You're kidding," she said, her beautiful face settling into a worried frown. "We thought he was dead—that the Bright ones killed him."

"Nope. They sold him back to the Ra'Ak. It's my guess that the Khos'Mirai convinced a few Ra'Ak to listen and told them to either go backward or forward in time so they wouldn't be caught up in what I did to the rest of them. Now, they're sending their Ra'Ak-enhanced armies out to destroy entire worlds, all while hiding from us. I'm still working on how and where they might be able to do that," I muttered angrily. "I think all these Ra'Ak-enhanced are quarter or eighth-bloods. Those would still have enough Elemaiya in them, Bright and Dark, to accept Ra'Ak DNA. All they have to do is go up and down the timeline, kidnap as many as they can find while deliberately breeding others and presto, you have sufficient numbers." I gulped my OJ. It was very good—fresh squeezed.

"So, they've been breeding them purposely, too," Kiarra nodded, her eyebrows drawing together in thought. "But where are they hiding? Where have they been, all this time? The Ra'Ak must be shielding them heavily."

"Kifirin seems to think the universes are in trouble, but he can't give me details. He says I have to figure this out and then find a way to deal with it."

"You wouldn't be able to find them easily if they were hiding inside a void," Joey suggested.

"A void?" I stared at him. He was Merrill's last vampire turn and reportedly a genius. Around five-eight in height, he had strawberry-blond hair a shade darker than mine and green eyes. Those eyes were trained on me while ideas formed behind them.

"Yeah. Where there isn't much of anything. Voids can be so large, it would be easier to find a single grain of sand in the ocean, I think."

"But what would happen if something was placed inside a void—something that didn't belong?" I asked. "What would that do?"

"Things would definitely be out of balance, I think," Joey said. "The largest void actually counterbalances everything else—sort of weighing what is empty against what is full."

"There used to be a gate, too, into that void," Griffin appeared at my elbow. "Hello, daughter. Amara says to give you a kiss from her," Griffin leaned down to do that. "The baby will be here soon. Therefore, you have to wrap this up quickly."

"But I closed the gates down to everybody except the Saa Thalarr and people like that," I said.

"The Ra'Ak have the power to open a new gate, although their gates stay open afterward, unless they deliberately close them again. The original gates had to be held open with power. They would also shut immediately after you traveled through them. What do you think that might mean, sweetheart?" Griffin blinked at me.

"That there's an open gate into a void." I said what I knew.

"A void is a very cold place," Joey offered. "If they've stuck a planet or something like it inside a void, it would be a warmer spot in a very cold place. Right?"

"Let me get this straight," I muttered. "They've placed a planet or something inside the void, where it shouldn't be. Just so they can raise their enhanced soldiers, after collecting them up and down the timeline, that is. And then they took them out a gate, while there was still a gate, but they had to create another one when I closed the gates against them," I said.

"It could work," Joey agreed. "Pretty sneaky—and smart, too."

"Well, daughter, I think you have it figured out, now all you have to do is decide how to eliminate the problem." Griffin leaned down and kissed me again. "That one is from me," he smiled and disappeared.

"I'll have to go to energy," I grumped.

"I can only give a little advice; I cannot interfere by my own word,"

Kifirin said, standing with me. "Look for the warm place in the largest void, avilepha."

"Sure, honey. And as soon as I figure out where the largest void is, I'll definitely look for the warm spot there." I patted his face and folded away.

~

"Is she going to be all right?" Kiarra asked.

"I do not know," Kifirin sighed and disappeared.

~

I should have asked Joey if he knew where I should start looking. I didn't see any flashing signs pointing in the proper direction or how far it might be before I got there. I had to start *Looking* with my head instead of looking with whatever served as my eyes while I was energy.

A void isn't easy to find; I learned that the hard way. I had to *Look* for cold spots after a while, until I found the biggest cold spot ever. Almost a billion light-years across, it might be much more difficult than looking for a needle in a haystack to find the minuscule warm spot in it.

Once I found the warm spot, then I had to figure out how to destroy it—after I determined whether it was the only place where the Ra'Ak were manufacturing their army.

No problem.

Except I didn't know what the fuck I was doing to start with.

~

Earth

"Mom, we're exhausted." Justin and Mack flopped down at the kitchen island three months after Lissa disappeared. Kifirin hadn't been seen, either. Grace had gone into labor shortly after Lissa began her search for the source of the Ra'Ak-enhanced and Kevis Halivar, Karzac's son, came into the world, voicing his opinion loudly upon arrival.

Griffin's son had been born six weeks later and Griffin and Amara named him Wyatt. Wylend approved of the name and immediately proclaimed Wyatt his heir. Amara was glowing and the child couldn't have asked for more loving or solicitous parents.

"Eat first, then get some rest," Kiarra placed food in front of her son, Justin, and her adopted werewolf son, Mack. "I know you're worn out, but we have to send you out again as soon as you get some sleep."

"The new guys are working out, at least," Justin mumbled around a mouthful of ham sandwich.

"Yeah. Belen picked some good ones. Two werewolves and three vampires. They're all death on those bastards." Mack bit into his sandwich.

"We needed more wolves." Martin folded in and sat wearily beside his son. Kiarra offered him a sandwich, too. Things were so tight that even Merrill, Adam and Devin were out tracking and killing spawn. Normally they didn't go out—they were Enforcers, but the problem had become so severe and widespread there wasn't a choice.

"I hope it's enough and I hope Lissa is able to do something," Kiarra sat between Mack and Justin. Justin nodded mutely and continued eating.

~

Refizan

"Decide now," Kifirin demanded. Gabron looked up at him. There was no other conclusion to draw—Kifirin wasn't joking. He could and would do what he said. This was the one powerful enough to create the Dark Realm on his own. Gabron often forgot that. Kifirin would always do what he thought best for Lissa. Unlike Gabron, who'd put his own concerns and interests first.

"So, either I come back to Le-Ath Veronis as someone else and then do as you ask, or have the memories of her taken away?"

"Your choice, vampire. If you choose to have the memories removed, I will remove them from her as well. Despite how you choose, I will remove all the damaging lies and recordings from all the worlds where they exist—you deserve the ridicule but she does not. This is a gift for my mate."

"She'll recognize me if she sees me again."

"No. I will remake you—you will be different. I have that power. Choose, vampire—either the brothels or a new name and a new life."

The Void

I'd found the void. It was larger than anybody thought. I also considered closing the Ra'Ak-created gate first, but that would tip my hand and alert any Ra'Ak to my presence. I had to be careful not to raise any alarm. I'd been energy for weeks now—hadn't changed and hadn't slept.

While I was energy, I discovered I didn't need sleep in that state. My physical body did, however, and in its finite shape, it only drained energy away. It did not replenish itself as it could in this form.

Now I was looking for what didn't belong in the void—a planet, galaxy or a space station. Whatever it was, it had taken a great deal of power to move it here. And cold? There wasn't a freezing cold such as this anywhere else.

The Ra'Ak had chosen this spot wisely, probably with help from the Khos'Mirai. All I had to do was find a single grain of sand (their relocated planet or whatever they'd chosen to use) inside a very, very large ocean of nothing. I went looking for less cold amid very, very cold, to find where the Ra'Ak had established their base.

It was a large, lifeless planetoid. Nothing grew anywhere on it and it had never supported life, until the Ra'Ak found it. A lifeless hunk of dusty rock; that's what it appeared to be, and the closer I got, the more it pulsed with the wrong energy.

It should never have been brought here. It upset the balance, although it truly was similar to a single grain of sand in all of Earth's oceans.

There wasn't anything on the surface—how could there be? This meant that whatever resided there had to be inside it. I filtered through layers of rock and dust until I found the core.

An artificial environment had been created there and two Ra'Ak had been assigned to maintain that environment, otherwise, the thousands of enhanced humanoids that slept in row upon row of coffin-sized cubicles would have frozen to death long ago.

More Ra'Ak in humanoid shape, all dressed in lab coats, were checking and injecting this sleeping subject or that. It looked like a frightening science-fiction movie, but those are generally removed from reality.

This was reality.

While I floated around as energy, more Ra'Ak came in with more captives. Some wore clothing that hadn't been seen or worn in centuries. The Ra'Ak really were tracking up and down the timeline to bring them in. I needed to take care of this, but I had one other thing to do, first.

I had to find the Khos'Mirai.

~

Le-Ath Veronis

"No, the Raona is away on business. I will have her contact you when she returns." Grant was weary of all the communications, written, oral and otherwise. Someone wanted to sign her to a recording contract.

A visiting guest, who'd scheduled his wedding in Casino City, wanted her to sing at his wedding. Talk-show magazines were begging to have her on. Fan mail was pouring in once more and Lissa was receiving all sorts of messages.

People asked her to bite them. People wanted her to bless their children. People informed her that they'd named the dog, the cat, or the baby after her. Grant was losing his mind. Flavio and Reemagar had taken pity on him and were searching for two more assistants. Grant needed them and quickly.

"Grant, I think we have someone." Flavio stood in the doorway with Davan and Heathe. Griffin had agreed to the suggestions, actually. Davan had been an accountant and he knew how to keep records. Kyler had worked with him for a while but he was bored. She mentioned it to Flavio, who spoke with Griffin and they'd come to the same conclusion—Davan needed a new job.

Heathe wanted out of the brothel business. He'd only worked there for a few months and was sick of it already. He'd placed his name in the job pool; Flavio interviewed him. Flavio liked him immediately, so he was hired.

Grant, who was trying to keep an eye on Toff, chased the child around his desk and picked up the load of fan mail that had been knocked off as a result. Grant breathed a huge sigh of relief when Flavio brought in the new assistants and put Davan and Heathe to work immediately.

~

More Ra'Ak in humanoid form were at the very core of the planetoid, where there were round tunnels carved out of the rock, each large enough for a sixty-foot Ra'Ak to slither through. I passed several Ra'Ak that were forty feet in length as I made my way downward. They were guarding something. It wasn't hard to guess what that something might be.

Two more Ra'Ak snarled and lunged at each other as I passed them by—none of them had a clue I was there. Part of that untraceable ability I had, I suppose.

What I searched for I found at the center of the planetoid. A circular prison held him captive, with bars all around and solid rock over his head and beneath his feet. He was chained, too.

Dark haired, quite young looking and perhaps a half-inch taller than I. I circled his cage in silent regard, studying him. If I'd been solid, I would have shook my head at what the scents were telling me. It was shocking, what I learned through scent.

Gathering more energy around me, I wove a shield around the Khos'Mirai's cage. To the Ra'Ak outside, it would appear that he slept —he was lying on the bare rock of his cell. Once the shield was in place, I turned first to mist and then to myself inside the cage.

"I wondered when you would get here," he sighed, sitting up and blinking at me. "They can't see or hear us, can they?"

"No. We're completely shielded. The image they see is of you sleeping."

"I don't mean to do wrong—most of the time."

"I can see that," I said, watching as he nervously twisted his fingers together. "But there is total chaos going on out there in the real world and you're sort of at the bottom of it."

"I know. I remember doing and saying some of those things, though I sometimes regret them later." He was now rubbing his arms —as if he were cold. I watched him carefully. The Ra'Ak kept everybody else warm, but didn't worry so much about this one. Mentally shaking myself, I shoved that thought aside.

"I knew what was going to happen to the others—the Elemaiya. That made me happy. Both Bright and Dark, wiped out with a single blow."

I could understand how he might feel that way—he'd been sold to the Ra'Ak twice. The other things he'd done, though—I didn't understand that at all. He wasn't sane—one look into those hazel eyes and anyone could tell. I moved backward as he stood, rattling his chains with the slow and deliberate effort.

"So, you saw that, huh?" I asked, keeping an eye on his movements.

"Saw it?" he laughed. It was nasty, that laugh. "I planned it. I knew you would come. Friesianna and Baltis just couldn't help themselves. They didn't forbid their subjects from breeding indiscriminately with any other race, but they never hesitated to kick out the undesirables, did they?"

The Khos'Mirai leaned against the bars of his cage. His dark hair was shaggy but not unnaturally so, and he was clean and dressed in something similar to a healer's scrubs. Bare feet stood on the rock floor of his prison and I focused on his toenails for a moment before going back to his face.

"They weren't particularly kind to their quarter-blood children," I agreed. "They are paying for their abuse now."

"Hmmph. You should have killed them, but no matter," he tossed up a hand. "They'll all die, eventually. You should have made them suffer more. I wanted to see that."

"I don't do suffering," I said.

"Such a shame," he dipped his chin and shook his head in confusion before lifting his eyes to mine again. "I lost sight of you for three hundred years. Why is that?"

"I can't really explain that," I hedged. Something wasn't right, but I couldn't put my finger on it. Still, he hadn't moved toward me and didn't appear threatening in any way. I hadn't seen anything from him that might be truly threatening. Yet.

"But you don't see," he laughed as his eyes filmed over in a strange glow. "I know I'm going to die. But I'm going to live." The grin he offered was unholy in its glee. Well, he was insane. Still, there was a touch of truth in his words. That frightened me.

"See me now?" His chains dropped away and he changed. Ra'Ak were frightening when they turned, but this—he was a terrible experiment gone awry. Half-humanoid, half Ra'Ak, with a Ra'Ak's scaled body, he grew and elongated on the opposite side of his cage. The scales covering his snake-like body were flesh-colored and poisonous. A flattened, humanoid head sat atop a thirty-foot body when the change was complete. His arms and legs, shrunken and stick-like, were still attached to the reptilian torso.

Ra'Ak have a terrible, gleaming beauty about them when they transform. There was nothing redeemable in this monster. "I knew you'd find me repulsive," he laughed. "I asked them to do this—to experiment to make a hybrid. I'm almost as poisonous as they are, if you touch me." Eyes that were larger and rounder than they'd been in his humanoid shape still glowed, although they were slitted, now.

"You know I killed bigger and stronger than you on Kifirin," I pointed out, watching him warily.

"Oh, but you didn't kill smarter," he snapped and rows of long, sharp teeth clicked as he bit off his words. I'd hit a nerve, looked like. "You can kill me—I've already said that. But you can't kill all of me."

"Look, stop talking in riddles and just tell me what the hell you mean," I snapped. Yeah, I was getting a little testy, too.

"Do you think," he hissed, his lengthy body uncoiling and beginning to move toward me, "that they'd be satisfied in creating just one of me? That's so limiting," he growled a laugh. "There are hundreds. Thousands. Who knows how many of me there are? And the best part?" His eyes glowed brighter as he glared at me.

"I'm sure you're going to tell me," I muttered, shocked and angered by his words. There were thousands, just like him? Could all of them do what the Khos'Mirai could do? Create havoc and destroy?

"Oh, yes. All of who I am—what I am, can do everything I can do." He'd pulled the thoughts straight from my mind—I hadn't shielded them as I should. "I am the collective me. You can kill me, but you can't kill ME."

"But what about the Ra'Ak?" I asked, stalling for time while I searched desperately for an answer to this new and horrible reality. "Aren't they pulling your strings? You're in their prison, after all."

"You take things so literally," he pointed out. "They've done exactly as I wanted them to do—for a very long time. Once I saw they wouldn't let me go, I began to work on this from another angle. They ask, I answer. You see they're still around after you thought you'd destroyed all of them. Not a problem if you can manipulate time, you see."

I almost said it before thinking better of it. Yes, the Ra'Ak could manipulate time. This aberration admitted that he knew I was coming. The Khos'Mirai had also admitted that he'd lost track of me for three hundred years.

Somebody had covered up evidence of my existence except to a select few during that time. I desperately needed more time to think and I didn't have it. Not here, facing down what may or may not be the original Khos'Mirai.

You're not thinking big enough. Or small enough, the voice filtered into my brain. Well, he was right. I wasn't. It had taken me months just to locate this Khos'Mirai. How much longer might it take if I used my usual, humanoid way of measuring space? How long would it take me to hunt down thousands of these monsters, when each of them might see me coming? Squaring my shoulders, I focused on the job at hand.

"Figured out that it's useless to fight me?" That many teeth definitely did not fit in so small a mouth as he laughed.

And then he struck.

～

Verbaan

It was a joy to rip into them—they moved swiftly but not swiftly enough. His canines shredded Ra'Ak-enhanced flesh as they attempted to land blows. A few did land but they were shrugged off as he decapitated one after another. He'd been powerful before but this—this went beyond his expectations. The reward at the end? Well, that had been promised long ago. It would be in his grasp—soon.

～

The Void

"Now what?" I sat on a stainless steel table with my head in my hands. The Khos'Mirai—this incarnation of him anyway—had been quickly dispatched, as had the fifty-odd Ra'Ak living inside the planetoid. Machines softly beeped around me as the Ra'Ak-enhanced slept in their small, coffin-sized spaces.

Before I'd killed the last Ra'Ak (who was still in humanoid form), I'd forced him to tell me how many clones of the Khos'Mirai they'd made. There were more than thirty thousand.

Thirty thousand, each with guardian Ra'Ak in attendance, spread across the Dark and Light halves of the universe. Each of those clones was busy creating an army of Ra'Ak-enhanced humanoids.

The Elemaiya, Bright and Dark, had unwittingly spread their quarter-blood children across the galaxies, seeding unsuspecting planets with the fodder the Khos'Mirai and his flunky Ra'Ak needed to kill everything. That didn't include the quarter and eighth-bloods the Ra'Ak had purposely bred.

Me? I'd killed a clone. Not the original as I'd hoped. He was still out there. I would have to find him and his artificially produced brothers and kill all of them. The prospect was wearying. What was it the voice had whispered? That I wasn't thinking big enough or small enough? What did that mean?

"Here." He handed me a tennis ball. "It's the one the cat plays with," he added, flashing me a grin. He'd appeared from nothing and was now sitting beside me.

"I thought you couldn't help me again," I grumped.

"I didn't say that. I only said I couldn't hold your corporeal body together while you did your best to blast it apart with power," he said.

"Picky, picky," I muttered.

"Besides, you can figure this out on your own if you stare at that tennis ball long enough. When you're done, send it back. The cat sort of likes it." He disappeared.

"What the?" I stared at the tennis ball. It was dirty; I could see that, with smudges everywhere. Muddy brown instead of its original yellow, the ball had bits of fuzz missing. They'd been ripped away by an animal that had played with it for who knew how long. What did he expect me to find in this? Under normal circumstances, I might not have picked it up to begin with. And then it hit me.

Andrallis

"Come." He was old—older than Wlodek—and he and the former Head of the Vampire Council fought together. These had no chance against the two of them. He laughed as he killed the aberrations; their smell informed him they were off.

Wlodek said it might be so and he hadn't been wrong. These had intelligence, whereas some of the others didn't. Wlodek said it was the difference between the enhanced and Spawn—Spawn lost their ability to speak and sloughed away their humanoid existence while the enhanced kept both. It was frightening.

"I'll kill you." This one was cornered but he brandished the weapon he held threateningly. His comrades had already fallen and still he refused to give up.

"You can try." The newly conscripted Spawn Hunter took the battle to the enemy.

~

It took a while. Forever, if you counted time as the very small do. Not long at all if you are much larger than that. Big enough. Small enough. I was now big enough, although it frightened me—more so than I'd been frightened when Kifirin first turned me to energy and spread me everywhere.

At least I'd thought of it as everywhere at the time. My vision had been so limited. I'd only seen a small portion of everywhere. Now, I was so large a presence as to be nearly immeasurable. The worlds around me were microscopic compared to the tennis ball my corporeal hand had held bare moments earlier. Things moved at such great speeds on those tiny worlds. Deaths, births, cataclysms—all happening in a blink.

Had the Khos'Mirai known how good my nose was? How I used that information to ferret out the smallest details about him? He'd probably dismissed it as unimportant. I used it now to sniff out his clones, wherever they hid. If I hadn't had his scent, I never would have found the others so easily. One by one, they winked out of existence, while guardian Ra'Ak and their enhanced warriors roared and cursed.

Like sparks leaving a campfire, the final handful burned brightly before turning to the Ra'Ak dust they were. Except for one. The last one. Who wasn't Ra'Ak at all. He was the true Khos'Mirai—the original.

I was weary, but this one I wanted to see for myself before he was destroyed. It took a great deal of effort and was quite tiring, but eventually I managed to condense what I'd become into a corporeal body.

～

"The others are dead?" he asked. The clone I'd killed inside the planetoid looked much like this one, and like him, this one was caged and chained. The difference was this; these chains and this cage were real.

The reason I knew? The first one's nails had been carefully manicured and there were no scars on his wrists from years of being manacled. This one hadn't been cared for so kindly and the scars on his wrist were only the beginning of the scars on his body.

"Your clones," I agreed, watching him carefully. "A few of the Ra'Ak and some of the enhanced, too. I couldn't get all of them, they were so scattered."

"They knew not to stay too close, just in case," he blinked at me in the dim light. We were on a dead world; one the Ra'Ak had killed long ago. The Ra'Ak had transformed an old underground bunker to keep this one alive and out of sight.

"Because you told them so," I pointed out.

"True. One of me told them, at least. I'm glad you killed what you could."

"You sound happy they're dead," I observed. His words sounded like truth, but then he wasn't sane. None of them had been.

"I want you to kill me, too," he said, picking at his chains. "I had to do this, you know. If I hadn't, I would have lived in this cage forever. They'd keep me alive forever. You understand that, don't you? I had to do something terrible so somebody would come after me—to kill them and then kill me. I was hoping the last one who pulled me out would allow her kind to keep me hidden or destroy me. The Bright

254

ones—they took one look at me and started negotiations with the Ra'Ak again. After placing the geis, of course. I did what they told me to do—I did not destroy their race. You and the other did that. Of course they regretted selling me back to the Ra'Ak later, after one of their foreseers saw that I would be at the heart of the destruction of everything." He laughed when he said that.

Like I said—not sane.

"They were doing their best to get their hands on the Ka'Mirai. I assume it was to get you back?"

"One of the reasons, sure. Wouldn't that be fun? They wouldn't kill me the first time around; what did they think I was going to do if they got me back? Just sit there and do what they told me from then on? I would have made them die. The geis had no effect on me after a while." He shook his head, his expression one of endless sadness.

"The Ra'Ak take bits of my flesh and mix it with theirs—did you know that?" he sighed. "It makes it easier for the DNA to combine and change the others. The enhanced. Don't ask what they do to create a clone." That information caused me to shudder. They'd been picking away at him for who knew how long? That would cause insanity, all by itself.

"Is there anything you want to say, or any messages you want to pass on, before I turn all of this to dust?" I studied his face—it seemed so innocent, somehow. Was that what the madness had done for him?

"My brother is dead, so there isn't anyone I want to say good-bye to. Except for you, that is." He blinked at me a time or two. "Thank you for bringing my death. It will be most welcome, I assure you." He lay down again on the bare floor of his cage and closed his eyes.

"Good-bye," I whispered softly and turned to energy.

It probably isn't a good idea to blow up an entire planet, especially if you're trying to keep things quiet. I merely caused the resident Ra'Ak and their enhanced army to explode instead, after I'd given the Khos'Mirai as easy a death as I could. Now, the small planet inside the void was my last destination.

Pulling just enough power to fold the small planet out of the void, I caused it and its sleeping inhabitants to disintegrate. There wasn't a particle left of anything that was larger than a grain of sand when I finished with it.

Then I went back and closed the gate that had been created, so nothing could ever get inside the void again. I sealed off the whole thing, too. The Ra'Ak were locked out, now.

Forever.

I also sealed it against time. I hadn't known I could do that, but I can. Funny, isn't it, having that much power? If I die in my physical form, then my physical form is dead. The most I can do is what the Nameless Ones on the other side do—maintain corporeality for an hour or so, but past that, it's all energy.

If my physical body dies, the only mate I can keep is Kifirin. For a while, at least. We are the same, he and I. I knew I wanted to keep my physical body—I wasn't through with it, yet. Wouldn't be for a while, I think.

Wending my way homeward, I zipped through galaxies, passing suns newly born or dying, planets of all kinds and colors, asteroids, comets, galaxies; some of them so beautiful I wanted to weep as I left them behind.

I even raced beams of light that rushed through space—many of them flying away from a star long since dead. Who says there is no life after death? That light flows away from you until it reaches a destination. Who dares to guess where that might be?

CHAPTER 15

Le-Ath Veronis

"I'm exhausted." I walked through my palace, gathering a crowd behind me. Gavin and Tony were the first until Connegar and Reemagar folded in, then Shadow, Garde and Erland were there.

Roff was still missing and that left a hole in my heart. Karzac wouldn't be there; he was caring for his new baby. Drake and Drew were still out taking down the last of the Ra'Ak-enhanced. I'd taken the long way home and they'd had almost eight months to track and kill what I hadn't gotten.

I wondered, too, how many Ra'Ak had gotten away and now threatened all the worlds again. The Saa Thalarr would have their hands full, if my guesses were correct. Grant, Giff and Toff came along; Giff's baby sac weighed heavily on her left side, held up by one of the slings designed for that purpose.

Two other vampires came with them, but I only recognized one of them. Davan was there. I smiled tiredly at him and he smiled back. Well, he was my uncle, after all.

"Lissa, you have been gone for nearly eight months and no word." Of course, Gavin would have his say.

"Well, it's better than the alternative," I said. "You wouldn't believe how big everything is, Gavin." I wasn't about to tell him how close we'd all come to destruction at the hands of the Ra'Ak and the Khos'Mirai.

"Are you well? Did things go as planned?"

"Things went pretty well, I think," I said. "I'll have to go see Kiarra —I have news for her."

"Lissy, please say you are not going to leave again, just as you're getting back," Tony said, his gray eyes begging me not to abandon him and the others so quickly.

"Kiarra is only a blink away. I've been billions of light-years from here. The news I have won't take long to deliver."

"So many things have happened while you were gone, Raona." Grant grinned at me. I loved Grant. He was always happy to see me. "Someone came and offered to help build the university and library you want. He's willing to put up part of the funding if we can raise the rest. I can set up an appointment for you, if you want."

"How about next week?" I asked. "I should be rested by then. I hope."

The crowd followed me all the way to my suite and almost followed me into the shower. Everybody who wasn't a mate was forced to stay outside. Actually, I was bathed and kissed and loved by my Larentii in the shower. It took all three of us shielding everything to keep the planet from flying apart from the energy sex.

Gavin, Tony, Shadow and Erland, who waited inside my bedroom, were included in the backwash of energy sex and all of them were knocked unconscious. My Larentii and I ended up on the floor of my shower, but I don't think any of us minded a bit.

"Why didn't we know you could do that before?" Erland demanded when I came out in Reemagar's arms, wrapped in a big, fluffy towel.

"You want energy sex all the time?"

"If it's like that, I'd pay," Erland sniffed.

"Don't you start," I swatted at him. He grabbed my hand and kissed it.

Everybody came for dinner, including Flavio and Roff. Giff didn't look at him; it was too painful, still. He should remember. He should. That was his child and she was about to have a child of her own. He should be supporting her—telling her what it was like. Perhaps I'd find another comesula to help her—one that had at least one child—so they could offer advice.

"When will you go to see Kiarra?" Gavin asked later. His fangs were gently scraping the spot where my shoulder met my neck—just above my collarbone. He knows I like that.

"I just want to rest for a day or two. Then go see her. It's news that can wait."

"Might I hope that we can spend time with you?"

"We haven't had any time off, have we? We used to talk about taking time off, but we never did. Where can we go for a few days and just be lazy? I want to float in a pool or sit in a hot tub, or just lie around and read and eat potato chips."

"I will feed you potato chips," Gavin murmured against my skin.

"I love you," I sighed.

"And I love you. More than you know."

Earth

The Gulf Coast was very nice. We sliced up fresh melon and ate it. We ate grapes, pineapple and peaches, too. We went out to dinner and had lobster and fresh shrimp hauled from the gulf that morning. We'd rented a four-bedroom condo, so there would be room for everybody. I did get to read and swim and eat potato chips. Gavin bought four bags.

"I want something like this for us on the light side of Le-Ath Veronis," I told Erland. He was enjoying himself, just as everybody else was. He'd hauled me off in the middle of the afternoon so we could do the horizontal be-bop before dinner. Garde got the night, after a late dinner.

Gavin, Tony, Shadow, Garde and Erland were all discussing

exactly how big our oceanfront property should be, what amenities it should have and how quickly they could put it up.

Three days of this wasn't nearly enough. I had no idea why we hadn't done it before. It was absolute heaven, just to be able to cozy up with one of my mates, or have a drink with any or all of them. Kiss them while they were half dressed in the morning or afternoon as I was flipping pancakes or making sandwiches.

Most women might have swooned at the bare chests and hard abs that surrounded me. If my Falchani, my healer and my winged vampire had been there, it would have been bliss to the hundredth power.

"We're building something just as quick as we can get it up," Gavin growled when we had to leave. Tony and the others had made preliminary drawings on napkins or anything else they could find.

They all knew what they wanted—enough bedrooms for everybody, a pool, maybe a tennis court, a big hot tub, a huge kitchen with a bank of refrigerators, plenty of closet space, big laundry room (my idea, they didn't care), a media room, screened-in lanai and a good stretch of private beach.

"And we'll be there nearly every off-day," Tony declared. Yeah, he didn't mind waking up in the morning next to me, with nothing on the agenda.

❀

Le-Ath Veronis

"Behave yourself, Raona," Grant grinned. I'd signed a stack of letters for him before heading off to see Kiarra. Heathe was the vampire I hadn't recognized before; he and Davan were my new assistants. Everything seemed to be running smoothly, so I straightened myself up and folded away.

"How is everything?" I asked when I materialized inside Kiarra's kitchen.

"Good—we're making headway." Kiarra offered me a cup of tea. I accepted.

"No new ones showing up?"

"No. Whatever you did seemed to work. We have containment, now. We just have to get rid of what's already there."

"Yeah." I agreed. "I just wanted to drop in and let you know what I found and what I did," I said. "I found the ones living inside a planetoid, about three hundred million light-years from the gate inside the void. That's sealed up now, by the way, and the entire area has been warded against the Ra'Ak or anyone else trying to get in."

"Good," Kiarra sighed. "I was worried about that."

"I have to tell you what I found, though. I learned a lot, from a very brief conversation."

"Does anybody else need to hear this?" Kiarra asked.

"Maybe Conner and Daddy," I said. Kiarra sent mindspeech to both and they showed up a few minutes later.

"What do you have for us, baby girl?" Griffin asked.

"Information on the Khos'Mirai," I said. "The minute I saw him—or scented him, actually, I knew who he was."

That raised eyebrows for sure. "Who was he?" Griffin asked.

"Saxom's brother," I said. That caused chaos.

"You're telling me that Saxom's brother was the Khos'Mirai? That's insane." Kiarra snorted when things were back to normal. At least she could talk about the schmuck without turning green, now.

"That's not all I learned about him," I said. "He was Saxom's twin. He and Saxom had insanity running through their veins. They were half Elemaiya, but one parent was Dark Elemaiya, the other Bright Elemaiya."

"Holy crap," Kiarra sighed. "The two races are never supposed to mix."

"Built-in insanity, like I said."

"All that time and we never thought to *Look*," A muscle in Griffin's jaw worked.

"He was waiting for me," I went on. "Both sides sold him to the Ra'Ak, did you know that?"

"I can't believe the Bright Elemaiya had him and they didn't kill him or contain him somehow." Griffin shook his head in confusion.

"He was glad they were gone—the Elemaiya, that is. The Bright ones knew they were doomed—somebody foresaw it. That's why they were desperate to get their hands on Fox. They wanted to change that."

"Too late now." Conner smiled tightly.

"Here's what bothers me," I said. "Saxom had to know what his brother was and where he was after a while. You guys were going after his captors. Why didn't he take advantage of the situation instead of doing what he did?"

"Perhaps he was working around all of us, instead," Griffin suggested. "After all, he managed to contact the Ra'Ak twice. Of course, his obsession with Kiarra probably interfered and his propensity for insanity didn't help either."

"I can only imagine what kind of nutcase he truly was," I grumped. "I sure had a hell of a time getting rid of his turns."

"Lissa, if I'd been aware of you sooner, I would have invited you to join the Saa Thalarr," Kiarra told me. "Griffin and Merrill were so tight-lipped where you were concerned, I never found out you existed until you went to help Dragon. You were hauled off immediately after that to take down Xenides. I never got the opportunity to ask you when it came time to increase our numbers."

"Don't fret over it," I waved a hand at the suggestion. "I'm probably better off, now. Not that I want to go back and repeat any of that shit," I said, handing Griffin a meaningful glance.

"Baby, that's all over, now. Someday, maybe you'll forgive your old man. In the meantime, your little brother is beautiful. Amara wants you to come for a visit."

"That's great, Daddy," I said. "But I don't even know where you live."

"You're here and you don't send mindspeech?" Karzac was upset, I could tell. He and Grace folded in and Grace had the baby in her arms.

"This is Kevis," Grace handed the tiny baby to me. He had the cutest, chubby little face. One day he was going to look like his father.

"He has your nose and mouth," I smiled up at Karzac.

"He'll have Karzac's eyes, too," Grace agreed. Kevis was asleep at the moment, so his eyes were closed. I had to take her word on that.

"Honey, you deserved this," I rocked the baby gently. He slept in my arms.

～

Would I ever tell Kiarra and the others about the Khos'Mirai's clones and what might have happened? Probably not. They had enough to worry about for a while. Still, it makes me shiver at what could have happened if I hadn't had a little help. The Ra'Ak planned to gather uninfected humanoids and raise them like cattle on a few worlds so they'd have a food source, all while their Ra'Ak-enhanced army destroyed everything else.

I doubt they'd informed their enhanced soldiers that they wouldn't live more than fifty years before they all died. The Ra'Ak would have everything to themselves if somebody didn't stop them.

I admit—I wouldn't have worked out a solution quickly enough if *he* hadn't come. It only took a nudge, but I'd sat there with that stupid tennis ball, staring at it until I looked past the surface. At all the things growing on it. Granted it was bacteria, but those were living organisms. Most of them were harmless. A few could be deadly if they encountered the right victim.

I'd removed the deadly ones—the Khos'Mirai clones. Now, the worlds represented by the tennis ball would have a chance. After all, the worlds had been pristine in the beginning. Before life was introduced.

Life is messy. Not all of it is deadly. Sometimes those things have to take care of themselves, without interference. It's only when things get out of balance that they need a little help at times. A hand to touch the scales and restore the balance so we might see something close to normal, now and then.

～

My life settled into a routine after my visit with Kiarra. I went to Council meetings. I signed letters, took calls, played Queen. Our beach house was being built and it was going to be nice. Kifirin folded in occasionally.

I met with the vampire who wanted to help build my university and library. He was old and had a lot of money. He wanted to put up half. I agreed to match his contribution. His one stipulation was that he be allowed to teach history courses or oversee that department.

That was fine with me; after talking with him, I decided he'd be good at it. He was nice to look at, too. Dark-brown hair, gray eyes and tall. He was around six-two or so. Almost as tall as Tony or Drake and Drew. His name was Aryn and had all his papers in order. He came across as somewhat scholarly, but wouldn't be opposed to taking someone down if he were threatened. He was vampire, after all.

"I am looking forward to this stage in my life," he informed me over a glass of blood substitute mixed with wine. "Even though the Alliance worlds are quite tolerant toward our kind, it is a great relief to walk freely on the streets at any time and know I belong there."

"I know," I said, smiling at him. "And when we get this university built, it will be open to all vampires, taught by vampires and run by vampires. We may open it up to a few foreign students, but they'll be screened carefully."

"The library as well," Aryn's smile was wider, now. "Imagine all the books that our resident vampires have brought with them. I hope we can convince them to share at least parts of their collections, so that all may have access. Some of those volumes are ancient and the information may have been lost to others. We will have it again and we can transfer all of it into permanent storage. I will be handing over most of my collection as soon as the building is completed."

"That sounds like heaven," I sighed. "I just want to go through the stacks and smell them, one day."

"You will have that day and soon," Aryn promised. Yeah, he wasn't hard to look at. Not at all.

It took me a few days to realize that I hadn't seen Rolfe. I saw Giff every day and her baby pouch was quite large. When I asked her about Rolfe, she pouted.

"They came to get him—Wlodek and Charles. They wanted him to help fight those things—you know—those things."

"The Ra'Ak-enhanced humanoids?"

"They call them Rees," Giff was giving me the phonetic pronunciation. REH could sound like Ree easily enough. I smiled.

"Giff, this means he'll be able to walk in daylight now and eat dinner with you when he gets back," I said. "That's their gift to him, for helping out with this. You just have to be patient."

"I know, but father still has no memory of me and I miss him. We used to do everything together and I wanted him with me, when the child comes." She patted the baby sac carefully.

"Well, we're both in that boat," I told her, giving her a hug. There was a hole in my heart where Roff belonged. I saw him now and then, usually following Flavio when they attended Council meetings or came to the palace. He glanced my way often—in a curious way, I'm sure. Each time I was the one to look away—so I wouldn't weep.

My Falchani came back after two more months had passed. I'd missed them so much and we spent a few wild nights together. Nope, no details, but we were all happy afterward. An invitation was delivered, too, addressed to all my mates and me. It was for dinner and a reception at Gryphon Hall, to celebrate the destruction of the REHs.

"Gavin, stop grumbling," I swatted his ass as I passed him. He was already dressed in a suit and tie. My twins had taken him, Shadow, Erland and Garde shopping. They'd all come home with some very nice things.

I was trying to dress myself—Giff and Rolfe were going, too, so Giff was having her own little tizzy about what to wear so the baby pouch would be nicely covered. Comesuli had eleven-month pregnancies—go figure. Of course, the babies did have full sets of teeth and could eat meat right out of the birthing sac, so there was that, I guess.

Kifirin showed up just as I was about to pull Gavin into the hall to join the others. Gavin hates parties, so this was a forced march for him. Kifirin folded all of us, this time.

All Saa Thalarr, Spawn Hunters and Healers were in Adam's huge ballroom, laughing, talking and drinking. As soon as my bunch showed (a few minutes late, of course) Kiarra called for our attention. She got us seated on chairs around the room first before going on to other things.

"I wanted all of you to come so you can meet our newest Spawn Hunters. They will be doing other things in between assignments, but they have already proven themselves admirably. First off, Jeral joined us."

That was a bit of a surprise. I knew I hadn't seen him around, but hadn't asked. I thought he was staying with Griffin, since they were brothers and were becoming close. Jeral walked in looking just the same, only he wore a confident smile on his face.

The transition had been good for him. He went to sit with Griffin and Amara, who were there with Wyatt. My little brother, I realized. I had a brother for real, now. The though made me dizzy.

Rolfe was introduced next, and I'd already seen the transformation in him. He didn't seem self-conscious about his height now, whereas he had been before, towering as he did over everybody. Now he wore it comfortably. I was more than happy for him.

"And now, for the ones Belen chose," Kiarra announced. Someone folded to her side, smiling. I was on my feet in a second. Thomas Williams was grinning at me as I rose to go to him. He took my hands and bent down to kiss my cheek.

"It's so good to see you again," he whispered.

"I know." I was trying not to cry. I'd watched him die on a dark night in North Dakota. His family had accepted me and I'd become a member of the Sacramento Pack after Winkler was forced to move my membership from the Dallas Pack.

Thomas went to sit next to Martin—they'd renewed their friendship, I could tell. I wanted to get the full story but that would come later.

I went back to my seat between Gavin and Garde. The next one to fold in had Gavin on his feet, though, and I'd never heard that sound come from him before. I realized why after only a second or two.

"This is Aurelius," Kiarra introduced the vampire. He had a lion's mane of dark-gold hair and he was a bear of a man—strong and authoritative. When Gavin went to him, Aurelius welcomed his son, crushing him against him and weeping.

That was a reunion I never thought to see. Garde pulled me into his lap so Aurelius could sit beside Gavin. They were both misty-eyed when they took their seats.

"You are Gavin's—the Vampire Queen?" Aurelius asked when he settled on the chair beside us.

"Yeah." I wanted to cry for Gavin, too—happy tears. "I can't tell you how glad I am that you're here," I said. "And I want you to meet Connegar soon," I added. Aurelius flashed me a brilliant smile and nodded.

"And now, last but not least," Kiarra was smiling as someone else folded in.

He was tall, black-haired, black-eyed, and moved with the grace of a werewolf. He wasn't wearing a suit, either, but had settled for jeans and a pullover. No socks were worn with the designer loafers and the grin that came was like a gift from heaven.

"Winkler!" I was shouting his name as I ran as fast as I could in his direction. He took the hit as I crashed into him and he lifted me off the floor, kissing me hard and fast. I was saying his name repeatedly as I kissed every bit of his face I could reach. He finally set me down and got my face between his hands, holding it still for one long, deep, *I'll-never-let-you-go-again* kiss.

Do you know how much I love you? He sent the mental message.

Not as much as I love you, I returned.

I think not, he argued, giving me a mental chuckle.

"Come on, baby, we're being stared at," Winkler lifted me up and carried me off to the side. Two more chairs were brought so we could sit down.

"The last announcement I have to make before we sit down for dinner," Kiarra called for our attention again, "is that there are Rogue Copper Ra'Ak out there again. The ones that were out planting REHs are now among the worlds of light and Belen says they're making spawn as quickly as possible. The Saa Thalarr and Spawn Hunters will be given schedules to hunt them down. We hope to contain them quickly, before they have a chance to spread again. In the meantime, enjoy yourselves. You've earned it."

"Let's eat," Winkler pulled me from my chair.

He was hungry.

Well, some things won't ever change.

The End